UNREAL CITY

BY THE SAME AUTHOR

Homesick

UNREAL CITY

TONY HANANIA

BLOOMSBURY

First published 1999
This paperback edition published 2000

Copyright © 1999 by Tony Hanania

The moral right of the author has been asserted

Bloomsbury Publishing Plc, 38 Soho Square, London WIV 5DF

A CIP catalogue record for this book
is available from the British Library

ISBN 0 7475 4578 2

10 9 8 7 6 5 4 3 2 1

Typeset by Hewer Text Ltd, Edinburgh
Printed in Great Britain by Clays Limited, St Ives plc

'So far as I know, no one has yet related his own delirium.'
                                        – Machado de Assis

CONTENTS

SIDON

London, 1992

February 3rd, Daybreak

I

As always I had dreamt of Layla.

From under her thick, damp fringe she looks down at the land she has never left as if at the first view of a foreign shore; wisps across her eyes, her lost face spun from the world into its own charmed orbit.

In those summers before the war she would come from the refugee camp with her brothers up the tracks through the maize and sunflower fields and through the wadis under the olive terraces where the watchmen had been posted to catch the Palestinians stealing from the lower orchards by our cousin the Bey who owned all the land from the mountain to the sea; at noon reaching the shade of the willows and tall bulrushes along the half-dried stream below our village.

By the silted sluices beneath the square where Ali and the other boys on the steps of the mosque threw peel and pebbles at passing strangers to the cover of the willows and holm-oaks they would bring the shrapnel and cartridge-cases for me to sell when I returned to boarding-school in England, in their chapped hands the polished florets glinting in the high sun over the groves, but I buried what they brought under the ruined pergola and waited only to see her narrow hips and dust-shot eyes peering back along the road through the valley to the silver ribbon of the sea.

At nightfall we would meet at the beach, the dusty enclave of shuttered villas and peeling eucalyptus trees cut off from the sea by the ring-road and low-rise tenements. The reed tables along the near side of the moss-floored square with its trickling majolica fountain, the other diners all tourists, the elderly women with their hair up, their jewellery flickering like fireflies as they turn to peer at each other across the candlelit patio.

You were already there always in your silk slip-skirt and halter-top, and though I arrived early you complained I had kept you waiting and played with your food and drank too much and giggled at the old couples like a schoolgirl on her day out.

And sweating in my linen suit I followed you to the small Maronite chapel on the other side of the square. A picked carcass of bare, low joists; in the gloom the altar like the mirror on a dressing-table.

We walked behind the pews, and up the short wooden steps to the narrow gallery. We leant on the cool balustrade, and looked down over the dim contours of the icons; when we kissed you pulled your head away, and turned your back, your fingers lazy over your hips as if over a sleeping cat.

You take a candle from the rack, and squat on the dusty boards, in the shadows your thighs white as sole-flesh; guiding my hand as I keel over you; the sudden outward thrust of your lips like a child miming a fish.

As you stiffen you bite my arm, coil yourself over my shallow chest.

And afterwards you say nothing, crouch against the wall, but grasping my hand so tight, as if at the outer rim of the jurd heights; in the darkness we cling together without speaking as one by one the old taxis drive out over the loose gravel beyond the square and down into the hum of the ring-road.

I wake to the cold light of the winter dawn.

This room of Leighton's always reminds me of the lowest

of student digs. On shelves improvised from bricks and planks, the books he could not sell, all their spines facing inwards as if in disgrace, chipped saucers and mugs do for ashtrays, and framed by a pilastered brass surround that has survived all efforts to wrest it down from the wall the dickering gas-fire casts long shadows over the pompous curlicues of the wall-paper which climb among ancient stains to the chipboard panels of the lowered ceiling. Around the scorched mattress two garden recliners with faded floral patterns, the sagging Parker-Knoll customarily surrendered to Verger, the swarf of tin-foil, matches, butts, dented plastic bottles and spent biros which Leighton carefully gathers from the subfusc carpet and deposits in the opera-red bin decorated with cartouches of maritime scenes whose contents are in turn decanted into one of the black sacks in the other room where they will collect until the spring when Leighton comes out again and spends his days down by the river or at the cemetery.

Above the buzz of Verger's Walkman I can already hear the cooing of pigeons through the soft wash of traffic along the Lower Richmond Road. Leighton stands, and pries apart the ravelled blinds that never pull up, and peers across the blistered shale drive into the thin light. The traffic is still moving fast, those late to bed and early to work making the most of the open roads, headlights bright, as if they can't quite trust the night not to close in again. Needlessly shielding his eyes he looks down to the head of the drive where two overgrown stumps which may have once supported stone urns or pylons mark the only entrance through the cracked brickwork of the front wall.

'Did he give you a time?'

If I did not know the house was empty I would think Verger was calling out to someone in another room. Leighton holds up a bare wrist to his bloodshot eyes, and with his fine hands gestures noncommittally, as if throwing aside an empty skin, and turns to huddle back over the fire. All these months, and it is still difficult for me to see him like this, his frayed poplin shirt with safety pins for cuff-links, the unwashed jeans soaked in stolen cologne, his arms as thinned and lucent as antique porcelain still being used for everyday, the old scar puckering again under brows singed by the flames of his pipe, his attenuated frame as if about to fold away like a rickety beach chair under the solid fact of his head, and yet he holds himself as he always has, with that same pained contraposto, seeking no passing comfort from the ragged padding of the recliner, his long noble face unflushed by the closeness of the fire which does not reflect in the rose film of his eyes. I will never get used to him now.

Before he can settle Verger kicks out with one of his air-cushioned trainers at the back of the seat. 'Did he give you a time?' he asks again, gentler now, and when he notices his trainer has become scuffed by the kicking, he looks resentfully at the recliner, and goes at it again until Leighton rises, and it slides away towards the fire. Leighton knows not to speak until Verger has unhitched one of his earphones.

'He just said to wait.' His voice when it comes is barely aspirated, so dry it seems hardly to carry at all.

The voice brings back my thirst, but there is nothing to drink here except the Lucozades which Verger keeps to himself under the folds of his puffer-jacket, and the stewed tea with UHT milk which Leighton brews with water heated on the Belling in the kitchen. I have yet to break my fast.

There is still not light enough to read, and Verger closes his eyes and does not sleep, and Leighton stands again at the window, and peers down to see if any cars have pulled in between the yellow aureole from the Shell sign and the mouth of the drive. I can hardly bear to look at him, not in the light, his face so firm and as it was through everything, the fine lattice-lines of age touched in without the intervening coarseness and pouching of the middle years. And when I do I am careful not to let him see me watching.

'You'd better've told him the right directions.' Verger kicks out again, but finds nothing to connect with this time; his trainer dangling in the air as he relishes its box-freshness. When he gets no response he draws out his phone from its lizard sheath, fumbles it up to his face, a bear with a biscuit, without unhooking the headset he strokes the digits with his wide fingers, the fluorescent dial glowing in the darkness of the room like the lamp-worms on summer evenings in the fallow fields behind the village orchards where they would have cut your white throat if they had ever seen us together.

Under the window, the crumples of foil over the carpet. He holds them to the light, pries them open, tentatively, like some strange fruit.

His narrow shoulders shuddering, but his hands steady as he lifts a square of foil, a flame splayed beneath.

No smoke rises. He grips his shoulders, leans back under the window, and rocks gently.

'Was that a car door?' Verger turns his thick neck towards the window. He can see nothing from the recliner.

'You told me not to look.'

'Did I tell you not to listen?'

Leighton's long legs drawn up like a grasshopper to his chest.

'We'll hear him down at the door.'

'We might not. He could stand and ring and knock and we wouldn't hear.'

'I would. I would hear.'

With an exaggerated effort, Verger pulls himself up, all his weight on his arms, as if on the parallel bars. He shuffles across to the window.

He looks down over the black shale, the sun rising through the dark arches of the gantries, the snow almost gone now.

His padded back over the blinds shuts out the remaining light. It was as if the sun had gone in already. His thick winter clothes made the room seem suddenly colder than it was.

Leighton down on the floor still, his knees like a caught spring to his chest, his eyes closed.

'You said he never comes when you watch.' The parched whisper again, as if he does not care to be heard.

'I'm not watching.'

'What are you doing then?' Leighton shifts, silently, crab-wise, towards the corner.

'Verifying he hasn't come yet.' When Verger kicks he finds only the wall. He looks down at the trainer, lips pursed with self-reproach; as if it were some living thing he had not meant to harm.

It used to be difficult to tell what he was thinking, an inscrutable Buddha's passivity to his bulk, but now that same mass made his every act seem fulsome and brutal, like a cartoon bruiser, a fighter run to fat, his face hard-set into its shallow grimaces, but opaque for all that.

That flamboyant drifter with his silk kaftans and scarab-beads and wild corkscrew hair, a livid orchid blooming through the terraces of Brixton, had nothing more in common with this rough-house dealer who had stripped Leighton of every last dignity other than his own strange name.

In those years long ago in Beirut wherever he walked in his Afghan and trailing loons across the broken city the amputees and street-boys followed in an antic cavalcade, but now he was as studiedly indistinctive as any other homey; the giant cocoon of the puffer-jacket; a baseball-cap drawn down against surveillance cameras.

His face has lightened with the years, from the blue-grey of old gravy to this sallow uncolouredness, though even when he was young there was always something strangely perishable and applied about his darkness. I had half-expected to come upon him one day without the colour, all fey and abashed, like a woman disturbed without her face on.

'And when does verifying become watching.' Leighton has shuffled further into the corner. Verger turns back from the window.

'A thing has to have happened to be verified.' He brings this out with a certain trumpery, as if that were an end to the matter.

He slumps back on the recliner. The Watchman propped on the soft crux of his lap; he brings this with him always: he will have no one looking over his shoulder.

The molten images swimming on his sleepless face like some old dance-hall effect. Ruins, a flotilla of ships, rivers; an effigy burning.

II

From the road the house looked much like any of the other large mid-Victorian mansions on that side of the hill between the service-station and the intersection, but it was wider than the others, and set back more, and had retained the stretch of wall which in the rest of the row, converted into flats, a retirement home, the offices of a local solicitor, had been replaced by asphalted forecourts for additional parking separated from the pavement by low-slung chains and tubs of bright perennials. Dead ivy and rusted downpipes hung down over the blackened brickwork of the façade, and over the flaking stucco transoms above the windows many of which had been covered with chipboard so that walking up the blistered shale drive between the high grass there was an intimation of that same unsettling licence one knows when close to the blind.

The hall was dark and cool, like a place sunk deep under water, a bottle-green dimness through the stained-glass of the fanlight and the panes above the stairwell drifting down across the black-and-white tiles and the cracked majolica pot that held the dead stump of an indoor palm. On a long counter at the back still lay the neat piles of playbills and crinkled tourist brochures, and above over the ribbed wallpaper dangled the dull emblems of motoring clubs and old hotel associations. Beyond this was a passage without windows, lit by striplights that were never turned off, a broken payphone to one side against which rested the heavy wooden sign that must have once stood at the front of the drive, the characters printed in that hopeful fifties sanserif, *Hotel du Lac*, a k scrawled in by some wag at the end.

Letters still came in this name and piled up around the door, but if there had ever been the prospect of a lake from the house it had long been obscured by the high walls and gantries of the container depot across the way. Up until eighteen months ago the place had been a benefit hostel, with Bengali and Irish families living on the upper floors, the lower half still in use as a roadhouse for commercial travellers, and before that the villa had served as a rest-home for elderly widowed gentlewomen, the name chosen by the owner perhaps in fond remembrance of some youthful summer by the Swiss lakes. If Leighton was to be believed, and his knowledge of local history was uncannily precise, the house had by a circuitous coincidence originally belonged to a distant relative on his mother's side, a planter retired from Ceylon, and sometimes he would claim that as a boy he had once seen a photograph of the villa in these early days, taken from the back, with maids in starched aprons standing in front of an elaborate conservatory filled with tiger-skins, high-backed rattan settles, mounted hunting trophies, but there were no surviving traces of this structure now.

When the hostel had been closed by the council due to the difficulties with the roof and the police, Leighton had stayed on with the vague consent of the Greek-Cypriot owner who ran a chain of boarding houses on the south coast and may have reckoned to save on private security by this arrangement. Every couple of months this stocky little man would arrive in his Range Rover and wander with a clipboard in the long grass at the front. I had soon learnt that no one else ever came to the house, unless of course by careful invitation, and this was how Leighton had managed things for a good while before I had finally found him again; though in the weeks after I had moved down from the communal house at the Ealing Husseinya it was already clear that Verger had begun to see advantages for himself in Leighton's isolation.

At first I could not get used to all the empty rooms. Through the day Leighton stayed by the gas-fire, reading his old books, and waiting for Verger. Before going out to my shift in the evening I would tramp about upstairs to keep warm, there was nothing left there, just the dark oblongs on the walls where bed-heads and wardrobes had once stood, polythene sheeting over the floors, brown puddles where the drips came in, a disparate collection of plastic tubs and basins which I would empty and put back under the more persistent leaks. As the weeks went by some of the smaller rooms would fill up with the sacks of rubbish which Leighton never took down, but if there were rats I never saw any; at night Leighton said he could hear scurrying noises above the lowered ceilings on his floor, and when I lay down during the day I would look up and listen, but I would hear only the old ringing in my ears from the summer of the siege that always returned when I was alone again. The place was so cold there was little smell from the sacks.

Sometimes Verger would not come, and when I returned from my shift along the drive in the early morning I would see Leighton, up there behind the blinds, wrapped in the old woollen blanket, a sentinel on his lonely parapet.

For weeks I never saw him eat. I did not understand how he filled all the sacks that slowly took over the rooms around him. Each morning I bought him cigarettes and newspapers, but he never asked for anything else from outside, and though he brewed his tea in the kitchen there were no signs that he ate or cooked there. The sink was blocked by a thick crud of soil and drowned grubs, and when I opened the drawers I found clusters of delicate aphids which the cold did not kill off. I would eat out whenever possible, and on the mornings I brought in food I took it directly to my room. There were no shops nearby, and the service-station stocked only pork pies, cold meats, pale rolls filled with halved sausages and bright-yellow mustard. I had never cared much for pork, and since joining the brotherhood I had always avoided it. Sometimes when I had forgotten to bring food and was too tired to go out again I would search the tall cupboards in the pantries, but all I ever found were catering-size jars of salad cream and Branston pickle, scabs of mould under the lids, and later when I went back to my bed I would dream of those nights I used to creep down to the kitchens at school and seek out the huge jars of mayonnaise and jam and ketchup that had not been locked away, and in the darkness I would delve in with a long spoon, my pillow in the morning covered in a crust of sweet-smelling stains.

After a few weeks just walking back after work into those large empty rooms brought on a nagging hunger, and when I was not fasting I would sometimes have an early lunch at a small Lebanese restaurant in Ravenscourt Park which I had first visited with Jawad from the Husseinya who did not approve of the place but kept coming back for the food. This was not one of the more popular Lebanese in the area, nor was it especially cheap, and I favoured it over the others only because it served Shish'Taouk in the old village way, mari-nated overnight in garlic and rosemary and sesame oil. Like most of the Lebanese restaurants in London the Al-Bustan was run by Maronites, emigrants from the first years of the

15

war, though the cook must have been a Shi'i from one of the hill villages above Sidon. I never went down to see him for fear of drawing more attention to myself; I was showing myself there too often as it was.

Along the walls were all the usual bric-à-brac, stylized cedar trees, brass coffee-pots, heavily framed paintings of Phoenician galleys, photographs of Beirut in better days; the same sullen match of gold on the handrails, the light-fittings, the trimmings on the tablecloths. The place was always quiet at lunchtime during weekdays. There would be a few local businessmen with clients, sometimes groups of overdressed Maronite housewives back from shopping trips in the West End, and I would sit in the same dark booth at the back, though the pale young waiter would always try to usher me to one of the tables nearer the window.

Despite my hunger I would hold off as with a certain deliberate and overbearing courtesy he laid out the standard spread of hummus, pickled beets, olives and radishes, careful never to leave too much of the white damascene cloth showing, and even when he brought the Shish'Taouk on its bed of steaming saffron rice the uneaten dishes remained to cover the empty sections of the table. The meat would catch momentarily on the skewer as I pushed impatiently with the fork, then come away softly, slipping down to form a rough cairn over the rice. Under the charred crust there was the sudden whiteness of the flesh, the sweet juices running over the gums and tongue, and I would close my eyes and see again the heraldic blue of the sky and the terraced hills and the distant margin of the sea, all that could never change there, and when I had finished and the pale boy wheeled over the trolley with the small glass bowls of milk pudding topped with rose syrup and pistachios reflecting infinitely back in the

16

mirrored sides of the tray I would wave him off before he came too close for I wanted nothing to take away the taste of what I had just eaten.

Sometimes I returned to the Al-Bustan in the evenings, though not to the restaurant itself. There was a bar upstairs with a late licence, and its own small entrance on to the street, a narrow cavernous room with low banquettes tricked out in mother-of-pearl, tinted mirrors along the walls, the bar area set back in a rustically plastered surround hung all year with fairy-lights and tinsel. The place was popular at weekends with Maronite businessmen and late-night drinkers back from the clubs, a trio of belly-dancers laid on for the brisker hours; on good nights they could collect up to a monkey in tips so they liked to have a driver they were used to. Most of them were Argentinians and Brazilians, not Arabs, but they looked the part, with spangles on their cheeks, long false eyelashes, rhinestone bikinis with long fringes and beaded tassels which rustle under their plastic mackintoshes as they come out to the car. Some of the girls would work several clubs in one evening, and often they would want me to wait for them outside before driving them back to the flats they shared in Bayswater and North Kensington.

The sun has risen, dispelling the last skeins of mist from the drive. Leighton stands at the window, the hard winter light through the woollen blanket over the blinds. He shivers, and hugs his shoulders.

Outside the traffic is hardly moving. I hear the grating of awnings, the soft thud of plaster on a full skip, the clack-clack of heels down by the bus-stop. Verger with his back to the window, the deep cope of his anorak up against the light.

'He never come when you watching.' Verger does not look up from the tangle of his fingers.

'But that's just a superstition.' In Leighton's parched whisper, a note of reproach, as if he were reminding himself of what he would later forget. He steps back from the window.

Down on the drive the blistered shale has begun to show again through the melted slush, like something coming slowly into focus. Through the blanket, the wedge of light falls over the rutted surface of the carpet, the dog-eared pages of the books on the floor, the mug-rings on their jackets. This was the hour I would come in from my shift. Through the open door, Leighton nodding over the fire, on the floor the cigarettes and papers I had brought in the previous morning, and softly I would pad back along the unlit passage to my room where on the bedside table I kept the clock turned upside-down, but I have not gone to work since Ali appeared to me seven days ago in the snowbound cemetery. I have remained within the confines of the house and yard, and I have fasted, taking only salt and water, and every second day an unleavened pitta heated on the Belling. I have shaved my head, using Leighton's cut-throat on the back and nape when I had run out of blades, the nicks clown-red with Mercurochrome through the thin black silk of the band Ali left knotted on the aerial, the dome of the scalp rising with a low sheen like egg-white into the only mirror above the basin, and on the brighter days I can see the faint lines of old scars that might always have remained hidden, and under the skin the black pinheads of hairs that will never grow again.

After the audience with Ali was over I had gone back and parked the car outside the garage at the end of the row of railway arches, leaving the keys behind the fender on the driver's side, the standing arrangement already agreed with

Jawad's Tehrani contact at the Husseinya. Over the course of the week they will have packed ninety kilos of Hexogen under the boot and along the drive-shaft and under the cylinder-block, binding it on with gaffer-tape, distributing the weight evenly so the chassis does not sag, the blue strips of jeta-sheet fusing linked from the engine casing to a switch under the console. I will find the car early tomorrow morning on the forecourt of the service-station below the house, but I will be in no condition to write then, and so I make my testimony now, while I have the strength.

I had never had to pick up from the cemetery before, though I had wandered over there often enough in the summer when Leighton camped out with his pipe and books in the long grass behind the church; in these months the gates were kept locked because of vandals, and it was hard to grip the old stones through the toadfoot and bindweed and drop blindly into the thicket of brambles and weeds which concealed the low iron-railings, but after coming in like this a few times Leighton had shown me how the pennant above Burton's tomb jutted over the wall at a place where the earth beyond was clear and giving to land on.

But that evening I realized I had forgotten which side the official entrance was, and I had to circle the church several times before I found it. As I went around I was held up in the traffic through the narrow lanes. The first snow had fallen that afternoon, but already it had begun to settle over the pavements and the parked cars, and the streets seemed that much darker for its sullen glare.

When I found the entrance it was off to the left of the church, beside a sort of cottage-orné, half-timbered, its gables swollen by the thickening snow. I suppose I had expected to find someone waiting, a widow come to lay fresh flowers, an old couple huddled in their coats after mass, but there was nobody by the gate, and I had tipped the seat back and read the paper again, the engine running, the headlamps on. But at some point I must have fallen asleep, and when I opened my eyes the motor had cut out, and the interior of the car was cold, and only the dim outline of the gatehouse was visible outside. As I started the engine the lights came up again, and I saw him, standing out in the snow, beneath the flint wall of the apse.

I slapped myself a couple of times on the cheek, then rubbed with my cuff at the inside of the windscreen. But this only made the figure appear more clearly, and he began walking slowly towards the car, and as he came closer I saw that the snow had hardly settled on his shoulders and over his beard.

I always lock the doors when I am alone in the car, but when I turned to pull up the lock I found that he was already sitting in the back. I was so struck through with fear that I could not make my mouth form words, but he reached his hand into the space above the gear, and when I kissed his fingers they were smooth and warm like polished olive-wood left out in the sun.

He sat in the back in such a way that I could not see his reflection in the rear-view mirror, my breathing so heavy that the surface of the mirror had condensed over. When I looked around he was sitting close up to the window, staring out into the darkness, and there was no moisture on the glass beside his face. He did not seem to feel the cold, though he was dressed for summer, his café-crème safari-suit with its buttoned-down epaulettes bringing up the sheen of an old tan and the scarlets of his paisley cravat. He had always worn the simplest clothes, but now he was got up like something out of

Somerset Maugham, though at the time I cannot say I saw anything strange in this.

We drove back towards town. All the while he was drawing softly on a pipe which he did not pass into the front. On each occasion that I had steadied myself enough to speak, the thick smoke caught in my throat, and I could not get the words out. Ali had never been to London, and yet this man had an exact knowledge of the streets, and pointed the way down short-cuts and rat-runs which had taken me years to discover.

Within a quarter of an hour we had reached the lower end of the Brompton Road. I rarely came to this part of town now. That must have been why it always looked the same, like a vacant set awaiting the next period production, an inscrutable rigour to the high windows, the clipped spheres of the bay trees, the lustre of black railings against the snow.

We drove across one side of the square. The far end was taken up by a private garden, with wooden benches around a small green and an en-tout-cas court, the net and posts rolled up under the wire fence. At the corner an unlighted house, the curtains drawn, the snow not yet cleared from the steps up to the door, beside the far wall an alley leading through an arch to the cobbled mews behind.

It was here he told me to cut the engine, his hand raised to the house above. I had turned the heater up full, but was still shivering as he walked out into the snow, and stood at the foot of the steps.

By the railings, a long stone trough, and below the door a box tree, and two untrimmed bays. I watched him place his hand into the trough, and cast a rain of pebbles up into the shadows of the porch, and from his jacket he drew out a blade, and crouching on the steps he cut down the box tree, and the two bays, their lopped heads drifting out into the snow.

My breath had clouded the windscreen again, and when I rubbed away the moisture he was no longer standing below the porch, but I thought I could see the outline of a figure moving up on the rooftop, stepping along the slates in the lee of the gables, and in the house beneath a deep glowing crimson though all the curtains were tightly drawn, the windows lit up like a paper lantern, and then the figure was lost, above the dark ridges of the chimney-stacks a bright cinder rising slowly into the snow-grey night.

By the sign of the pebbles, and the sign of the fallen trees, he had shown this house of the writer to be a cursed and unclean house, haram, for on the plain of Badr the Prophet had cast pebbles at the tribe of Quraysh, and cut down the palms before the fortress of Nadar. In this house the writer had mocked the customs of his fathers, and aped the manners of his conquerors, and betrayed the religion of the Prophet, and forgotten the tongue of his people. The fruit of the groves and orchards of his fathers was lost in the sweet vapours of his pipe, and the labours of the fellahin and aghas on the lands of his forefathers spent in forgotten nights of pleasure, and among his company of flatterers and revellers he was reckoned the sleekest pig in the sty, and when his lands were wasted he had lived from the coining of base jests and by making an entertainment of the sufferings and foibles of his people, and as his people were hunted down like rats and the world turned its back he had hidden himself in the study of idols and painted illusions, and when his groves and orchards were felled by his enemies he had abandoned himself to the kayf and fannas of his pipe, and as his city burnt he lost each night in dancing and his days in idle reveries.

I walked out along the frozen pavement, and stood below that rooftop from which the bright cinder had risen into the sky, and high over the square the sky rent suddenly like a sheet in passion, and from the gash of light the great golden escalator of the miraj was brought down to my feet, and I was lifted up, and from its wide steps I looked down on the house of the writer, and the glow within had grown brighter, its walls of fire, all within a crucible of molten brass, and foundering on that burning sea a man in rods of iron, his garments of fire, his only food that of the zaqquam tree whose fruits are the heads of demons which devour the bellies of those who eat them from within, and over that cursed sea the scorched pages spun and eddied in the parching winds like embers over an autumn fire.

The miraj lifted me over oceans and mountains and wastes of sand and above the plains of Kerbala, the high dunes sown with the sun-blanched bones of the martyrs, and I was brought down among a grove of palms. I wandered in the shade of a single and boundless tree. I saw the boughs laden with giant pomegranates, grapes fat as melons, dates broad as breadfruit, and the branches bowed down to the hands of those who passed beneath, and from the fruits of the tree burst silken robes and dressed fowls and beasts richly bridled, and the soft grasses in its shade were watered by streams of milk and wine and honey and the pebbles in the fountains of coral and emerald. The spreading of this tree was so great that the freshest relay of horses would not span its shade in a hundred years, and the roots of the tree were set among the high pavilions of the Prophet on the mountain. On the gentle slopes of thornless sidr and talh I saw the dark-eyed houris with cheeks as pale as the buried eggs of ostriches bearing the fruits and waters of the streams in ewers of gold, and though these groves cast a dark penumbra my eyes were not able to withstand the radiance that rose from the thrones on the higher reaches of the mountain, and I turned back to the lower gardens of roses and jasmine, and wandered through the wilderness of palmettos and wisteria and ruined pergolas to the clearing in the orchard where Harun and Asad are waiting still, their pockets heavy with the shrapnel and cartridges they have brought up as gifts from the camp, and we tumble through the wild poppies and lilac and chase through the high grass of the terraces to the spring in the hollow where Layla squats with her comics under the willows, and the boys lie naked in the shallow stream, and from behind the bank I watch her eyes through the damp strands of her fringe peering out over the valley as if she had once lost something there, down along the road winding through the olive orchards.

In the pale light under the window, Leighton studies the surface of each square, a relief map of clefts and wrinkles.

His palms, the tips of his fingers. Black from the burnt underside of the silver-foil, as if he had been giving prints. He drops the crumples back on to the rug.

His face to the blinds, dark whirls of snow-damp along the empty drive.

Below the window, the old woollen blanket with crests sown into the corners drawn up to his chin, his head bowed, the room still, only the dickering of the fire, shadows flinching from the hardening light through the blinds, and if I close my eyes I can hear above the more constant hum of the traffic vague clutches of the distant call of a muezzin carrying through the keen winter air from somewhere towards Mortlake, long recorded syllables drifting unheeded over the slate roofs, container depots, frozen streets, lost to the gonging of scaffolding as the builders start up across the way.

Aaal-lah -a -aa Akbar . . . Aaaal-ah -aa-Akkbar
    Wa-ah Muhammaa-d rasuu-ullillah Ima shaha-ada
    Rassuu-ullillah

From the tea-chest I take the straw mat, the thick twine of the compass I have bought from the camping-centre rubbing my nape, my eyes unfocusing at first from the fast, from the slippery linoleum of the stairs through the rotten door into the back yard; on the face of the compass, the flèche-point. I brush a clearing in the frozen slush, roll out the straw.

Over the walls there are sodden espaliers with nothing growing on them, and dried trails from the overflow drains, pigeons on the sheltered window-ledges with feathers ruffled against the cold. Before I had the compass I would ask Leighton who knows most things to point me in the right direction, and he would stand shivering in his ragged dressing-gown among the dead plants on the glassed-in porch, and hold out his bony arm towards the chicken-wire fence, his hand jerking like a water-diviner while I aligned the axis of the mat.

Out here I can hear the traffic more, and as I kneel the dampness seeps up through my jeans, but I no longer feel the cold. Once the garden of the house would have run right down to the spreading beeches at the bottom of the bank where now there are narrow allotments between sheds with tarred roofs and a row of lock-up garages, the backs of which form one end of the lower part of the yard, a crust of pigeon droppings and dank moss over the wall that never sees the sun, thick creepers hanging from the silted guttering above, but I do not look there until I have completed the sura of Qadr, and three times the sura of Dawn, and then only into the middle thicket which holds within its dark and errant terminus a figure of the long-ordained deliverance begun that night three years before when I had stopped at the roadblock south of Sabra on my way down from the mountains . . . For weeks there had been no petrol in the western sector, but I still had supplies hidden under the duckboards in the pool-house and had let a couple of the boys waiting at the Amal checkpoint siphon from the cap-hole. Squatting in the road, they had sucked on the rubber pipes to bring the fuel up, grinning as they spat on to the ground. There had been shelling again that day, old women carrying the bodies on planks and broken doors covered in sheets of polythene towards the market, only a few generators still working on rue Bustani and I had not noticed the mass of silent young men walking from the direction of the ruined stadium, holding up flags and hastily made placards illegible in the half-light of the street. Carrying the bottles high over their heads, the boys had disappeared into the crowd, and as I edged the car away I could see the fires being lit. All the parks and the pine forests around the hippodrome had been stripped years before, and yet these were the flames of wood burning.

I stopped for a moment, and looked back, a group of Isfahani workers from the Makassed hospital lowering card-board crates from the loading-step of their aid truck, the books all with the same cover, pages ruffling and snapping in the wind off the empty beach, and the books burnt well, throwing up banners of light against the pocked walls, single sheets rising, dancing above the shuddering of the fire, the young men drawing back from the heat, shooting off tracer into the darkness, above their shaven heads like a buoy on troubled waters, a giant effigy whose face I could not see, bobbing uncertainly towards the flames.

Already the faces of the martyrs are beginning to fade from the giant hoardings that stand at even intervals along the cratered roads that lead south from Tyre and Tibnine into the abandoned villages of the borderland. The sun has taken the hectic bloom from their cheeks, blanched away the darkness from their hair, from their young beards. They could almost be Europeans now, their features rendered with the same cheap panache as the film-stars on the billboards along rue Hamra, calloused with rust, blistered by the heat, and like sunflowers tired of time the heads sag down over the dry earth. Soon they will be uprooted to make way for the bright emblems of soft drinks and engine-oils whose foreign colours fade more slowly, as have the portraits of the martyrs in the southern suburbs where there is no sleep for the gnawing of bulldozers through the humid nights, the sky barred with cranes and girders and the streets filled with dust and the cries of the workmen who once fought over these same shelled-out lots where the ruined walls still bear the faces of martyrs framed by garlands of roses and jasmine and black tulips, at their shoulders the streams and fountains of paradise and in their eyes the high pavilions.

I look down into the Perspex casing of the compass. There is my dim reflection, as if in a puddle or pavement, but I cannot see it well on a shattered wall among fountains and black tulips, a comical imposture there, as if at one of those seaside stands I had put my face to the body of Winston Churchill or Elvis Presley.

When I get up my head swims. I reach out my arm, steady myself against the rotten trellis.

An even light through the dust on the bookcase, on the foxing of the wallpaper. Leighton crouches by the fire, the blanket over the blinds. His feet on the tea-chest, Verger slouched low in the armchair, a half-drunk mug of tea at his side. Under the lee of the wall the snow still lies thick, the slush on the street not yet melted, and above the heads of the workmen on the scaffolding the sun has risen silver-white through the mist. It will be a fine day.

III

Last night I had another strange dream.

For several years I had been writing a play about the civil war, villages were divided against villages, brothers against brothers, no savagery perpetrated without the sanction of religion, enemies intimates, and intimates enemies, each man a stranger to himself.

But as the performance of the first night was about to begin I had tried to rise from my seat in the wings to give some final word of encouragement to one of the actors only to find I had been gagged, my hands and feet bound to the chair. And above the footlights there suddenly appeared a garish marionette, his features not entirely dissimilar to those of my own person, his limbs shaking and twisting to the evident amusement of the audience.

The footlights went down, the curtains rose, but still this figure did not leave the stage. He held the attention of all the house, swaggering and blaspheming and uttering every profanity like the good clown he was.

With every shake and swagger the audience became more fractious, and desperately I signalled to the stage-hands in the wings, but they too had eyes only for the puppet, and it was not long before I began to nourish a great hatred for this mechanical which had provoked such disorder in the house.

Finally I managed to free myself from the fetters, and rushed out on to the stage. As I pulled the thing down the audience hooted and bayed and in my anger I broke its limbs and trod them into the boards and stamped on the glass eyes, and as I did so the crowd beat drums and fired fusillades into the ceilings and in the confusion old enemies took every opportunity to snipe at each other across the theatre.

But then the lights went down, the curtains fell, and lifted, and I saw that I was bowing low. And as I left the stage, the playwright rose from his seat in the wings, and came out to enjoy his share of the applause, and as we passed he patted me on the head. 'Well done, old boy,' he said, 'you played that little part convincingly tonight.'

For many centuries the royal courts maintained ape-houses and menageries of wild beasts. So our narrow littoral has long been indulged by the world: a memento of the savagery to which man may revert. But in a land from which the basest has always been expected, acts and events which elsewhere provoke outrage and alarm soon pass entirely unremarked. Prophets, generals, Caesars, saints, all have long been forgotten, their memories effaced by the march of pimps, playboys, traffickers, warlords, militiamen, our cradling of mysteries and religions reduced to the faith that war and poverty are step-mothers to the mullahs, arid soils bearing poisoned blooms, but I will witness that my own conversion has been the only child of fate, and my own poverty a most recent circumstance.

I had returned to London with no money after the war, and had avoided all my old acquaintances. Within days of my return Salah at the Husseinya had arranged for me to work several shifts a week at Excelsior Cars in Turnham Green to supplement my benefit payments. To begin with I had been convinced that one night I would find myself picking up someone I had known in the old days, but this fear had passed as the months went by.

At the communal house in Ealing I had only to contribute a small amount each week towards food and bills, and at Leighton's I took care of the gas and electricity, to keep them connected, but there was no rent to pay. Jawad and Salah and the others at the mosque did not like to use the telephone, and so it hardly mattered that Leighton had refused to have the payphone repaired down in the hall.

It was not until the last year of the war that my father had finally severed the drip-feed of an allowance that had sustained me through almost a decade of occasional and underpaid jobs in the art world. When I had been in London I had made my withdrawals from a bank in Hanover Square where he had set up an account in my name for this purpose. The sum would differ from quarter to quarter as a result of the arcane inflationary calculus devised by his accountant who administered these payments from Douglas on the Isle of Man. At home in Beirut I would have to arrange for the sum to be telexed through to whichever of the banks was working on the headland that month, and go with Jaffer and two of his gunboys to make the withdrawal, always concealing the money in a different place when I returned to the house, though sometimes I would forget where I had hidden the envelope, and I would have to search for hours through all the cubby-holes and hollows I had constructed down the years.

Our contacts had been whittled down to almost nothing in the end. In the last years of the war the telephone rarely worked at home, and he had never kept up with the changing numbers at the Bey's house off the Brompton Road where I had always stayed when in London. He would send cards, one on my birthday, and another at the Christian new year, but due to the vagaries of the wartime post these would come at moments remote from the event in question, as if I were now living by some long-extinct calendar, so late sometimes that they would seem almost premature.

The cards themselves were in the American style, with photographs of the new family set into a laminated surround, on the inside a page of gushing commentary on the progress of my half-siblings through summer camps and grade-school; sometimes there would be the same photograph on both cards, but faintly different news; they must have sent the same picture to all their friends; usually they would be posed on an open verandah, in descending order of height, though once or twice the shot had been taken down at a marina, with them all got up a little self-consciously in Keds and windcheaters and floppy caps ringed with nautical motifs, tritons and anchors and knots, the children hanging goofily off one of the struts to the side, or squatting low on the sun-dappled boards, coiled to spring once more into their own unpausing world. I kept these cards, but rarely looked at them; they would travel with me through the roadblocks and the museum-crossing and through the lunacy of the airport, and back again.

There was something almost self-effacing about how tanned my father had become, his burnished face an easy match for the recreational tones of the polo shirts she had gradually eased him into over the years. Beside his learnt informality there would always be a hint of unfamilial elegance in the way she came across; despite the heat she kept up a tailored, buttoned-in discipline about herself, with studiedly expressionless make-up, halter-tops with high roll-necks, skirts that fitted closely while at the same time appearing strangely demure: she had that knack some women have of seeming perennially fashionable without ever altering their style, and of wearing tight clothes and giving nothing away. Sometimes when I looked into the photographs I would wonder if she was not unfaithful to him in some systematic, brutal way he would never know about. I pictured her assiduously using up his absences, waiting, all pinched and pent-up as he fumbled in the driveway with his books and faded lecture notes.

He wrote the cards in English now, though the grand diagonals and lateral flourishes betrayed the animus of the hand I recognized. Elaine and the kids added their names at the bottom, out of scale and at acute angles to the page, as if they were signing autographs. Sometimes he would enclose a cheque, written on their joint account, but I had never opened a dollar account, and so I would have to make it over to Jaffer or one of the Armenians with their insolent rates of commission still operating on rue Bliss.

I had never resented my father's lack of communication; even in later years when it had just come down to the quarterly payments and the cards and the occasional phatic exchanges over a bad line I could never hold it against him for he had behaved in such a way that it had always seemed that his long disengagement had only tactfully mimed those sleights by which I had slowly slipped the knot of his care. In the years when I was still at school in England after my mother's death it had not been convenient for us to see very much of each other. During the holidays the increasing student unrest on campus had made it difficult for him to give me his full attention, though he had done his utmost to keep me diverted when I returned home, buying a television and taking me twice a week to the latest American films at the cinemas on rue Hamra, and at the weekends to the old picnic spots in the mountains.

When I got back for the summer he was always there waiting at the terminal, and it would be that time in July when he had begun to wear his seersucker suits again, and I would feel strange hugging him now that I was almost his height. By then he was using his driver less, my corduroys and school shirt sweaty against the hot leather as he revved and changed gears clumsily on the journey back into town so that I could pick up whatever I needed before we took the coast road down to the summer house in the hills above Sidon where Uncle Samir and his younger second wife were living all the year round since the shipping business had failed.

The semester was already over, and the house near the campus had been closed for the summer. When we reached the drive he would wait with the engine idling in the shade of the carob trees as I ran up along the verandah with the keys. It would be dark and cool inside, the furniture shuffled out of its usual places so that I would let my eyes adjust to the half-light before making my way through the dim outlines of the dustsheets smelling faintly of naphthalene. The rugs had been taken up and rolled in the attics until the end of the summer, and everywhere on the bare marble floors there were the thin white spirals of the poison left down for the brown-tail caterpillars, like atolls on a still sea, and all the doors to the bedrooms off the corridor would be locked except mine.

The room would be as I had left it, but things dominated there which I had never really used, above the wardrobe the thick wedge of the surfboard, the tennis and paddle rackets in the wicker basket by the door, the faint embarrassment of the posters, past attributes of a youth that had never happened quite that way, like visiting the house of some historical personage and finding the study filled with improbable pipes and spectacles, the books open at the likely passages.

Never knowing what to bring, I would gather up tapes, the air-rifle, alligator shirts and flip-flops, and hurry back through the empty rooms, over the darkened walls the white light through the slats of the shutters like the filigrees of some vast ornamental cage, and out again into the bright afternoon, the car waiting under the carob trees.

It would be evening when we reached the village in the hills. Fireflies on the unlit drive, the murmuring of cicadas on the dark lawns. Aunt Mona would already be in bed, on the porch Uncle Samir waiting with the hurricane lamp, his breath heavy with garlic and arak. When he held my father there would be tears in his eyes, and tired from the journey I would fall asleep in my clothes to the hum of the press turning down in the valley.

The house was large, with nowhere comfortable to settle, dark passages smelling of damp chalk and boiled beets leading out from the diwan to the kitchens and the sleeping quarters where all the windows were locked and taped over because of Aunt Mona's asthma. The diwan was still hung with the old bokharas and salvers and Berber rifles from Ottoman times, in the alcoves precarious arrangements of dried gourds, at the centre the dry basalt fountain with the spouts set into the mouths of carved lions whose gaping eyes had frightened me when I was younger, though this room was never used to sit in, but as a junction to the other parts of the house which had been filled up with all the furniture Uncle Samir had brought back from the city.

Their old maid Zainab had also come down with them from Beirut as Aunt Mona had refused to have any of the village girls in the house, and all day she would shuffle from room to room dusting the mother-of-pearl settles and the puce upholstery of the empire chairs which stood in un-homely ranks over the worn tiled floors like pieces waiting to be auctioned off, and in the hot afternoons she went out and cut down any wild flowers that were encroaching on the house, though sometimes she would sneak sprays of barwaq into my room, and their heady scent would linger on there until the end of the summer.

After a week my father would leave again for his lecture tour in America, and a restless silence would descend on the house broken only by the shudder of the tractors coming up from the fields and the high-pitched squabbling of Zainab and the Maronite cook Khalil who suffered from ulcers and paced about in the vine-covered yard outside the kitchens to escape the fumes of his own cooking. Aunt Mona and Uncle Samir slept in different rooms, and during the day my uncle would keep to his own wing of the house where he constructed his model triremes from matchsticks and balsa-wood while listening in to Radio Monaco and the World Service. I would rarely see Aunt Mona except at mealtimes when my uncle wearing his tweed jacket and double-knotted woollen tie despite the heat would patiently await her entrance while the food grew tepid on the hot-plate. She came to the table sore-eyed and heavily made-up, remote and dopey from the antihistamine, in different clothes for every meal, slacks and cashmere cardigans at lunch, though never the same pairing, and in the evenings long silk dresses and pale waisted kaftans, a large man's handkerchief like some monstrous growth tucked in above the elbow.

After dinner they would sit together beside the deep fireplace filled with arrangements of dried reeds and gourds, and over their liqueurs play silent games of polyglot Scrabble and read back-copies of *An Nahar* and *Paris-Match* which

Khalil brought up from the seafront hotel in Sidon, and Aunt Mona always turned in first, bending to let my uncle kiss her on the forehead before walking slowly back to her room.

Having been brought up a martyr to the social isolationism of her family Aunt Mona had adapted naturally to this solitary and withdrawn life; while it was customary for old Levantine clans to claim some tenuous descent from one of the crusader dynasties, her family had always maintained their stemma had remained untainted by crusader blood and mixed only in the most circumscribed circles, and even before the collapse of his company had never quite approved of the match with my uncle despite my father's position at the university and the growing political influence of our cousin the Bey. But if Uncle Samir missed his cronies at the yacht club, his lunches at the St Georges and the Bristol, he rarely let it show, humming and grinning through his empty days as if this country retreat was something he had long been looking forward to.

In the mornings I would sit with my schoolbooks in one of the cool alcoves in the diwan, and in the hot afternoons lie out in the long grass behind the dusty planes and date-palms which lined the seaward side of the drive up from the village road. From here the wrought-iron pergola led down to the paved terrace overlooking the coast, but the way was blocked by a thicket of acacias and spiked palmettos, and I would have to clamber along the fallen-away edges of the hill to reach the far promontory which had never been completed after the land beneath had been sold off.

Through the drooping wisteria over the pergola I could look across the old mulberry terraces where the quinces and pomelos which Uncle Samir had planted to sell to the restaurants in the city had not taken, down to the road and over the last of the olive groves to Abu Musa's hut. There was little to watch on the road, just the tractors bringing up the dried tobacco sheaves, and the black Lincoln of our cousin the Bey trailing its clouds of dust up to his house above the village, and at weekends the tourist bus climbing slow as a blindworm around the hills.

Sometimes the bus would pause at the turn above the house so the tourists could take photographs of the prospect over the orchards to the coast. The view was actually better a little further up from above the village, but the driver would no longer stop there since the fellahin women had begun to surround the bus selling shawls, straw hats and pickled fruits, Ali and the other boys spitting and flinging pebbles down from the steps of the mosque.

From the cover of the dried tobacco sheaves carried from his grandfather's hut beyond the river it was Ali who had always cast the first stone, his older brother Jaffer and the other boys following with their volleys of watermelon-skins and pebbles before sloping back into the shadows of the sandstone porch.

When he heard the bus Uncle Samir would go up through the garden gate above the kitchens and invite all the tourists in for coffee. While Aunt Mona hid in her rooms, these elderly ruddy-faced Americans and Scandinavians would troop across the vine-covered yard into the diwan where Zainab brought the squared-off rows of demitasses and the plates of baclava and chopped nougat with pistachio on an unwieldy brass salver which none of the visitors would ever help her with. Some wandered around peering intently at all the frowsty furnishings as if they were in a museum, while others would look for price tags, no doubt suspecting that Uncle Samir and the driver were in league to fleece them.

Most of the tourists seemed bewildered as Uncle Samir

38

went round at the end with his folder, showing them the names of all the young men who had emigrated from our village over the years and never been heard of again; the black-and-white photographs, where they existed, pasted underneath, some going back to the twenties, small and indistinct, cut out like paper dolls, others circled within stiff family groups, wide-eyed and hopeful, with moustaches waxed for the occasion. When they saw the folder many of the tourists would head straight back to the bus, presuming it was some kind of trick to get money out of them, though some would attempt to be helpful and give the addresses of local congressmen and church groups.

When I was younger I had tried to devise ways of profiting from these weekly invasions. If no one was looking I would pick on an old couple and offer to guide them for a small consideration to a secret statue in the lower gardens, but once I had taken the money I would run away over the drive and hide in the clearing at the end of the promontory. From here I could see the whole coast laid out beneath me like a vast map of itself. The hills hatched with the ruts of the dried wadis reaching across to the Palestinian camp of Ein Helweh like a great quarry scar, their folds betraying the sunken course of the Awali down from the milky turban of the mountain and the falls at Jazzin to the distant shadow of the lemon and orange orchards above Sidon, the dark huddle of the town over the thin claw of the mole, off the refinery to the south the tankers no more than black pin-pricks on the silver ribbon of the sea.

Before I was born we had owned strips of land right the way down to the sea road, zucchini, maize and sunflower fields worked by sharecroppers and fellahin from the village, but now most of the sahel was given over to cashcrops, the polythene-covered runs of tomatoes, peanuts, carrots grown by cultivators from the town using chemical fertilizers, and since the collapse of the company many of the groves around the house had been sold to our cousin the Bey, but from the hidden promontory it all still looked the same. The white walls of the terraces, the white earth. The sahra huts between the olive trees, and further up the tobacco plots on the hills.

In the early summer the limestone mountain over the village became charged with the heat of the high sun and as the parched air rose from the white earth and the wadis, the cool westerlies blew in from the sea through the willows in the valley and the poplars and the tall date-palms along the drive, down in the fields the winnowing-frames like giant tambourines against the windbreaks. Within a week the skies were empty of colour and clouds, and the dry trade winds drove up from the southern deserts and chafed the hills, and it would be as if everything had slept too long and woken with sand in its eyes, leaves and glass and lips all coated in a fine layer of dust, and in the fellahin quarter they would hang wet sheets over the windows and the boys would run naked in the shallow stream, and in the village they called this wind the cleaver.

Sometimes in the high summer the sharqiyah blew through the mountains from the Syrian deserts, gusty and bitter like the blast from a lime kiln, chasing the dead leaves and tumbleweed up the steps of the mosque, and sucking the sap from the baladi and the tobacco plots on the hills.

The clouds did not return again until the Nile broke its banks at the close of the summer, high and lonely at first like stray weather balloons, and then it would not be long before the wet maritime winds would carry in from far over the Atlantic, the black cloud-banks over the mountain bringing the first of the rains, the water seeping down though the porous limestone and out through the hilltop springs to irrigate the olive and tobacco terraces, the surviving clouds drifting eastwards across the deserts to break over the green mountains of Oman. With the rains came the first teeming flights of white storks and rose-coloured starlings following the line of the coast from the north and the slow-flying button-quails whose call was like dripping water and the hoopoes with their horned crests nesting in the drainage-holes under the road to the village, and on the telegraph wires and the plane trees along the drive the little bee-eaters perching like targets in a fairground range, their white eggs buried in the sandy banks of the stream below the village where the boys from the mosque would always find them.

When the clouds lifted I went out to the promontory and watched the distant vapour-trails of the Phantoms over the camps to the south slowly dissolving into the darkening sky like sperm into water, and as the light faded over the valley I would remember the angel Azrael who had fetched the seven clods of earth from which man was framed and had parted the souls from the bodies, and suddenly I was afraid, and I would run back into the silent diwan and play forfeits until the fear had passed.

IV

If I climbed down through the olive terraces below the promontory and walked upstream along the half-dry bed between the hills I could reach the village without being seen from the house. Uncle Samir had never liked me going up to the village, and now that I was older he had made it clear that he thought it no longer appropriate for me to be seen roaming around the orchards like one of the village boys.

During previous summers on the cooler days I had been allowed to go down through the terraces to the warehouse where they kept the electrical olive-press and up as far as the ridge of tobacco plots below Abu Musa's hut, but no higher than the first turn in the river-bed, although I always went on to the lower edges of the village, and sometimes further up to the hill above the mosque. Zainab would not let me leave before I had taken a supply of pittas and sambusek-pastries stuffed with warmed cheese, and setting out with this gingham wrap tied to the olive-staff over my shoulder I would feel like some pantomime Dick Whittington, and discard it once I was out of sight of the kitchen garden. But now there was the expectation that I should stay up by the house and spend at least the mornings studying; I had assured Uncle Samir that none of the other boys in England would open a single book throughout the holidays, but he had taken this as the ruse of a slacker and at every meal he would bark through his sea-dog beard about the cost of the school fees and my mother's unbetrayable wishes and so whenever I went into the gardens I had to take the Kennedy's Longer and Loeb cribs and as the summer wore on the print faded in the sun and the pages became brittle and calloused in the winds, and through all the year to come I would keep their ruin close to me.

When I came down from the last terrace to the river-bed I would shake off my sandals and walk barefoot over the warm rocks, keeping to the middle where the current still flowed. In the shadows of the willows the surface of the water was sticky-black, puckered by the flitting insects, nearer the banks the dead pools swarming with flies, but above there were more willows and the water ran quicker and deeper at the place where the village boys came when the sand winds blew, and higher up the river crossed the old road at a shallow ford where the fellahin women brought their bright washing under the shade of the eucalyptus trees with peeling barks white as rice-powder.

If I saw smoke before I reached the ford I would clamber up to Abu Musa's hut through the terraces of dead mulberries, and as I climbed above the first turn of the river I could see down to the shadow-lines of the gangling poplars on the plain, the cattle cropping the fields after the harvest, between the hills the shimmer of the new asphalt road. Beyond the first of the tobacco plots the roofless shells of the old cocooneries which I would hurry past holding my nose though the stench of the rotting worms were only a memory now, the broken stone walls encrusted with the hardened droppings of the small black bird the villagers called the tatmuos which would come up in the autumn from the cold fields to nest among the ruins.

The hut was taller than it appeared from the river below, the earth floor streaked with the thin lines of sunlight through the walls of roughly matted straw, the sloping corrugated-iron roof hung with the drying tobacco sheaves. Sometimes Ali and Jaffer would come to help their grandfather thread the floppy leaves on to the iron skewers before they were bound and hoisted up to the hooks on the roof, but that year I never found them at the hut, though I continued to walk up the river-bed every couple of days hoping that I might. Ali must have been fifteen that summer, and already he was sitting apart from the other boys we would pass on the steps of the mosque as we drove up to the house of the Bey above the village, reading in the shade of the sandstone porch or staring out to where the river disappeared between the hills, and Jaffer had begun to spend his days helping his father up at the hidden plots on the mountain, though sometimes I would see the trail of dust from his scooter as he headed down to the coast, the sideburns he had copied from the gangster films like inverted commas around the mask of keffieh and dark glasses, his billowing shirt open to the waist, the sheen of his platform boots flickering in the sinking sun.

When he heard my call from the doorway Abu Musa would come out from the back of the dark hut, slowly parting a way for himself between the long strings of dead leaves, like an actor emerging between curtains and drops, and I would not know what to do with my hand after he had kissed it, sensing it would be rude to put it straight back into my pocket, but wanting to rub away the tingle from his bristles. I would sit on the straw stool and try not to stare as he brought through the green tea and the small glasses which were too hot to hold except by the uppermost rim. When I was younger Abu Musa had seemed like one of those fabled beings positioned by the ancients at the extremities of their world, and I had climbed up to the hut knowing I would be frightened by his oldness and the tic which shook his head so violently that I thought one day it would spin away still speaking across the floor, but to my disappointment this never happened though in later summers I would avoid watching him too closely because I did not want to believe that Ali and Jaffer would ever come to look as he did then, bent and broken-down, with burlaps of loose skin for a neck and the rutted cheeks beneath those burning, sunken eyes.

Seeing that I was hot and thirsty after the climb through the terraces he would carry the earthenware brek out from some shady place at the back of the hut, but Uncle Samir had made me promise that I would never drink unbottled water outside the house, and so I had always to refuse it, though I longed to lift the cool pitcher above my face and let the thin spurt of water play over my dust-crusted lips and eyes. But I would console myself with the cooling cadences of his voice as he told me all the old stories about his youth as a rat-catcher in the cellars of the Bey and the torchlit searches for the treasure of the caravans that had sunk under the marshes in the years before the coast road was built down on the sahel and the journey he had taken long ago to the land of the locusts where the women and children had bellies round as balloons and ate the grass and weeds in the fields and sold themselves to the beys for a single pail of milk, and as I listened to his tales I would not dare to look up higher than the baggy folds of his shirwal which he wore still in remembrance of the years when he had exercised the Bey's horses down on the plain and hunted gazelles and jackals and foxes and porcupines in the mountains with the old Bey who had died the week I was born though I felt I knew him all the same from the photographs that faced out to sea on the mantelpiece in the dining-room we no longer used where he stood at the median-point of every gathering in his tall tarboosh and pressed linen suit, his murafiqin and other followers a pace and a half behind, some in lesser tarbooshes, others in loose keffieh, all posing stiffly with their chests out as if lined up before a firing squad; Abu Musa must have been there somewhere in the back row, but I had never been able to pick him out.

When Abu Musa was no longer spry enough to hunt in the mountains and exercise the horses down on the sahel, he had been appointed by the Bey as an estate bailiff to weed out the cheats among the olive-grove watchmen and settle land disputes with the sharecroppers on the plain, but ever since the events of that year when there had been blood between his son Musa-al-Tango and the new Bey's murafiq he had been relieved of his duties and reduced to tending his smallholdings of tobacco and zucchini. On the day the new Bey had made Fawzi-from-the-mountains his murafiq over Musa-al-Tango there had been bad words between the two men under the old plane tree in the village square, but it was not until almost two years later that the incident would occur which all the village had come to view as the beginning of the conflict between their two houses.

In the week the inspector from the tobacco-regis came over from Nabatiyeh and sat on his three-legged stool on the steps of the mosque to price the loads that the smallholders brought in from the terraces Fawzi had been driving the Bey up the hill outside our drive when he had found the road blocked by Musa-al-Tango leading his ass heavily laden with the dried tobacco sheaves. There were certain sections of the hill where the width of a car almost exceeded that of the road and the driver would have to pull up over well-worn verges to pass the tractors and asses, but this was not one of these widened stretches, and Musa-al-Tango would later insist that the load

46

on his ass was so broad that there had not been sufficient ground to move aside.

We had heard the continuous hooting from the house, but there was nothing unusual in this as all the cars hooted as they went up the hill, and even when there were no obstructions the drivers of the few cars in the village who each had their own signature toot would sound their horns simply out of bravado and to signal to their friends and wives that they were drawing near, though Uncle Samir had repeatedly tried to put a stop to this noisome practice on account of Aunt Mona's nerves, and for a couple of weeks after he had raised the matter in the Husseinya we would hear only the tractors on the terraces and the turning of the press down in the valley.

On that afternoon the hooting had been followed by distant shouting, and then the reports of four rounds fired in quick succession, and a few moments later we had seen the ass of Musa-al-Tango running alone past the end of the drive with its load trailing behind in the dust. I was still only a young boy at the time and had never seen an ass trying to gallop, and I had begun to laugh until Uncle Samir shouted at me to keep quiet and rushed down to the road only to see the Lincoln passing by, and Musa-al-Tango running behind it, both his fists raised, cursing in a language I had never heard before.

It remains unclear whether Fawzi-from-the-mountains had been acting on the orders of the Bey when he had opened the window and fired under the hooves of the ass, but when the following night Musa-al-Tango found one of the hounds of the Bey in his store-room and shot it twice through the neck with his hunting-rifle, no one in the village was in any doubt as to what this act presaged. At the end of that week, the tenth day of the month of Muharram, all the men of the village commemorated the death of the martyr Husein on the plain of Kerbala by marching in white shrouds up from the square, the young fellahin striking themselves with knives and bi-cycle-chains in imitation of the sufferings of the martyrs, the women sitting on the walls, cooling them off with hoses and tending to their cuts with iodine, but that day no one from the house of Abu Musa came out to join the parade other than Ali who every year would watch from the branches of the plane tree over the square.

Towards nightfall a man in a white shroud was seen driving the Bey's John Deare seven times around the square and through the alleys above the mosque, drawing in his wake a bier of matted straw on which the dead dog lay. The tractor was followed by several of Fawzi's cousins who had come down from the high pastures for the march in the morning, and an excited column of fellahin and village boys. Within minutes of the procession arriving at the door of Abu Musa's house a scuffle had broken out between two of the cousins and a family of fellahin who they accused of stealing from their orchard on the Nabatiyeh road, and after some shots had been fired into the air and several windows broken the crowd had dispersed into the night.

For some weeks nothing further had happened, and many in the village had begun to hope that the matter would be forgotten. But then on a morning at the end of July one of the cousins from the mountain had been found lying face-down in the dry wadi above the turning to the sea road, bleeding from shots to his neck and jaw. Like Fawzi this cousin had a full moustache and wavy black hair, and always wore his sage-green hunting-jacket whatever the weather, but he had been a half-wit from birth, and barely able to feed himself, and had never posed a threat to anyone other than himself which was why he had never been allowed to carry a gun, and for several

48

years after the attack the Bey would pay for his treatment at the American University hospital, though he would never fully emerge again from his coma.

After Musa-al-Tango had fled, Fawzi-from-the-mountain and his cousins from the high pastures had let their herds loose over his maize fields on the plain, and burnt his crops at the threshing ground, and dumped rocks from the jurd on to his smallholdings below the village, and Abu Musa was too old to fight them off, and Ali and Jaffer still too young. Musa-al-Tango had returned from an exile of five years in Buenos Aires to find his family treated as outlaws within the village, avoiding the roads around the house of the Bey, working hidden plots of poppies in the rocky places on the mountain where only the blue irises and the stone-pines grew.

I had learnt a little Spanish at school, and sometimes when I came across Musa-al-Tango on the terraces below the village we would exchange a few words, though neither of us could penetrate far through the thickness of the other's accent, and so I would never understand his excitement when he whispered to me afterwards that this was our secret language in which one day he would disclose a truth that others would try to keep from me.

If I had left the house early enough so as not to be back late for the evening meal in the sealed dining-room I would carry on along the river-bed until I reached the ford, and then take the old road into the square in the lower part of the village. Before heading further into the village to search out Ali I would rest a while under the spreading plane whose silver-white leaves shaded most of the square. I would lie back on the rough bench nailed at the bottom and peer up through the blinding light above the holes in the trunk stopped with tar to prevent the hornets nesting and the sun-blanched posters of the Bey from the last election which no one ever took down and the branches higher up where the blooded bridal sheets were hung after a wedding in the village and over them the ceiling of silver-white leaves which shimmered like fish-scales even on the stillest days.

All but the highest branches had been blackened by the smoke from the sarj on the other side of the square where the village women baked their bread on thin iron trays over strips of smouldering broom. There among the mossy rocks beneath the level of the road was the spring where the few village cars were washed and the women filled their pitchers and jerry-cans and where towards nightfall the fellahin brought their fat-tailed sheep to be watered.

As I walked up I would pass the small hardboard kiosk, the two shelves at the back stacked with cigarettes, lighters and Chiclets; a large tin Pepsi sign over the roof, but no cold drinks within. In the shade of the plane tree behind the old men would sit out over their trictrac tables in the coolness of the wet street as the sweeper passed slopping out water from the sheepskin on his back. On my first visit to the village at the beginning of every summer they would all rise fractionally from their straw stools and salaam as I went by, but they did not acknowledge me until it was almost autumn again when they would stand up over the low olive-wood tables and call on Allah to protect me on my long journey to the north; to them I must have seemed like the kites and the swallows, a figment of the summer winds, my parting a harbinger of the hard winter to come.

To reach Ali's house I took the rutted chalk path that led along the nearer edge of the fellahin quarter. The first row of houses with unpainted breeze-block walls, most no more than a single room, with quilts and mattresses over the floor, a paraffin-stove against the rear wall, in the small yard a donkey or chickens, and plastered-mud vats for grain, meal and straw. Further up some of the houses had two storeys, and small balconies lined with geraniums in tin cans, through the open windows the smell of fried onions and coriander. Half-hidden in the shadows of the doorways young girls in long white scarves with faces pale as newly dug potatoes giggling shyly as I passed, but I never met anyone else on this stretch of the path. Most of the men in this quarter worked as hamals and mechanics down in Sidon, or in the labour gangs building the new runway at the airport on the coast to the north, and did not come back until the weekend, and those who had saved enough to buy their own tractors hired themselves out to plough and harvest down in the Bekaa and the plains of Aleppo and did not return to the village for many months.

Towards the end the path became steeper, the houses separated and taller, those of the emigrants overlooking the rest, with straw booths on their flat roofs where the old men sat out with their narghiles in the cool of the evening. Many of the fellahin had left in the harsh years before the war, prospering as pedlars and hoteliers in West Africa before returning to build these grander homes. Sometimes from those narrow paths between the whitewashed walls I would glimpse children with dark faces and kinky hair running away in their plastic sandals down the silent alleys.

Ali's house stood on its own above the fellahin quarter, its back hard up against the hillside so that from the raised verandah you could see anyone coming out over the scrub-land between the village and the mosque, above on the hill the roman-tiled gables of the house of the Bey half-hidden behind the white almond blossom. In the years of the exile of Musa-al-Tango the rooms had been almost bare, with makeshift divans and low tables over the untiled floors, but since his return they had paid for electricity to be brought up from the valley and during the day there would be striplights on in all the rooms and strings of white fairy-bulbs hung along the arches of the verandah, their light barely visible in the brilliance of the afternoon.

In the hall, the glossy calendars open on the wrong months, at photographs of Bolshoi dancers and Alpine valleys. On the smoked-glass tables, lit up like game-show prizes, the sea-shell models of cottages and fishing-boats, and the large stuffed bull.

When I came up the steps Abu Musa would already be sitting at the back of the verandah, calmly puffing on his water-pipe, and I remember always being disconcerted by this, though I knew he must have a secret way through the hills to the house, and as I entered he would greet me with a great profusion of ahlan-wa-sahlans and hamdalilahs as if it had been many months since our last meeting, and I would pretend to interest myself in the knick-knacks and the view, avoiding his eyes in case his tic suddenly erupted, though of course when it did I could never stop myself from looking.

When I called Ali's older brother Jaffer would usually be working up on the mountain with his father, but sometimes I would find him preparing to go down to the coast on his scooter, and I would pester him to take me up to the cave under the falls at Jazzin where the dwarf emir had hidden from the Turks to which it was said only his family still knew the way, but when I spoke he would always laugh and push me aside. As I watched him carefully polishing his eagle-head buckle and his stacked boots as if he were about to be passed out, I did not dare to ask him why he did this when they would be coated in dust again by the time he reached the village, for even then there was a coiled violence to the care he took with himself which I did not wish to tease out.

Sometimes that summer Ali would not be at the house when I called, and though his mother and Abu Musa must have known that he had begun to spend more time alone at the mosque they would always tell me only that he had gone to buy something in the village or on a kassoura into the hills, and so I would have to wait, knowing he might not return, and as I sat looking down over the valley his mother would bring out a bowl of lebneh with olive-oil, and warmed mountain bread to scoop it up with, and sometimes a plate of Shish'Taouk which we never had at home, and on the way back through the village and along the river-bed the sweet essence would linger over my gums, and when I returned I would have to brush my teeth so they would not smell the spices on my breath.

It must have been during one of these hot afternoons on the verandah that Ali's mother had first told me of the old village belief that the last of the beys would redeem the crimes of all his forefathers, but not wanting to betray my wanderings beyond the boundaries prescribed by Uncle Samir I had never dared to ask anyone at the house what she had meant by this.

If I still had time I would go back the long way, walking over the open hillside, coming down to the mosque from the lane behind so as to avoid the village boys on the steps, though by that hour they had usually gone down to wheel around the square on their bicycles and scooters. From the lane I would cross between the stucco turbans and broken columns of the beys' tombs to the entrance at the side of the porch which overlooked the leafless plane tree and the paved esplanade where the tourist bus used to stop on its way up to the ancient ruins in the mountains. At one end of the entrance there was a stone table where the dead were washed, and beside it an open bier of rough planks leaning upright against the wall that used to frighten me as we drove past the steps of the mosque, but once I had entered the dark shadows under the three arches of the porch I was invisible to those still sitting below.

The inner door was never bolted, though no one ever came there much other than on Fridays when the young sheikh would drive over the hills from Nabatiyeh to lead the prayers, and on those rare occasions when the Imam and his bearded followers drove up from Tyre and all the men would come in from the fields and the terraces and sit beneath the raised mizrab to hear him tell them in his reedy Persian accent that they would never again know a time of plenty until they remembered their faith and the sacrifices of the martyrs. But I had always been away on these occasions, and would hear of them only later from Ali, and from Uncle Samir who claimed the Bey was intending to put an end to these visits.

After the dust and heat of the walk it was almost cold inside, and I would feel the sweat cooling in the small of my back and hear the flies buzzing against the dirty windows set high into the walls as I padded barefoot between the dark swirls of the threadbare bokharas and reached up to touch the brass chandeliers which dangled like giants' pendants from the gloom of the barrelled ceiling. Ali would always be sitting in the same place, under the small gallery at the back, his legs crossed, his Qur'ān open on his lap, though it seemed too dark to be reading there.

It was only when I came closer that I would see the ellipsis of his smile, his teeth in the shadows white as fish-bones, his fingers trailing over the letters as if over braille. Sometimes we would hardly talk at all. He did not ask me about England, about the Bey and the city as the others did. He never seemed interested in these matters, and when he spoke it was of Kerbala and the martyrs and of that past I had never understood but which lay there under everything like a great sleeping beast we had all mistaken for an island.

That was the summer Zainab had told me how she had heard in the village that Ali had wanted to make the pilgrimage to Mecca, but when the Imam had visited the mosque he had dissuaded him, telling him that the Shi'i were in danger in the holy places and that his time should be spent studying and preparing to help his brothers in the south, but I did not question Ali about what she had said, and when she spoke of it again I had not listened.

And when I remember those summers now I do not think of Ali, at least not at first, but of Aunt Mona and her sore eyes, and of Abu Musa and his stories of the lost caravans and the land of the locusts, and of Khalil crying when he thought nobody could see him, and of the white almond blossom on the hill where there are only ruins now.

By the end of the summer I had found Ali's talk increasingly difficult to follow. He had begun to affect a Persian accent. He spoke in riddles, his eyes puffy and bloodshot. I did not like to look at the wispy hatchings on his cheeks and chin.

I do not remember much of what was said between us; what I do remember seems too strange to make sense of, and all mixed up with what came later.

When I asked him about the origin of Abu Musa's tic he had told me the story of the giant hunter Nimrod, and how he had raised up a tower to peer at Allah in his heaven, and ascended in a chest borne by four monstrous birds into the skies, and fallen to earth, and been plagued by gnats which had entered into his nostrils and ears, and the pain had been so fearful that his only release had been to beat his own head with a mallet.

And when I had pestered him to tell me about the crimes of the old beys, or to show me the way up to the cave under the falls at Jazzin, he had solemnly vowed that on the appointed day we would go together to the cave, but that day he said would come only when our vow had long been forgotten.

V

I am walking up the lane to the house of the Bey. It is the middle of July, and already the sand winds have blown away the wild barwaq between the bare grey rocks and the last of the almond blossom from the hill beneath the new drive.

Under the date-palms nearer the house, a line of long American cars, all black, too dusty to glint in the high sun. The drivers in their black-framed sunglasses, standing apart, smoking.

I cannot tell if they are watching me. The trees casting their narrow strips of shade over the treacle sheen of the new drive, my head down, watching for snakes as I step across the cracked earth along the border where nothing has been planted yet.

As I get closer I hear the hiss of the sprinklers. A faint beat of music from the back of the house near the kitchens.

Along the wall at the front there are iron bosses and rings sunk into the sandstone blocks, like an antique dock left behind by a long-receded sea, but they are too hot to touch, and so I do not climb up, but go round by the steps. At the door a younger driver in fatigues is leaning over the neck of one of the stone lions, and when he sees me he pulls himself up abruptly as if I had caught him in some private clowning, and shuffles away towards the line of cars.

As I pass I put my hand into the mouth of the lion. I have done this for as long as I can remember, and now I do not like to miss it out, though the lions look less intimidating than in the old days, their faces less fierce than those on the basalt fountain in the diwan whose features had been sculpted from the last of the mountain lions to be captured by the old Bey in the forests above Aleppo.

Sometimes I would leave pebbles and acadiniah stones on the little pad of sand in the hollow jaw, and the following year when I returned they would always be gone, but it is enough now that I touch the hollow, and run on.

The first hall is empty and cool. On the low tables, the clusters of empty coffee-cups, untouched bowls of figs and sugared almonds, the flies circling silently.

I slip some of the pale-green nuts into my pocket, and go through into the manzul, but there is nobody there, only a young maid I do not recognize, and she watches me without speaking as she leaves with her tray, her reflection shifting like a mist-light among the brass salvers over the high walls.

I follow the trail of smoke, the murmur of voices above the hum of the air-conditioning. Along the glassed-in courtyard with its palmettos and stumpy cacti, down the passage hung with bucklers and rocaille mirrors which I do not look into. At the end the panelled doors to the diwan, and out of the glare through the glass Fawzi is leaning back against the wall, the butt of his automatic above the high waistband of his flares. I hear throats being cleared, the scraping of feet over marble. From somewhere further within, the voice of the Bey, fitful and disembodied, like a lost recording being played again after many years.

'Our guests have become bears in our vineyards.' Bears, mad dogs, jackals. These are the names the villagers use now when they speak of the Palestinians from the camp above Sidon who have been setting up checkpoints on the road down to the coast, stealing olives and fruit from the terraces, practising with their katyusha-rockets in the wadis up on the mountain. That morning I had watched the black Buicks and Chevrolets of their leaders slowly climbing through the hills, and I had followed the cars to the house, knowing everyone would be too busy to notice me as I crept in to be alone with the painting.

But as I cross the end of the passage, Fawzi still as a statue in the shade under the wall, the panelled doors are half-ajar, and the old men sitting between the embrasures under the high windows turn and see me standing in the archway, my knees stained with Mercurochrome, my eyes watering and bloodshot from the dust on the hills.

I am a little disappointed by the Palestinians. I had expected guerrillas in fatigues and webbing, but these swells in their vivid ties and crumpled suits look no different from all the other politicos who come up from the city to visit the Bey, the long-faced quawajis scurrying between them in their pointed slippers bringing the cones of tobacco and charcoal to the pipe-heads, those further in around the Bey half-hidden by the ranks of tall narghiles with their bulbous bases of crystal and damascene glass.

I hold my throat so I will not cough on the smoke, and draw more attention to myself. Through the hanging clouds I can see Uncle Samir reclining on a divan at the back of the room, and I am surprised at this for since the unpleasantness over the sale of the land below the gardens my uncle has never called at the house of the Bey. But then I notice the paisley foulard, the gold trimming on the abaya, and remember that the Bey has been working up a beard to appease the growing religiosity of the village in the wake of the Imam's more frequent visits from Tyre. With his scarabed hand he beckons me across the hall, leaning over stiffly so I can kiss both his cheeks, and for the rest of the day the scent of his old-fashioned cologne will linger over my cracked lips; medlars and cedarwood.

As I stand there, with all the politicos and carpet-guerrillas looking on, the Bey launches at me in his grandiloquent English, and I have to pretend to be interested as he asks about the boat race and the season in a raised voice so the others will hear, but I know nothing of this England, only the private world of my school and those distant symmetries glimpsed through the condensation of the taxi window on the road to the airport, overpasses, hoardings, the glare of sodium-lights across frozen fields.

I wait for him to answer his own questions, as he always does, and then for the set-piece about his salad days at Cambridge, the balls and the hacking on the flats and the rowing and the three dances with Princess Marina, but by this time he has returned to Arabic so as not to lose his audience and I am no longer listening to what I have heard so many times before; the last time I had come to the house Uncle Samir had told me afterwards how the boys at Trinity had treated the Bey as just another showy wog for bringing his valet and keeping a sports-car parked in Grantchester for weekend sprees up to the clubs in London, using him, then cutting him in later years.

As the Bey stands and mimes the steps of some half-remembered waltz, the old quawaji enters from behind in his brocade waistcoat and shirwal baggy enough to catch the holy spirit falling to earth and as he beats the grinder into the stone bowl a few of the coffee-beans spin off like unstrung worry-beads and roll out under the divans and empire-couches along the walls. I see my chance, and back away, crunching the beans under my sneakers as I step down again into the dark of the passage.

By imperceptible degrees the house gradually excises all traces of the Orient from within itself, the traditional Ottoman manzuls and receptions shifting into the café-rococo of the corridors and the club-regency of these inner chambers. Here in the study there are scuffed leather armchairs and canterburys stacked with *Punch* and *Country Life*. It feels like England in a heat wave; a scent of dead flies and horsehair, of things coming unstuck. The view down over the bare hills and terraces above Ali's house suddenly remote and fantastical, like a wrong drop.

For a moment I thought he had moved it, but then I saw that it was just that the secretaire had been brought nearer the door, the anglepoise and the dried asphodels obscuring the gilt oblong of the frame.

I push aside the lamp, the flowers, draw the velvet curtains against the glare. The heavy frame makes the face appear smaller than it was, as if faintly burdened by the pompous weight of shells and scrolls and acanthus leaves. She seems to know that it does not suit her, the clouded cornflower eyes raised, a fractional consternation, but so as one would hardly notice, as someone might raise their eyes when come upon in unsuitable company, discreetly signalling they are there on sufferance.

She must have already realized it would not be a great likeness, her subtle essence foundering in that commercial-gallery manner of the early fifties, the livid hues and heavy impasto, a style that has not dated well, though the painter had honesty enough not to hide her disquiet, and somehow I trust this picture more than all the old photographs with their stressed smiles and lost light.

He has drawn her from the waist up, in a shallow niche, the background indeterminate, flecked through with what could be wreaths of smoke or the arabesques of a worn tapestry, her face upturned a few degrees, as if about to twist away from the plane of the canvas in some violent contraposto. She was still a girl then, and there is an air of fancy-dress to the pearl choker, the sparkling pendants, the lizard-green gown that surely could never have been that colour. This must have been the year she arrived in the city, and he has painted her high on all the attention, the cheeks flushed with memories of gallantries, the eyes lit with the reflection of some distant conflagration.

I suppose the Bey would not have had the picture made if he had meant to keep her, though even in those high-rolling years of the fifties she must have seemed quite a catch, an English girl with stormy-blue eyes, a trophy to show off at the yacht club and on the terrace at the St Georges Hotel. My father would have known her then too of course. They would have gone to the same parties, on the cruises along the coast on the Dido-Sidonia, on the same skiing trips up to the cedars. He would have seen her playing Desdemona at the Trianon in those performances Uncle Samir still spoke about when she had died so beautifully that everyone had called out for an encore, and all the time he must have been waiting in the wings, and yet I do not remember him ever speaking of those years; they had been an agony perhaps.

She had come out first with the British Council, and stayed on to run the theatre company, and it must have been so easy for everyone to forget that her mother was a Palestinian when she looked as she did and had only ever learnt kitchen Arabic like all the other English girls in the city. Her father had been Governor of Haifa before the war, but she had been schooled at a boarding-convent in North Yorkshire, and the Levant had probably never quite lost its adventure for her.

She had already been ill when they married, but then there had been several years of complete remission. Her condition had worsened again only gradually. When she would not go back to London for treatment, they had done what they could for her at the university hospital. For several months at a time she would seem to recover her strength. Nothing was ever said in front of me, and I was too young to understand. Resting was just something mothers did, like smoking through ivory holders or drinking from glasses with long fluted stems.

When my father worried about her, it was in practical ways, warning her not to drive too fast, not to go through areas where there had been trouble, not to wear her skimpy dresses into the traditional districts. Though in the last year she always wore loose silk kaftans and stagy hats: bombazine turbans, velvet berets at a jaunty angle. I would put on her wigs, and stroke them until they gave me shocks, and stomp about unsighted by the long fringes.

I was already away at school in England at the end. I do not remember much about that time now, just coming back and finding the doors to her rooms locked, and the scent of too many flowers, and her photograph everywhere.

After I leave the house, I clamber up the dried wadi above the last of the terraces. Nothing grows here among the scree and rocks. The place is bare and desolate, as if many plagues had once passed over the hills.

In the spring, for one or two weeks, the earth turns crimson with wild anemones, but they soon perish in the desert winds.

A few lonely clusters surive in the lee of the wadis until the summer. When we walked here together Layla used to tell me the flowers were dyed with the blood of Adonis, seeping up from the underworld.

The villagers call these hills the jurd, the dead place; they do not come here. They still remember the raids of the men of the high pastures, the wells poisoned, the orchards and fields stripped as if by locusts. But there have been no further raids since the Bey chose Fawzi as his murafiq whose family are from the mountain, though sometimes at night I still see the fires of the watchmen in the olive terraces.

The olives are the blood of the village, demanding little, yielding much. In the years the government-regis will not take the tobacco sheaves, the villagers must survive from the olive harvest; what they cannot sell they feed to the asses and goats: the crushed stones serve as fuel, the oil they use instead of butter which cannot be preserved in the heat, to burn in lamps, to anoint the brows of the dying.

Higher up I pass the ruins of the charcoal kilns once used as shelters by the the mountain goatherds, and the standing stone that marks the end of the Bey's domain, the rocks white as sun-dried bones, the soil between eroded by the heavy winter storms.

This is as far as I come. When the sun is still behind the mountain on a day without sand winds I can see all the way down the spring-line to the grey hives of the other villages, the darker streaks of the rivers and run-offs like veins in an old hand, and below the black smudge of the coastal marshes where entire caravans had sunk and disappeared. And on the hill above where I would not go, my three lonely stone-pines, their thin trunks and spherical heads against the bare rocks like a shy of giant toffee-apples.

Less than seventy years ago there had been woods over all these hills. Firs, junipers, holm-oaks, pines. But the Turks had taken the timber to build their railways, and the goats had eaten away the remaining seedlings. The old fellahin in the square still remembered the woods, and they told stories of wild boars and Syrian bears coming down from the mountain, taking their livestock and children. Sometimes only an arm or a leg would ever be found; Abu Musa had heard the tale of a handsome young hunter gored on the mountain by a wild boar and of the river to the north which still ran crimson with his blood every spring.

Sometimes from the rocks below the pines I would hear Jaffer riding back across the wadi-tracks from the plots up on the mountain; by then he had changed his scooter for an unsilenced motorcycle which went no faster but had a deeper putter.

He would not stop when he saw me, his wheelies rucking up clouds of dust over the bare hillside. I would watch him slowing with the distance. The sky empty of buzzards and vapour-trails, his open shirt billowing behind like a spinnaker in the wind off the mountain.

VI

As the hill steepens, I cut the engine, let the jeep freewheel.
Ali huddled over his book, I cannot see his eyes. I tuck my feet
under the seat, I will not touch the brakes until we are past the
press.

As we glide down, the hills are quiet; the murmuring of the
cicadas, the slow putter of a tractor high on the terraces.

Every week now Ali leaves the village. Since Khalil has
become too unwell to drive I make the journey into Sidon to
stock up with provisions. I give him a lift to the coast, then he
hitches along the sea road on one of the fruit lorries to Tyre;
he has begun to help at the relief agency set up by the Imam
for those villagers who have fled the Israeli bombardments on
the border.

On the days I did not go down to Sidon I mooched about
the house; pretending to revise for my exams, day-dreaming
about her knowing eyes, her sour lips. I no longer took walks
into the village.

As we passed the first poplars I reached down again for the
rubbberless pedals. In the widening river, the jumpy reflection of the bone-shaker. The ripped canvas roof, the chicken-
wire over the headlights, but to me the most splendid vehicle
on the road for when I let Layla's brothers borrow it they
would leave us alone for hours.

On the drive to the coast Ali never spoke about his work
with the Imam. On every journey he made me promise I

would not go back to England. Then he fell silent, peered down at the Qur'ān on his lap, his eyes screwed up against the sun and the dust. Even in the high summer, his face pale as a convalescent on his first faltering outing.

As we came down out of the hills, he would pick at his thickening beard, though there was nothing caught in it. His lips so dry and cracked I longed to run a wet finger over them; for a time I had left a tube of Layla's lip-salve on the console, but he seemed never to notice it.

On the high cambers and ruts before the new asphalt road, the Qur'ān jerking out of his hands, snapping shut; he would not try to find his place again, but read on wherever the book fell open.

On the turns around the hill we would meet the Lincoln up from the coast; sometimes I would pull on to the verge only to see Fawzi was already making way. The tinted windows in the back were always up so I never knew whether the Bey was inside; as we passed, Fawzi staring through his silver-rimmed sunglasses at Ali's huddled figure, the arm hanging out over the door flicked up into a limp salute.

I had not yet learnt the short-cuts through the orchards, and so we would come down into the new town through the edges of the Ein Helweh refugee camp. As we slowed at the checkpoints, sore-eyed children ran alongside the car with Chiclets and Gazousa, further back the old women standing in the metallic haze of the road, holding up chickens, halves of watermelon; I never once saw a car stop to buy. The Fateh men waved the traffic through from the shade of their straw huts, rarely looking up from behind their papers, but sometimes there were tailbacks where the Popular Fronters stood sweating in their chocolate anoraks between the concrete blocks they had dragged into the road and Ali would walk out across the fields to the coast, his thin back slowly disappearing between the bowed black heads of the sunflowers like a living thing passing among shades.

Though I had driven around the perimeters of Ein Helweh from several different points, from the Tyre roundabout, from the new market, I still had no true understanding of its proportions and topography. The upper parts of the camp spread up to the first line of hills, but at this time the hospital and the new mosque had not been built and none of the breeze-block houses were of more than two storeys, no landmarks visible from the road with which to take bearings so that when I came down through the checkpoints I had no sense of where Layla's home might be in relation to where I sat waiting; if I tried to picture her she seemed only as close as the centre of a maze to one outside it.

I had only ever visited the camp at night, with Harun and Asad, Layla's brothers. I do not know if they deliberately took a different route each time through the ramifying alleys, but it always seemed so, and even if I had been bold enough to enter the camp alone I would not have trusted myself to find the place by day.

When I had finished at the market I would seek out the boys at the old harbour on the headland, leaving the jeep at the ridge, walking out over the empty lot, the storks clattering off the pink-tiled roofs to pick at the rinds and rubbish, the pie-dogs snoozing in the shadows of the wild figs, down into the still air of the narrow sandstone lanes above the front which smelt of pitch from the upturned boats below on the beach, and of brine and rotting fish.

The lanes came out on to the cobbled promontory where the tourist buses parked across from the small arcade, the blinds of the souvenir shops down against the sun and the dogs, behind their murky windows the rows of brass trinkets and olive-wood camels, outside on the sandblown pavement the racks of faded postcards. It was here that Harun and Asad would wait with their olive-staffs and fake tourist-cards, offering to take groups to see the headless lions on the broken causeway and up to the cove where it was said Jonah had been debouched by the whale.

A couple of years back Harun had won a refugee-bursary to read ancient history at the American University, but he still worked the front with Asad during the summers, though there were fewer tourists now the shelling had started again along the border, and those that came often brought their own guides from the city.

If the boys were not out on a tour I would find them in the shade of the arcade, sometimes further along the beach under one of the boats, peeping out at the broad-hipped diggers in their slacks and sun-hats grubbing for potsherds among the fallen columns. When they saw me they would pass their pipe up through the narrow gap between the upturned prow and the sand, and to be polite I would take a small draw, quickly expelling the bitter smoke so I would not go all sloppy and boss-eyed when I was alone later with Layla.

Climbing out they would greet me in the old way, with a roll of kung-fu kicks and air-punches to the stomach, as they used to in the days of our mock battles in the olive groves when they would creep up through the terraces to bring me the dirty magazines and cartridges which I would swap or sell on the next term at school; the year the boys stopped coming to the house they had offered to cut me in at the front, and I had forged a guide-card on the ancient sit-up-and-beg Underwood kept in the study my father no longer used, marking on the government stamp in sepia ink with a fine-nibbed

Rotring, but now that most of the tourists had stopped coming I had given up on this plan, and I could no longer remember where I had hidden the card.

Later as the sun sank into the sea we would drive back through the new town and into the warren of alleys across the lower part of the camp, the skewed headlights picking out the huddled water-tanks on the flat roofs, twisted girders against the darkening sky, the lines of white sheets hung between. As the going got too narrow we left the jeep in the small clearing where the children played under a water-pump, and walked the last stretch between the windowless backs of the houses, their peeling door half-hidden by the dusty wisteria over the path. Above the low yard beside the house, the unlit alleys climbing in long black ridges to the foothills, the pale glow over the roofs where the old men smoked their narghiles out in the cool of the evening; the car lights breaking through the shadows like torches after something that has long moved on.

Inside there was electricity, on the chromed cabinet against the wall a string of coloured bulbs hooked around the fish-bowl television, the heap of leatherette cushions underneath over a tiled floor smelling faintly of disinfectant, nothing else much in the room, the mattress where the boys slept, the tidy tower of history books, on the whitewashed walls the usual repertoire of holy texts and prints of old Jerusalem all heavy with that reproachful air of things no longer attended to.

Sometimes we found their half-blind uncle squatting beside the television, just listening to the sound, and when he heard us he would shuffle off in his slippers lined with newspaper to the room at the back where he would sit silently until I left; he had come up with the first refugees from Galilee in the days when the camp had been no more than rows of white tents in a scrubland of wild dogs and jackals.

But usually Uncle Munir would be out playing trictrac, and would not return to the house until much later, and so we had the place to ourselves, though Layla would stay in her room to begin with, fussing with all the clothes she had to hide at the weekends when their mother came back from Beirut where she worked for Aunt Mona's family at their house above the Sursuq quarter.

The arrangement was that I was left alone with Layla while the boys took the jeep for a cruise into town, but before they left the boys would share a pipe under the cabinet, their faces up close to the bulbous screen, over the walls the dim reflections of the ghost towns and deserts and wide horizons from the dubbed westerns.

Harun preferred to watch with the sound down, but Asad could not bear to miss out on the fusillades and the whip-cracking, and would treaty for a burst of volume when it came to the shoot-outs. Suddenly the room would be filled with Hebrew voices, like Arabic spoken through a muzzle, Asad ambling between the doors with his crab-cowboy gait, lasso-ing the air, performing quick-draws from his turned-out pockets, blowing away the imaginary smoke from the tip of his finger.

Layla would say little until they had gone. She brought the stale crisps and popcorn to the low table, Asad dunking in with his bruised fingers. She stood back in her tight jeans and halter-top by the door to her room, picking at the stickers of marigolds and elephants, holding her freshly painted nails to the light.

She did not meet my eyes while they were there. She would catch my gaze only for a moment, then quickly look down or away to some other corner of the room as if there was someone else there still requiring her attention.

Her eyes always faintly bloodshot, though I never saw her with the pipe. The greyness tinctured with a clouded cobalt that stole away their hardness, and made her seem feyer than she was. When I watched her face she would smile weakly, and seem about to cry, the whites of her eyes viscous and flushed as if from some sudden pressure within.

Her room was small, and slightly damp, even in the high summer; but always clean, smelling of spearmint, dried barwaq. By the narrow bed, one lamp on the floor, draped over with the poplin shirt she sometimes wore knotted at the waist; the mirror stuck with transfers of Bob Marley, none of whose albums she had ever heard. On the back of the door, the poster of Farrah Fawcett whose fly-back bangs she had imitated with only partial success; her long fringe hanging limply down, shadowing her cheeks, hiding her eyes from the side.

As I lay on the low bed, my shoulders against the puckering of the wall, she would bring the two warm bottles of Amstel, setting them down for me to open, the glasses so small they disappeared under the over-running froth. She went to the stall in the alley for the beers. I waited by the window, the shimmer of her top bobbing in the shadows; as she passed the hopscotch-grids on the corner the younger girls calling her name after her down the alley.

When we were alone together, she never spoke of her friends. Harun had told me that the other camp-girls teased her for dressing up when her mother was away though I had often seen banat from the camp peering in through the windows of the Maronite boutiques in the new town; the girls waiting at the bus-stops below Ein Helweh wore heavy make-up and shiny belts and pumps with their fatigues, but they all belonged to the guerrilla training programmes which

Layla had given up; I suspected this was the true cause of her isolation.

At first I would be nervous of touching her. She would sit above me on the cane chair, the froth-beads like spittle over her thin neck, the faint tracks glimmering in the draped lamplight. When she thought I was not watching she would flick her pointed tongue over her lips, like a fly-catcher.

I had to pretend to know all the answers to the questions inspired by the magazines her mother brought down each weekend from the city, describe films I had not seen, the personal habits of actors I had never heard of, invent cities I had never visited.

When we had finished the beers, she would switch off the lamp. She knelt on the floor with the silver Dunhill I had stolen from the house to give to her, lighting the candles on the wax stalactites of the wine bottles which had been lifted by the boys from the tourist restaurants on the front; after she had sold the lighter on, she would spin me the sad little tale of how she had lost it, as she had with all the other gifts I had stolen for her from the house, and I was honoured she had kept it for so long. Every object in those rooms had been robbed or foraged from the town, and the place seemed all the more innocent for this, like a childhood den from which everything will have to be returned when the playing day is over.

The candlelight hid the uneven tinting of her bob, her raven roots, the fine pocking under her little ears. In that light, with her heavy fringe and sour lips, like a younger Jeanne Moreau; though it would be some years before this resemblance would work its particular tyranny on my imagination.

Only the thought that the boys might return gave me the

courage to touch. My whetted fingers on her hooded lids, over the fine corrugations of her chapped lips.

I told her she was beautiful; but not too often or she would think me insincere. She liked me to speak to her in English, but she did not understand many of the words.

She would not move as I undressed her, like a child being difficult at bedtime; only lifting her thighs as I pulled down the jeans which bunched at her ankles so I would have to kneel to peel them away. She did not help by raising her legs, her limbs all limp, as if she had lost the use of them.

When she was naked, she would peer down at herself, glazed doll-eyes fixing over her slouching body. Her skin pearly in the uncertain light, like unripe grapes, her narrow shoulders shivering as I ran my fingers along the back of her thighs where the chair had left its shallow cuneiform which I would finger with all the attention of an epigrapher without light, then press away.

When the tape stopped, we did not get up to change it, from the next room we could hear the gentle bubbling of the narghile, the clicking of worry-beads. Without meeting my eyes, she would reach down and touch me with short, brusque strokes, watching what she was doing, with that same dead gaze; her other hand in my mouth so I would not cry out.

And when I touched her I would put my hand in her mouth, and if she bit too deep I would reach for the fruit bowl by the bed, and she would bend her head down and lift out one of the apples with her teeth, clenching it hard in her little mouth in that way puppies have when they will not give back the ball.

This was in the days before she would let me fuck her; sometimes just as the boys were about to get back she would let me go down on her, opening her legs and arching her back, her gaze to the ceiling, the cruel moue of her lips parted a little apprehensively as if about to be hand-fed something she had never tasted before; when she finished she would push me away from her silent quivering, and I would lay my head in the soft hollow of her belly, my knees aching from the damp floor, and her taste would stay with me all the way up through the dark hills to the unlighted house; tangy on my gums, like mountain yoghurt, pistachio shells.

Once, when I had drunk too many beers, I had forced myself into her; she had peered down to where our bodies met with that same look of histrionic indifference of the fighters in the westerns when they had taken a hit, but there had been no blood; when I saw that she was sobbing I had begun to cry too, and she had held my head to her small, hard breasts, then pulled me away and lain deathly still, her shoulders to my face, the milk-teeth ridges of her spine showing like a fossil through her chalk skin.

The following summer we would meet in the afternoons at a small hotel above the north harbour. I paid for the room by the month in the hope that she might not return too often to the camp. Since Asad had let slip on the front that Jaffer had been calling with gifts when he visited the house, I had wanted her away from Ein Helweh. Almost every week Jaffer was coming down to the camp in his father's old van, strutting about under the water-tower while the shebab unloaded the parcels from the back, and afterwards calling at the house with cuts of meat, baclava, afioun-balls for the boys.

I had not told her that I knew this, only that I no longer felt safe coming to the camp since the Bey had voted with the Maronites in parliament for the army to move against the

Popular Front and the other leftist Palestinian groups. It was during that summer that I began to avoid the outskirts of the camp when coming down into the new town, taking the short-cuts along the tracks through the orange and lemon groves which the other village cars had been using for some years.

To reach the hotel I would leave the jeep below the market, tipping one of the Chiclet-boys to watch over it, walking through the old quarter, the shopkeepers sitting out in their slippers in the shade of their half-shuttered doorways, down over the alley of the butchers where the flies swarmed above the viscid blues and purples of the offal in the gutters which would not be sluiced away until the evening.

The hotel was small and quiet. There was no lobby, a narrow hall; zigzags of eau-de-Nil tiles over the walls beneath the stairwell. The only person I saw there was the Armenian concierge who sat knitting behind a wire fan in the back room.

On the stairs, fly-papers hung from the empty light-sconces, the corridors smelt of dead ants and damp loofahs. As I went up I would hear the distant crying of babies, a muffled hacking through the closed doors, from the floor above the reedy pulse of her cassette-recorder.

That summer she was always playing The Harder They Come which I had bought for her at the airport. I remember suspecting that she may have played it only when she knew I was calling, and once I had arrived early and sat listening on the landing, but that day there was building work nearby, and I could make out nothing until it was almost the hour I usually came, and by then the noise had eased and I could hear the lilting plaint of Johnny-Too-Bad drifting like old smoke on the unlit stairs.

The room was kept spitefully clean. The tiled floor always

76

shiny-wet from her mopping; I would take my shoes off at the door, leaving them on the bristle mat marked with the anchor-and-chain crest of a larger hotel up in the city where sometimes I used to have lunch with my father.

She had not brought much up from the house to make the room more homely; behind the plastic curtain in the corner, a butagaz-ring to brew the coffee on; under the window overlooking the air-conditioning unit on the wall opposite, three pots of white geraniums.

On the floor, the wax-encrusted candles from her room; above the bed two ragged posters of the Moulin Rouge; when I had told her that the room reminded me of the bistro on the high street in the town in England where I was at school she had begun crying and torn the posters down; the rips taped over roughly, the lime-green of the wall showing through from behind.

We would fuck while the coffee brewed, and sometimes again before I left, but usually only the once at the beginning. She seemed to like to do it before we had begun to speak. When I came in she would pad over the wet floor in her bare feet, and stand on her toes to kiss me, and then with her little feet perched above mine we would shamble precariously over to the small bed.

Though there was no need to now, we still did it silently, as we had at the house. She would only let me into her if I lay on my back, my shoulders caught against the brass bars of the bedhead, her fingers clawing into my chest as she rode about blithe as a child on her hobby-horse; when she stiffened her head thrown back like a seal nosing the air.

Afterwards we would stand, sharing a cigarette, by the open window. Our bodies pressed against the sill to catch the flecks of iced water spat out by the air-conditioning grid on the wall opposite. It was then she would ask me to tell her about England, and knowing what was on her mind I would go back to the bed, and she would pretend to busy herself with the coffee, cursing when she overpoured into the demitasses I had filched for her from the house.

She would bring my cup to the bed, then face the wall, leaving her own cup untouched, saying nothing, and in the end I would lie and tell her I had decided not to go back, and that if I did it would be only to collect my possessions; but she had heard all this before, and standing by the curtain in her poplin shirt she would begin to sob again; sometimes she would spit on the floor at my feet, then kneel rubbing her palm over the washed tiles until it bruised, begging me to take her back with me before the war came down on the camps again.

And I would want to get away from her, but would stay kneeling beside her for what seemed like hours, waiting for her panic to blow itself out, longing for the cooling air over the hills.

When I left the sky would be dark above the mountain. As I came out into the sandstone alley, I would have the sense that someone was waiting at the head of the steps that led down to the harbour front. I would double back through the alley of the butchers to where I thought I had seen the man standing, but there was never anyone there, just the boys playing on the level between the two runs of steps, further down the old men smoking in the half-shuttered doorways.

I waited there, looking back between the shebab in their stained aprons washing down the gutters, but I never saw anybody entering or leaving the green-tiled hall of the hotel. I would return to the jeep only to find the food I had bought had gone bad in the heat of the afternoon, and I would have to throw the bags out into the empty lot; below the new market the glow of the braziers where the Chiclet-boys roasted peanuts in the evenings. I would have to stop at the reed-hut restaurants on the coast road to stock up again, returning late to the village.

On other evenings I would walk with Layla down the steps to the front. We would avoid the upturned boats where the boys hid with their pipes, and wander with our ice-creams up along the headland.

When we had not argued she would lie with her head in my lap, her nails pressed into the palm of my hand. From the stone parapet we would look down over the sea-slicked rocks and the black water; when the blood-orange sun had set, the tanker-lights coming up, their brightness trumping the stars.

VII

It is the fag-end of the summer. Today we have seen the first clouds drifting up from the south, high, dark, lonely, like weather balloons. There is little breeze off the sea. Along the front, the reek of wrack and rotting wood, back in the sandstone alleys the air still and rank as an old dog's breath. We will not see many more tourists now. The last buses have stopped coming, it is almost time for me to leave again.

A black Mercedes taxi with city plates crosses the cracked esplanade, and halts at the boarded-up kiosk, beneath the arcade. Nothing else is moving along the front. The tourists do not get out. Keeping their tinted windows up, they peer out under their floppy sun-hats towards the ruined castle on the causeway; Harun watching from his straw mat in the shade of the arcade.

One of the rear doors opens, hastily, an ashtray is emptied into the road; the old couple holding their liver-spotted hands to their noses, their eyes narrowed with disappointment.

As they look out over the causeway, shots ring out from somewhere further up the beach, probably only the Chiclet-boys banging off rounds. The couple in the back gesture to the driver to move off. The car begins to turn. Harun drops his pipe and book, and waving his faked tourist-card above his head, he staggers down towards the road.

'MesDamesMeinHerrenMiLadiesGents. I am your guide to the marvel that was Sidon.'

When they see him coming, the old couple pretend to ignore him, the driver shooing him out of the way. Half-tripping, half-running, he scrambles over the bonnet, pressing his card against the windscreen, shouting to the driver that he will give him a cut of the tour if he stays put, salaaming fulsomely to the occupants; his luck is in, the driver recognizes him from a visit earlier in the summer, and turns to endorse him to his nervous passengers.

Bowing like a coachman, Harun holds open the door. A small portly man in a flared safari-suit steps tentatively into the glare; after him the old couple in slacks and baseball-jackets; then a youth in patched denims and scarab-bracelets, with hollow cheeks, bloodshot eyes, long dirty-blond hair, his sun-blanched brows crested by the puckering of a fresh scar.

The others have begun to amble down towards the ruins, but the youth falls behind on the esplanade; staring out over the harbour, the sea darkening inkily to the lacquer of the horizon.

'MiLadySirs. Please. This way to the marvel.' Harun shepherds the unsteady figures back into the shade of the arcade; along the row of half-shuttered shops to the stall of Abu Munir where he gets twenty per cent of any business he brings in. As the tourists look on with bemusement, he gestures grandly towards the trestle table, as if drawing the curtain from some great panorama; the piles of fruit softening in the heat; on racks behind the apples and bridled water-melons: dusty ceramics, straw donkeys, olive-wood camels.

'LadyGents. What is oldest in Sidon?' The old couple are peering back at the fallen columns, the ruined castle in the sea.

'But those were built last week.' Harun smiles, plucks out an orange, an apple, juggles them uncertainly from hand to hand. 'MiLadySirs. The fruit.'

'What do you take us for?'

'Fools?'

While the small man begins slapping back the pages of his Blue Guide, the old couple shuffle uncomfortably; the youth laughs, the sound filling the arcade, shrill, reverberant, like cymbals meeting; Harun waits, until they are listening again.

'Before the Turks and the Franks came, before Persians, Greeks, Babylonians, before the wild tribes crossed the seas into your islands, the orchards were here. The first Canaanites built temples to their lost god on the waters to the orchards, vast and naked terraces of limestone on the waters.

'Each spring when the hills were scarlet with anemones the Sidonians drew their god through the orchards in effigy to the sea, and to springs, and drowned him, and as his lover Ishtar had once wept the women wept and rent themselves and covered their hair with earth and waited for the return of their loves from the waters.'

Harun speaks quietly. The couple listening now, leaning back against the rusted railings, their caps pulled down against the listing sun. The youth growing older every time I look at him; he is fingering one of the apples, rolling it on his calloused palm.

'Is it a medlar, a rush orange, a colocynth perhaps?' The voice is not what I had expected; a public-school drawl, uninflected, incurious.

'We call it an apple.' The young man bites into the rusty-dark fruit.

'Strange. It has no taste.'

'Nor will it until it crosses the Euphrates. We feed them to our pigs and mules.'

Baring his yellowed teeth, the young man munches the

apple down to the core. He lobs it away towards the sea; it falls well short, bouncing on the tin roof of the kiosk. The others watch it roll and come to rest, then turn back to Harun who sits on the edge of the stall, still holding the orange, the apple.

'In the cool penumbra of these orchards the first crusaders, merchants, adventurers, delinquents, pitched their pavilions on the road to Jerusalem, dispatching men to plunder flocks and herds. In the orchards they were troubled by serpents and scorpions, and the townsmen came out to them with balm and theriac picked by rope-climbers from high crevices on the mountain, but the following year the Franks returned with a fleet of sixty ships, a siege tower of branches, mats and ox-hides drawn on pulley-wheels against the missiles of the townsmen, victualled with water and vinegar to quench the evening fires, and on the forty-seventh day the town surrendered and passed over into the dominion of the Franks.'

Harun leads the way slowly back across the arcade, the old couple at his side, the young man loping along behind, rolling a cigarette, his head bowed; I go after them down the stone steps; Harun's words, disembodied, drifting high over the bobbing sun-hats.

'Of the art of war the Franks learnt on this coast the use of the crossbow and portcullis; of the tambour and naker and kettledrum; of signalling by carrier-pigeon and by bonfires; the discipline of sapping; of the siege catapult and mangonel.

'Damask, fine atlas; they harvested the fruits of our silk-worms; sendal from Tyre, six-threaded samite woven with gold.

'They came to know the service of perfumes and spices, and the foods that still bear our names; carob and sesame, rice, lemon, apricots, shallots and scallions.

'The sugar that the Persians brought out of the Ganges valleys they took as physic from our plantations to the south where today from the coast road you see the refugee children in their rags sucking out syrup from the canes.'

They walk over the pebbly beach; between the upturned boats, to the first of the fallen columns. The small man with the stick, out of puff, hunkering down against one of the repitched hulls.

'And what did you Johnnies learn from us?' He is English also, ex-army perhaps, his voice clipped and level.

'To build strong castles.'

There is a pause in the proceedings. While the small man brings out a pocket Instamatic, ranges it on the fallen columns, the couple unwrap crumpled sandwiches; the boy in denims smokes his roll-up, coughs like an old man.

Harun beside the upturned boat, shuffling the pebbles under his sneakers; from the hull he throws his arm out in another grand arc, as if casting a net, his hand spanning the fallen columns, the causeway, the oily waters.

'The chroniclers tell of a city of teeming bazaars, mighty walls circled by a sea of orchards, of labyrinths, marble colonnades, caravanserais seven storeys high, of giant chains across the harbour mouth to fend away the sea peoples.

'The Franks garrisoned their prize with two towers on the mole, this causeway, the castle on the water, but could not hold Salah-al-Din from the city.

'When after ten years the Knights returned from Cyprus they stabled their horses in roofless halls and warmed themselves by fires of fallen cedar beams; in later centuries travellers who passed along the shore found only ruins and the black tents of the Bedouin.'

We follow Harun along the beach, past trenches reticulated with lines of white string, conical piles of potsherds, the sand above tufted with yellow grass. They are all looking up beyond the shingle to the long bone-white ridge which blocks the view back to the town, the headstones above dropping thin shadows down over the weeds and poppies and criss-crossed tracks; above the mountain the sgraffito of fading vapour-trails.

Harun stands at the edge of the white ridge, holds up a handful of the white earth; as the group come closer they see his hand is filled with small white shells.

High on the ridge a gang of Chiclet-boys are playing king-of-the-castle, two at the top by the railings of the cemetery waving purple banners, jeering; the others running at them up the steep slope. A further banner is lying at the foot of the ridge, tied to a rotting stick; Harun kicks it away.

The old couple and the small man are watching as he scrapes out handfuls of the white shells, letting them drop through his bony fingers on to the sand. Harun must have stopped here hundreds of times, but as he speaks again I have a sense that for him the place has not been bled of its strangeness.

'One morning when Helen was strolling on the beach in the years of her captivity at Troy she saw the mouth of her dog run purple with the juice of a shellfish; she so admired this purple that her suitors would bring her as gifts clothes of no other dye.

'This shellfish could have been no other than the mollusc on which the Sidonians built the empire which first brought light into the lands of the west.

'The discarded shells of the mollusc have made this white hill where the townsmen now bury their dead. These boys who play on the ridge still fix the juice of the mollusc with lemon to dye their banners.

'From this harbour the Canaanite traders took their precious dye to the Rhine, to Tarshish, across the Euphrates to India; their colour became the universal sign of majesty and divinity for this was the purple worn by Homer's kings and the emperors of Rome and the pharaohs of Egypt; by the high priests of the Jewish temple and the Aramean prophet at Hierapolis and the priest of Jupiter at Magnesia and by the first cardinals of Rome; the birth chambers of the Empress of Byzantium were draped with cloth of this dye; only with the fall of Constantinople did the secret of the dye's making pass away to the west.

'This first Semitic tribe who wandered out from the desert and made the seas their lake, the Greeks called the people of the purple, the Phoenicians.

'Their triremes they built of cedar logs floated down the drainage streams at floodtime; while others followed the coast they steered by the stars across the open waters, over the sea of darkness to the Azores and the isles of tin, concealing their passage so the Roman ships followed them in vain.

'To serve their trade they founded Carthage and Cadiz, Hippo, Malaga, Odessa, Barcelona; their anchors they forged of silver from the deep mines of Tartessus.

'In three years they passed around Africa, from the Red Sea to the Pillars of Hercules; Herodotus tells us every spring they planted wheat on the shore, and during the journey witnessed the sun setting on the starboard side.

'Through their ports came copper and turquoise from the mines of Sinai, silks and spices and slaves from India and China; over the old caravan road across the deserts from the incense lands of South Arabia, Sabean traders brought myrrh and balm and sandalwood, beryls and pearls gathered by captives from the shark-troubled coasts of Malabar and Ceylon.

'To the new world in the west the Sidonians brought cotton and glass; first cast, then blown transparent. On these wild shores they planted rose and palm, plum, almond, pomegranate and olive; returning with laurel, oleander, iris, ivy and narcissus that still preserve their Greek names in the east.

'By their enterprise they leave the names of carob and cassia, jasper, hyssop and nard; of cumin, chicory, crocus and mandrake; of saffron and sesame, gypsum and naphtha. Their caravan knew no frontier.

'When the Hebrews entered the land of Sidonians they came as Bedouin of the desert; of the Canaanites they learnt to plough and write, their temples they built of the cedars of the Canaanites; they worshipped in the high places of the Canaanites, and their first-born they called Yahweh after their own god, and the son born after they called Baal after the god of the Sidonians, rider of clouds, sender of rain and thunder.

'By their myths the Greeks inscribed the Sidonians at their origins, for fair Europa was the daughter of King Agenor of Sidon, and by Zeus in the guise of a bull she was borne away from a mead on this shore, and from their coupling was born Minos of Crete, first king and legislator of the Greeks.

'To search after her, Agenor sent his son Cadmus whose name is from quadam, one of the east; Cadmus brought the Phoenician invention of the alphabet among the Greeks; founded Thebes with dragon's teeth where the acropolis still bears his name; mined the mountains of Thrace for gold.

'To the Greeks the Sidonians taught the measure of time and space, the duodecimal division of the day into hours, the year into months; the sexagesimal division of the circle into degrees, the hour into minutes; without the gifts of the Sidonians we would not recognize nor quantify nor smell our world.

'But as the Greek states prospered, the Phoenician cities fell under the rude satraps of Persia. When he heard that Arta-Xerxes had mustered his hosts in Babylon, King Tennes of Sidon betrayed his city.

'From the walls five hundred elders came out bearing olive branches, and were cut down by the hosts of the enemy; the remaining townsmen vowed to die as free men; so none might flee they put to the torch every vessel in the harbour, and all their temples and gardens and palaces, and it is said on that day forty thousand took their own lives.

'But in those years the might of the Phoenicians had long passed away to their colonies in Africa. Over the sea Carthage had fastened such a hold that they vaunted the Romans could not wash their hands in its waters without their leave. For fifteen years the opium-addicted Hannibal harried the Romans on their soil, taking the fight to the walls of Rome itself.

'After he had died by his own hand a fugitive in Asia Minor, the Romans fell hard upon his city. For seventeen long days Carthage was put to the torch until the site lay buried under a high mountain of ash, and the plough was passed over it, and the ground on which it had stood cursed for ever.'

I drive Harun to the water-tower above Ein Helweh. Under the rusted struts of the tank, the usual gang of boys from the camp reposing over the caisson; he tells me to wait in the jeep, the fifty-lira tip from the tour in his fist as he walks across the rutted mud to the one he knows.

And as we pull away I see the white van in the hollow on the other side of the track; from behind the tower Jaffer striding back over the mud. Aubergine flares, white shirt open to the waist, his silver buckle flashing Indian-signals through the slanting sun. He looks over at the jeep, and waves, but does not come across.

On the steps to the arcade, the public-school hippie, hunched over his roll-up. He speaks in a throaty Maghreb-Arabic. He will hitch to Tyre in the morning; Harun warns him to go no further south.

At sunset we sit with Asad and Layla at the reed-hut bar beside the main road. The plastic tables covered in newspaper, the sea air stirring at last, though heavy still with frying-oil and diesel from the service-taxis and fruit-lorries along the sandy driveway to the sea. In the striplights over the hut, Layla's unmade-up face drawn and pale, her long fringe hiding the deep pouches under her eyes; she coughs weakly, tells me she has a cold. I have not told her when I am leaving, and now it is too late.

As the others order more beers, with the unwarmed mountain bread dunking at the hummus and moutabal, Harun goes out through the trucks with his pipe on to the darkening beach. But I do not stay.

They will have set a place for me up at the house, they will be waiting for the shopping. They no longer like to leave the village with all the roadblocks on the way down.

I kiss Asad on his unshaven cheek. I kiss Layla on her clammy forehead. I walk back up to the road; the sweet smell of the fruit through the tarpaulins of the parked lorries.

89

I sit for a moment without turning the key, my eyes shut against the undipped headlights going north; listening for the wash of the sea.

VIII

It is raining as we reach the house of the Bey. The new drive glossy in the wet, a beetle-patent over the parked cars; the clouds dark on the mountain.

We park, and go round by the steps. There is nobody under the porch, on the verandah; the lions basalt-black in the rain. We can hear the water running down into the valley. I wait until he has gone ahead before I reach out and touch the damp hollow of the maw.

We walk quickly through the first hall. We are late for the ceremony. On the low divan, the drivers sipping their demitasses, kalashins propped between their knees; they all stare up at his long matted hair.

Under the inner arch, Fawzi in his sage hunting-jacket; one hand to his chest, the other gesturing towards the door. The rain driving against the windows around the courtyard; the palmettos splayed out by the gusting, shivering, claw-like. From the other side of the yard, the low chanting, half-lost in the wind.

I had only come for his sake. All winter he had strayed no further than the front, buying what he needed from Abu Munir. He had taken the room next to Layla in the hotel above the harbour; working on his Burton translations with Harun, not losing his cough.

Asad had treated him as a guest, never cheating him on deals from the camp. Layla had washed and cooked for him, nursing him through the fevers. At the weekend Harun returned with books from the university library; Nefsawi, Ibn Batuta, the poets of the Ignorance. He would take no money for his tutoring.

The Englishman had hitched overland through Aleppo, Isfahan, Kabul; he had lived a year in Bombay; on his travels he had followed each day of the Ashura festivals, and Harun had arranged that I drive him up to watch the martyr play at the house of the Bey.

That winter my father had taken up a visiting-professorship at Stamford. The house by the campus had been left empty.

In a month the Englishman was to be joined by a coloured friend coming on from Istanbul, and needing the money I had offered to rent them the town house on condition that the rooms of my mother remained closed and that I could come and go as I wished. The fighting had started up again between the Maronites and the Palestinians around the camps to the south of Beirut, and everyone was saying that things would be worse this time, but the Englishman had accepted my terms without an Englishman's haggling, agreeing to take the house for six months, with the option to stay on if my father did not return.

Later we would learn that we had both been to the same brutal boarding-school in Hampshire, but he had left the term I arrived and we could not pretend to remember each other, and we never spoke of the place when we were alone together.

Beyond the yard, the door to the hall is open. There are more people than I had expected. Between the tall windows the politicos and mountain notables lounging on the gilded couches, the murafiqin standing behind in their black smocks; the city women in their tailored suits and Hermes head-scarves on the divans along the inner wall.

We squat down on the cool marble. At the far end we can

92

see a raised platform, there within the huddle of the faquieh the Imam seated among his followers; his grey cloak and tall black turban, his long, handsome face; a giant of a man, the only figure who seems in scale to the height of the hall.

On the floor before the platform, the Bey is standing in his gold shirwal and white turban, arms crossed over his padded chest. It is that scene when the heads of Husein and the other martyrs of the family of the Prophet are brought from the plain of Kerbala to be paraded before Yezid, the tyrant of Damascus; I have never known the Bey take any other role.

Over the floor to the feet of the tyrant comes Zain, the son of Husein, played by Ali; shuffling, half-crouching, his arms outstretched in stock lamentation, his beard thick and un-kempt now, his eyes watching me across the room.

Above him stands the old quawaji in his brocade waistcoat and baggy pantaloons, holding up the pitch-fork, mounted on the spikes the papier-mâché heads; their necks painted red, their eyes wide as mouths. As a boy I had spent hours searching the house for these heads, and never found them.

The Bey knows his lines, but Ali must read from the book.

The Bey embellishes, hams it up, smirks at the politicos, makes eyes at the city women. Bobbing around with his arms crossed, like the Cossack dancers in the downtown revue, his slurred words lost in the shadows of the high vaults.

'Lo. Cup-bearer, tarry not,
For the revolution of the spheres has no pause,
My minstrels come near,
Smite timbrels, the sistra sound,
Bring forth pipes and klaxons; tocsin-bells ring out
For Husein and his kin are slain on the plain of
    Kerbala.'

The quawaji waggles the heads. The Bey swaggering over towards the divans of city women.

'Come, nightingales of my rose garden,
Let your hands be dyed with henna,
Let there be bells on your ankles,
Uncover thy locks which are as bouquets of hyacinth,
Make a meadow of lilies with thy cheeks,
Burn ambergris, and fill censers with pure musk.
Come, Cup-bearer,
Beat your drum, make haste,
Full vinolent will be our days,
Rend the veil from the face of the lady of the jar,
Cast me like a drake in a river of wine
Thick as the blood of ravens
For Husein and his tribe are slain on the plain of Kerbala.'

Ali shuffles forward. He reads without raising his head, the book covering his face.

'But rather cast me like a drake among archers
To hear this sugar-eating parrot thus mock our holy name
For my soul is so pierced it will not suffer these bolts
    of insolence,
I will make the dark sky my winding sheet,
And blacken the days with my smoky sighs
For our princes have been as gazelles beneath the
    lances of hunters.
I will cast earth upon my face
And lay my head among the rocks and serpents
Hear only the tolling bell of passing caravans
And for forty days light a taper by the tomb of my father.'

94

Ali does not read well. He spells out the lines without relish; with the same forbearance of those who recite the Hadith among schoolchildren.

He can only have come with the giant Imam who must have asked him to read; afterwards he will stay close to his followers for Fawzi will not have forgotten the blood that is between their families.

As a child I had sat at the feet of my uncle and listened in delight to the mannerisms of the martyr plays; in the lower gardens I had danced to their measure, I had shouted the lines up the dry river-bed and stolen the florid refrains into my school compositions only to see them scored in red marker by my Attic masters.

Some lines I would repeat until they became strange and senseless and were changed into a call whose origins nobody could recognize and those fellahin who heard me among the terraces believed they had heard the crying of djinns. But now the speeches I had so grossly corrupted seemed unleavened and straightened to my ear, like unfermented liquor. I left my guest, and slipped away unnoticed to the study.

All was the same as ever there. The scent of worn leather, dead asphodels, the rain and coming darkness at the window masking the view down over the hills.

I pushed aside the lamp, the flowers; the dried petals that had settled on the frame. She seemed stiller than I remembered; more set and wooden, a spirit hardening into her tree.

I ran my fingers over the clouded eyes, the pearls at her neck, the bunching of the emerald gown; when I lowered my hand there was no dust on my fingertips.

Afterwards I went back and found Ali in the dark of the corridor, waiting for me, his part over. We embraced without speaking, the wiry roughness of his beard like a loofah against my face, scouring until my cheeks sang.

I do not remember much of what we said. I would wish later that I had. As usual he did not speak of his work with the Imam, of the new roads and schools and irrigation-lines the movement had been building in the lands to the south, but only to relate his visions of Kerbala and the martyrs and of that past that towered unheeded over all of us like the mountain over the village.

I see every detail. The curious symmetry of his blackheads, the comical wilderness of the beard; his eyes dull with certainty. But it is as if I had come away from a play remembering only the staging. The words do not return and I am left to parse a silence that never fell between us.

I drive the Englishman back through the village past the low wall of the graveyard, the crumbling turbans on the tombs of the beys, past the steps of the mosque, the paved promontory where the tourist buses no longer parked. Under the leafless plane tree we stop and wait for the procession to pass.

The rain has eased. A line of women walk ahead of us on the road, some carrying sponges and plastic buckets, others with bandages and cotton-wool. The younger women with their white veils up to their eyes, and as they turn we smell the iodine and rose-water.

From the path over the fellahin quarter the last men come through, those at the front still striking their breasts, their rhythm faltering, faces upturned to the brightening sky. Further down, above the cries, a dull pounding like the beating-out of kubbeh in the kitchens at sunrise.

The procession is longer this year. Through the square we

pass the youths showing off their bloody chests, slumped against the kiosk the row of shirtless older men with yellow-black bruises over their narrow ribcages, and there are many I do not recognize, mechanics and tractor-drivers returned from Sidon and the Bekaa, their hair flecked with the white rice-grains thrown by the boys from the branches of the plane tree.

I had hoped to take the Englishman back to the house, to give Uncle Samir company, but there is not enough time now. I slow at the corner below the ford and point up to the unlit verandah. But he is looking down at the new guards at the bottom of the drive, the cousins of the cook Khalil; the kalashins across their laps, their feet up against the brazier they sell chestnuts from on the corniche in autumn in the city.

The road down seems rougher than it used to be, but perhaps this is just because the jeep rattles more. We pass the still press, the turn where the Bey will have the boulders rolled across if there is more trouble on the coast.

Every week the Palestinian roadblocks climb a little higher into the hills. We see the first below the poplar-line, the Popular Fronters in their chocolate anoraks smoking behind their truck, their hoods up against the spitting rain.

We turn off on to the dirt-track, and down into the cover of the orchards. There is the smell of the damp earth; tunnels of thin, bare branches leading out into the sullen twilight on the plain.

It is dark when we reach the front, the rain passed, the first stars in the clearing sky. We do not go looking for Harun and Asad. They will have already returned to the camp. They no longer stay in the town after nightfall.

The month before I returned the mutilated bodies of two Palestinian boys had been found in a ditch below the old aqueduct on the Tyre road. Every week there are firefights between the Maronites and the camp-dwellers around the new market, along the highway above the new town.

We go down across the beach, our shoes scraping on the shingle, on the wet sand; like something being dug up. The Englishman leads the way, along the ridge where the up-turned boats lie in summer, to the near side of the abandoned dig where there is a polythene tent to shelter in.

We sit on the dry crates; at our feet shrivelled peel and old newspaper. Leighton huddled over the pipe, his back to the wind. Along the shore the lamps among the reed-huts, the distant rumble of the fruit-trucks heading north; a wide, white avenue of moonlight over the dark waters.

As the new moon creeps over the mountain, a spade is struck into the ground, a pit dug, a bonfire lit there for the ten days of Muharram.

In the courtyards of the villas in the hills, the dustsheets pulled down from the tabuts, from the semblances of the tombs of Husein made from ivory and white stucco; in poorer houses of lath and plaster, farded with mica and tinsel. Those who cannot afford a tabut keep a night-light floating in an earthen pot or basin sunk into the ground.

On the first day the banners of Husein rove through the alleys, his horse in effigy; the followers with peacock-tails, ivory and sandalwood, aftabi-banners blazoned with gold, and the figure of the sun.

The procession on the seventh night marks the marriage of Karim and Fatimah, the bridegroom under a silken umbrella; in place of dancing girls, the young men chant funeral dirges by torchlight.

The tabuts are carried on the tenth day to the cemetery,

and to the sea. Households merging in cavalcade through the narrow lanes to the esplanade; musicians with pipes, cymbals, high horns, followed by the arms and ensigns of the martyrs; the caparisoned horse, models of the sepulchres of Ali and Fatimah, of the seraph-beast Buraq on which the prophet had journeyed from Jerusalem.

Men come with censers of burning myrrh, clove-wood, gum benjamin; the tabuts shaking on their poles, on the humps of the camels; a train of faquirs and clowns. All thronging through the narrow lanes to the front, naked men joining the route, some painted as tigers and leopards, some with spears and clubs.

The tabuts carried out into the waves. Streamers, bright trimmings, floating after them on the wash.

It seemed a world away from the empty shore beyond the tent, the shuttered shops behind waiting on an uncertain summer.

I followed him back to the steps below the arcade. He was coughing, his hand held to his chest, as if to salaam. I listened for the gulls over the causeway, but could hear nothing though all the front was silent, the doorways shuttered, the level on the steps where the boys played deserted.

I remembered our first afternoons. Her dying-fish twitching. The rub of her salty skin, the gentle heft of her against my eyelids.

I let Leighton go on across the clearing to the hallway. From the head of the steps I watched the pale lights through the slats of the iron shutters, the shadows crossing.

When I heard the footfalls in the hallway, I lowered myself below the wall. From the unlit doorway, a figure staggered out into the alley, wiping his mouth with the back of his hand, his shirt unbuttoned under his coat, his aubergine flares dragging on the wet cobbles. Jaffer walked quickly, without looking round, up towards the market.

I waited there on the damp stone, for an hour or more perhaps, my head between my knees. I had not eaten since the morning, and when I retched the trail was watery and colourless as the rain.

As I walked back to the jeep with the sick-stench on my gums I remember looking down the alleys for some sumsum to take away the taste, but all the night-stalls had closed early, the Chiclet-boys long returned to the safety of the camp; the flickering lines of the recently erected streetlights rising over the new town into the black band of the foothills.

London, 1992

February 3rd, Noon

I open my eyes.

The room is empty.

Down on the stairs, I hear the soft tread of sneakers; the clacking of the loose parquet on the landing, like pieces being put back after a game of chess.

Out in the hall, hurried footfalls. The dull report of latches being drawn. The swish of traffic through an open door.

I try to stand. The pain in my stomach, dense and hard, as if it could drop down through the floor.

I reach out, to steady myself. To the chest. I feel nothing, but do not fall. Slowly the sense starting into my dead fingers; I stub at my scalp to draw the blood back.

On the empty recliner, the Watchman playing on in the darkness. The colours swimming with imaginary warmth; I bend over the small oblong of light, my fingers too numb to work the controls.

It must be a premiere, a charity gala. Beneath a spangled portico, women in low-cut gowns walking with men in dinner jackets between ranks of flashlights; some couples pausing on the wide steps, others hurrying in with heads bowed.

Between two taller women, stepping from a car, a man with a close-cropped beard; his tallowy pallor as if about to melt in the glare.

If it is him, it must be old film; that beard had been an experiment I had soon regretted.

The screen shudders. Above shaven heads, a giant effigy bobbing like a buoy on troubled waters, and the crowd turns, and there over the flames my own face.

I drop the set on to the torn cushion, draw my chair towards the window.

Downstairs there are voices; a door closes. Then silence again; the lisping of the gas grill.

Under the window; Leighton crouching, fighting for breath.

I had not seen him come back in.

He must have found the pipe downstairs; with his smoke-blackened blade, he is scraping at the ridges in the smutted chamber.

On the glazed level of the fire-surround, he taps out the blade. Thin grey flakes, like dead scalp-skin, gathering over the low sheen.

Spreading out over the surface, a single, viscous drop of acetone, colourless as rain. The flames dance high on the tile. I smell the singeing of his hair.

Over the pin-holed bouche of the pipe, the powder slipping away like sand in an hourglass.

A wavering flame, his lips to the gash in the flank of the pipe; the smoke-genie spinning in the chamber like a speeded film of clouds passing overhead.

His eyes closing, he falls back against the wall.

Over him Verger stands and looks down to the drive. In the shadows behind, the Watchman playing on; the rainbows circle the ceiling.

'Who was it downstairs?'

My own voice, strange to me, recoiling from itself.

Verger glancing up from his lap, picking away the orange pod of an earpiece. The even light of the winter noon over the wedge of pitted rug; the mugs and ashtrays there as permanent as the monuments of the city.

'No one.' He looks to the window, but can see nothing.

In the corner, Leighton still crouching, his bony legs shuddering under the loose jeans.

'We could call in, while we wait.' His pleading, spaniel eyes.

Verger puts back the earpiece; his head nodding to the beat, his air-cushioned soles pushing at the chest.

When he speaks his words are without edges, like a call underground.

'No one's phoning no one.'

Leighton scratching his arm, sipping from the cup, swallowing with some difficulty.

'No one leaves neither. Till it's all sorted.'

Down in the yard, the slush is melting. From the gutter, a black trickle over the walls, the pigeon-ledges, the rotten espalier.

I find the driest place, roll out the mat. I do not need the compass now. The mist has lifted. I can see the beeches, the brewery chimney on the river.

Sometimes he longs for me; he knows that I will not neglect him in the end. He does not replace lightbulbs, he keeps the curtains drawn. He does not sit at his desk at the window, but below the sill among the joint-stubs and bottles of vintage wine.

In the square where the bay trees never grow, he gropes through the house, searching for what he has mislaid. A corkscrew, his lighter, a printing cartridge. Every work, every petty task, a final act. Considered, cherished.

A rare beauty to what others would pass over. The angle things fall at; the dust spinning; the nicks on his scalp.

Through the slit between the brocade curtains, he looks down to the cobbled mews. It is empty. He wonders if he will see the summer, the white blossom on the cherry trees; the balmy late afternoons over the court whose lie he knows so well now.

DARK STAR

'To dream like the vulture, you must first learn to eat corpses.'

– A Bedouin proverb

I

It was always the large houses that were most claustrophobic.

Deep within themselves they concealed spaces that never betrayed the world beyond. Tack-rooms, forgotten pantries, priest-holes; dead passages, sunless courts. Interiorities which issued nowhere but into an indefinite extension of their own cribbed finitude, as Piranesi drew in his carceri; annexes to annexes: a closeness infinitely ramifying.

But our villa beside the campus was the antitype to these country houses I had visited as a schoolboy. Every room drowned in the mote-rich light, even the inner corridors giving at their ends to the smudged meeting of sea and sky. The wide verandahs on every side but the rear so that at any time somewhere there was shade; the slow-retreating shadow-lines telling the hours across the warmed terracotta of the tiles.

Between the web of the carob trees, the grey line of the corniche, its drop hiding the narrow strip of beach, the palms and tamarisks on the promenade scratching over the china-blue horizon. Across the dried lawns welted with crabgrass, the old swing and the dying cedar sunk like wrecks in the tall esparto of the lower terraces. Through the wizened branches the white blocks of the embassy compound, and all beyond unsighted by the outcrop of Ein Mreisse until again the view opens to the bay and the toy-scale marina where later I would watch the bravado water-skiers crossing on the days there was fighting up in the bourj.

Above the peeling poolhouse, the unfinished rooftops of the city climbing to the dark flanks of the mountains; their milky turbans lost under the bright unbroken clouds.

But that April after my final term at boarding-school when I came in by taxi from the airport, the corniche flooded with the rains, I had found the place still closed up as if for summer, all the shutters down, the rattan recliners and tables brought in from the verandahs. Inside the furniture under the dust-sheets, a scent of incense and stale sweat, the kelims and bokharas half-unrolled against the walls as if in a bazaar. Through the darkness the black man padding ahead in his long white umbaz and tourist-souk slippers, a weak coughing from the end of the corridor, billowing reels of silk hanging down from the blades of the ceiling fans to make a pavilion of every room, a circle of oil-lamps around the mound of pouffes and bolsters where Leighton perched puffing on his hookah like the caterpillar in Alice, on the lectern of his knees a volume of the *Nights*, his yellow turban fastened with a single teardrop pearl that seemed to drain the last light from his glazed eyes.

In the days that followed I would grow accustomed to the mole's life they had made for themselves in those rooms, my sight adjusting to the shuttered dark, the pale arcs of the lamps. Along the corridors the dim glow of the reed-baskets, the tiles that lilted underfoot, the rustling of an Abu Brace. Despite the shadows I knew the measure of every room and object and remembered those afternoons I had returned from the airport with my father and had longed to stay on there forgotten through the summer crawling with the ants and brown-backs over the cool marble streaked with the thin white archipelagos of poison.

Leighton rarely moved from the study. He had all he

needed there. His volumes of Burton, his translations from the Farsi; the sixteen books of the *Nights* stacked square as a stand for the pipe, a bowl of dates and black olives.

Along the shelves behind, other books he left unread. Tancred, *Eōthen, Travels in Arabia Deserta*; lives of Hester Stanhope and Lady Jane Digby; a manuscript of the *Perfumed Garden of Sheikh Nefsawi*.

Beneath the empty cabinet where my father had once displayed his Phoenician glass, his collection of pipes, in descending order, like a horn section. Tall hookahs, hubble-bubbles; a cherrywood tchiboque the length of a trombone; slender narghiles with chambers of rose-water; at the lower end the chillums from the Hindu Kush, the more workaday bongs and stems.

Against the opposite wall, enshrined in a penumbra of oil-lamps and incense-sticks, the heavy gilt frame circling the face of Burton, the features smoke-foxed, hard to make out. Down the cheek a long scar, the love-bite of a Somali spearhead from the first expedition to the source of the Nile. The lower face concealed by the beard, twin-pointed, mosaic; a walrus moustache over the lips, the wing-collar like a ripped envelope, his skin grey-white as Portland stone. The black eyes still imperious under the crumbled hang of the brow like marble settled beneath sands.

Under the portrait, Leighton reads, smokes, spits among the olive stones. Twice an hour, the turban unravelling; a mummy bandage. His long hair spilling over the unbuttoned umbaz; his shallow chest, sunken nipples.

It was weeks before we could hear the fighting from the house. In the mornings the students would be laughing and

111

calling to each other across the tables outside Faisals Café, and the shops along Abdul-Aziz would stay open until noon, and it was only when I came to the place where the old man still sat under the racks of plastic sandals and straw hats above the empty beach that I could hear the muted reports of the mortars down in the southern suburbs, like sap bursting on a fire.

Sometimes in the night we would be woken by the distant hooting of the cars along Hamra bringing the wounded up to the university hospital.

On the pavements the rubbish lay uncollected; we no longer heard at dawn the cries of the sweepers passing down the hill with their wide brooms and olive-branches.

Each morning when I ate my apricots under the shade of the hibiscus I watched our elderly neighbour Monsieur Tannous come out from his porch in his apron and oven-gloves, a camphor handkerchief over his face. He brought his old-fashioned oil-can with a long spout. The rubbish pile smouldered through the day, the grey smoke drifting across the verandahs.

I no longer took our rubbish down to the street. When the flies massed in the kitchen, I dragged the bags to the disused cistern in the lower garden. At night the cats broke into the bags, and in the mornings the lawns were strewn with plastic bottles and cartons, and those passing assumed the house had been abandoned, and cast their own rubbish over the wall.

Though I ran two lengths of chicken-wire above the breccia, the bright litter continued to gather on the lower lawns, though in time it would disappear under the tall weeds and grasses.

We no longer heard at dawn the call of the barwaq-seller on the corner of rue Bliss, only the hoarse cries of those

112

wheelbarrow-men displaced from their customary routes in the southern suburbs. As the sun rose over Sannine I watched the women on the balconies of the new block above the corniche drawing up their baskets filled with okra, water-melons, sun-blackened bananas.

When the shops on Ein Mreisse and Abdul-Aziz were closed and looted, people feared to leave their houses. We saw more wheelbarrows on the streets than cars, creeping between the smouldering rubbish piles, in their wake the scrapping Chiclet-boys, a silent train of pie-dogs and feral cats.

In the heat of the afternoon when the dogs were asleep and the streets empty the vendors of sharab and lemonade passed ringing their brass castanets. But the old-timers only rarely made the journey in from the suburbs; the tamarind-juice man with his cracked cymbals; the Sudanese peanut-shabb with the chimney he fed with old newspaper so it seemed the nuts were being roasted as he passed; the hunched sheikh of the sesame cakes who I had always approached out of sight of the house, slipping my ten piastres through the bars into his gnarled hand, watching intently as the old man shook the hollow dough, punching it with his thumb, filling the hole with thyme and salt, the warm pastry sticking to the floor of my mouth so that its sweet essence would linger on through the hot afternoons until the shadows lengthened on the lawns.

When the sun set the sahlab-seller still waited with his lantern. From the verandah I could smell the pans of sugar-milk and cinnamon forbidden to me as a boy; the charcoal-fumes drifting up with the smoke from the rubbish mounds along the beach below the promenade.

113

By early summer the old air-conditioning units had begun to fail. The nights became too close to spend in the house.

We dragged our mattresses up to the washroom on the flat roof. Leighton making another pavilion for himself under the sheets strung over the clothes-line; hanging up two hurricane lamps though the sky was bright enough to read by.

When he turned off the lamps we had a cat's view over the rooftops of the headland. The unfinished blocks rising like broken steps to the dark hallway of Mount Sannine. The clutter of sandbags, derelict furniture, washing hung out between the twists of girders; to the east the hotels above the bay lit up like fairground rides. Above their lights the black megalith of the new Murr Tower; without its scaffolding as stark and elemental as the Ka'bah.

In the mornings Verger took advantage of the short-lived breeze over the corniche to go out for provisions. He brought back mountain olives and tinned ravioli from Smiths-Stores on Hamra which had employed Palestinian guards; on the days Samedi Patisserie was open, baclava and sweetbreads in a glossy cream box tied with scarlet ribbon.

As Monsieur Tannous looked on from his porch he weaved his way between the smouldering fires in his flapping kaftan and cricket cap, no longer trying to shoo away the street-boys who followed him back from the corner, thrumming their lips, dragging their knuckles on the cracked pavements.

Black men were almost unknown in the city, remembered only as afreets and soldiers. The haggard, half-starved Senegalese abandoned by the French in their makeshift barracks in those final days of the Mandate when all the mulberry trees were dying and the brothels silent and empty, the deserters harassing the local fishermen, scavenging at night like cats among the rubbish; in the year the Sixth Fleet had landed the

114

only casualties had been the two black marines caught by a riptide off Ramlet al-Baida, their naked bodies knocking between the rocks below the Sidon road where the people stopped to look down from the sherbert and ice-cream stalls.

When he did not return by noon I would go looking for him along rue Hamra. Beyond Bliss the pavements blocked by the rubbish mounds and the pitches selling whisky, cigarettes and crates of beer looted from the warehouses downtown. Outside Smiths-Stores and the other open shops, the broken armchairs of the lolling militiamen with camphor handkerchiefs over their faces like movie outlaws.

If I could not find him, I would eat quickly at one of the two restaurants that had not closed. The Café de Paris still served a single plat du jour; at the Socrates the chicken stuffed with rice and mincemeat was now the only dish on that once prolix menu. After lunch the streets would empty suddenly, those few still out quickening their pace, looking over their shoulders, staccato-walking like men in antique film. I would pay one of the waiters to go out and flag down a taxi, and on the way back I would crouch low on the seat so that from the streets the car appeared empty.

Leighton had told me that Verger was a child of the Brixton slums, and knew how to look out for himself, but I could not help but notice how unsettled he became if Verger did not return by noon. Through the study door I would hear the crack of impatiently turned pages, the plop of hard-spat olive stones, the squelching of his sweaty feet pacing the bare floor.

Sometimes Verger did not return until evening. On those days he brought back no provisions. There were sweat-rings down each side of his kaftan, his face sheeny with sweat, pores wide as pock-marks. But on those evenings Leighton received

115

him with surprising indulgence, making room on the divan, plumping up the bolsters.

Those were the nights they would sit up smoking their afioun-pipes, and I would go alone to the washroom on the roof, and turn my back on the lessened lights of the city and the distant hooting along Hamra, and read my art-history books under the gently swinging hurricane lamps; the fly-blown Thames & Hudsons I had scavenged from the pavement bookstalls; Gombrich, Panofsky; the Penguin Vasari I had brought back from London; all on the reading list for my first year at the Courtauld Institute.

When my eyes tired from the poor light I would look out over the still glow of the horizon band, the far lights of the tankers drifting north towards Tripoli; as a boy I had run bets with myself on the time of their crossing, as I had with the trails of brown-backs over the verandah.

It was then I would think of my father, and the routines he must already be drawing up against the past. Each even-bright morning stepping between the sprinklers and the kotah-palms from his motel room in Palo Alto; the seersucker suit, the worry-beads clicking behind his back. His old-world gait over a landscape without memory; a scarab-beetle across a child's sketch.

It was unlikely he would be returning now with the fighting spreading from the camps around the airport, not before the new year by which time he would know if they had offered tenure. Through February and March he had phoned the house in London every weekend, making me promise not to go back, offering to fix me up with portering at Sotheby's, a temporary position at one of the Cork Street galleries, hanging up suddenly as the call got too expensive. When he knew I was determined to return, he could only speak of what I should not forget to bring back; the Persian miniatures, the remaining bokharas; all the Phoenician glass he had not already taken which lay embedded in boxes of sawdust in the cellars.

I had arrived at the airport to torrential rain after a delay of seven hours at Heathrow. In the customs hall the deuxième-bureau in their cream suits and dark glasses like a receiving line of cruise-ship entertainers, outside the troops huddled under the sodden tarpaulins in the lee of the personnel-carriers. There had been no roadblocks and few cars along the flooded avenue de la République, the southern suburbs around the camps silent under the driving rain though the papers in the airport stands had carried reports of firefights at the sports stadium and further shelling along the border.

When I had tried to take a taxi south, the driver had told me the highway above Sidon was blocked by the burning tyres of the leftist demonstrators; earlier in the week there had been mortar exchanges between the army and the Palestinians over that same stretch of the coast road. I had phoned from the house by the campus to find the lines to the village were down, and though I got through later to the hotel on the front the new concierge had never heard of Layla and her brothers from the camp.

The following day I had gone to the history department on the campus only to be informed that Harun had not returned that semester. When I had called their mother at the house in the Sursuq quarter I was told Aunt Mona's family had already left with all their regular staff for Paris.

And three months later the telephones were still down. For weeks I had tried calling out of the city. To Uncle Samir, to the Bey, to the maktab at the Ein Helweh camp, but like the hidden water-courses the calls only came up at the towns and resorts in the mountains north of the city. With patience it was still possible to phone abroad, but not to neighbouring streets. Monsieur Tannous had heard rumours that gunboys had broken into the exchange south of the city on a hashashiyeh and played havoc there.

It had become a city where nobody could know if they had been forgotten. We all lived in that room the philosophy master at school had described which disappeared when the last to leave closed the door. Those who cannot tell if they have been remembered must exist a little less.

I refused to forgive Layla her disappearance. Though I had strung her along for three summers with gifts and visions and promises my guilt had nurtured a tenderness for the hopes I could no longer bear to sink and now I punished her betrayal by remembering only what had least embodied her. A craze for liquorice, the suede jacket she had never worn, her platinum phase.

I had already punished her in anticipation of her betrayal, and perhaps she would never have betrayed me had I not. When I had beaten her I had used words on her she could not understand and the spittle in her eyes had dried like sleep and afterwards the penitent nuzzling in her hollow belly and the salt tears licked away until at last she would reach down and stroke my hair with the disdain of someone flicking straw off the coat of a soppy dog.

I had never told Ali about her. He must have heard the talk in the village. The Imam had offices above the city in Baabda, but whenever I managed to get through they would only say that he was working with his brothers in the south. I bought the newspapers that carried photographs of the Imam. Al-Safir, Amal.

I have these pictures still. The Imam at a rally of workers at

Karantina; his black turban high as a float above revellers. The Imam at bomb sites in border villages: towering above the bearded boys with kalashins and shy eyes; Ali was never among them.

By high summer the water supply had become irregular. The incense no longer covered the smells from the drying pipes, the sweating walls, the rubbish down in the gardens.

Leighton burnt camphor-crystals in the oil-lamps. The abayas damp with patchouli; their hair sprayed with Flit to keep the flies off.

Since the beginning of the summer the maid and the gardener had not returned from their mountain villages, and I no longer had the money to repay what Leighton owed them. We did what we could, burning the rubbish in the cistern below the poolhouse, mopping up the puddles in the empty pool where the mosquitoes bred. At night we lit moon-tigers across the verandahs. We draped nets soaked in Autan over the windows.

Though the air was fresher on the roof it was difficult to sleep there now. As the electricity supplies had become more erratic the generators installed on neighbouring roofs hummed and droned through the nights. To the south we could hear the distant crump of the shelling; in the hills the mortars like hollow clapping.

Since the fall of the government, the fighting had gradually begun to encircle the city; on leaving the parliament building, the first act of the prime minister had been to hand out automatic rifles to his followers from a van parked at the gates. On the darker nights we could make out the shell-flashes over the camps and slums to the east; Shi'i, Kurds and Syrian migrant-workers bombarded from those surrounding Christian districts that had once employed their labour.

By day Leighton read less, but still did not leave the study, practising his Arabic on the newspapers Verger brought back from the pavement stalls. He used the crumpled pages as a cuspidor.

We saw photographs of the Maronite brothers on the parapets of their mountain monasteries, kalashins held aloft, their soutanes tucked above their belts; when his laughter turned to coughing the pipe-stems tapping on the cabinet.

We saw photographs of the Imam at his hunger strike against the violence in the mosque downtown, each morning taking only salt and water, and a dozen sesame seeds.

These were the months when the fighters still wore masks. They returned each week to their jobs without revealing their new vocation.

Most battles were begun by accident. A dispute in a bar over a pinball machine between a Christian and a Moslem ignited seven days of shelling on the hills. One morning in August the brothers of a Christian girl importuned by two Iraqis came out into the street firing into the air to avenge their family honour, and soon the entire neighbourhood was exchanging mortars and rockets and shells falling over all the plains of the city.

That evening when I laid the moon-tigers on the verandah, I could see two thin columns of black smoke rising from the port warehouses and office buildings only two kilometres to the east of the house. The others had noticed nothing; I did not show them what I had seen.

Some nights I went down to the poolhouse, built a bed for myself from the lilos and recliners in the room where the garden furniture was stored. There I could not hear the generators, only the cats rooting among the rubbish. I had lost the wax earplugs brought from London, but improvised with pellets of foam picked out of the cushions.

If I still could not sleep I went in search of Verger. From his brass pillbox, the grains of Nembutal, thin and hard, like uncooked rice. Then I would sleep through until the following afternoon and when I woke it would take an eternity to cross the upper lawns and verandahs as if the world had been flooded and every movement under the pressure of a deep ocean.

But soon I grew accustomed to the pills. By nightfall I missed their warm armour; the ponderous freedom of the diver from smell and noise. In the daylight I saw the grains were not white, but the pale blue of the winter sky over the village.

By August the flies had reached the study. At dusk Leighton left the house, strolling down to the corniche as the second breeze rode up from the sea carrying the smells of frying farriden and roasting peanuts from the stalls on the promenade.

He walks stiffly, like an invalid, his back stooped from the opium constipation. They no longer stare at his filthy abaya, fruit-stained like a bib, his long hair too matted to lift with the wind; the sahlab-seller under his lantern; the shawarma-man perched on the generator which turns his spit; the old Druz cross-legged on the white sheet spread with candles, torches, gas-lamps.

He walked out to the same point each evening, that same

stretch of the corniche beyond the embassy compound. There the air was freshest, the rubbish not smouldering in mounds, but thrown among the rocks for the gulls to pick at.

It was the hour when families and courting couples and old men clicking worry-beads came down to escape the stench and noise of the city. Leaning over the pitted balustrade he turned his back on them all and looked up to what was still visible of Ein Mreisse, the unlit terraces below the roman-tile roofs and the serail on the hill, seeing only what Burton would have seen.

A Saint Bernard, two Yarboroughs, two bridled bull-terriers; a Kurdish pup, a camel, a white donkey, three goats; a pet lamb, a Persian cat; chickens, turkeys, geese, guinea-fowl and pigeons; a stable of twelve three-quarters and half-breeds (thoroughbreds would have implied corruption); later a black panther cub which slept by their bed, trapped in the desert, the gift of a Palmyran sheikh; in time the panther ate the remainder of the menagerie, and was in its turn poisoned by the villagers.

A garden of apricot, lemon and orange trees. A basalt fountain in the patio. Potted flowers on the flat roof.

Sherberts, lemonade, tchiboques and narghiles served on high divans.

Each week a colourful salon attended by orientalists, beys, sheikhs; notables of the seventeen sects of the city; by Lady Jane Digby El Mezrab who had run away from her husband, the Governor-General of India, and gone through six 'husbands' on the continent before winding up in Syria as the wife of a local Bedouin chieftain.

All this Burton had lost and remembered as he walked

alone along the seafront on that night he had been recalled in disgrace from his consulship in Damascus. Abandoned by his servants, unaccompanied even by a single Qawas with staff and pantaloons to show him out with a final semblance of state.

He pictured his return to England as Ovid his exile. 'I will become a neglected book gnawed by a moth.' 'A stream dammed with mud.' 'By Phalaris clapped into the belly of a brazen bull.'

'This is where he would have come that last evening.' Leighton peering back longingly at the darkening shore; his pupils small as pinheads. I do not have the heart to tell him the promenade was built in the late forties, and planted only then with these palms and tamarisks which against type have not taken well in the sea air though their roots are said to reach down to the underworld.

Burton could never have paced his final hour here. In that time we would have been walking out on the waters.

II

By the end of September the air off the sea was cooler, less humid, the scents of the rubbish receding.

Each morning I kicked away the rags and scraps lifted by the stronger winds over the verandahs. Like a tide the night washing strange wrack over the gardens. Watermelon-skins, comics; a brek.

In the tall grass: cartridges and unopened tins and broken mirrors winking in those first unwarming sun streaks above Sannine.

These were the weeks of the rentrée when the neighbours came down again from their summer villas in the mountain resorts, but that year with the fighting on the outskirts many families had taken their holidays abroad, and had still not returned. The streets around the hill remained quiet.

After midday little traffic passed the gates. I saw only Chiclet-boys on short-cuts to the promenade and the maids left behind to mind the houses. The wheelbarrow-men no longer called until they reached the new flats down on the corniche.

During the days we avoided each other. We kept behind the invisible partitions we had drawn across the rooms.

Leighton in the study, beside him on the book-tower his mezze of bowel foods. Prunes, acadiniah, mountain yoghurt.

Verger out on the front verandah, the old Grundig always at his side. The dial sliding in his fingers like a Ouija-cup, summoning the spirits of his past.

124

All afternoon he watched the street through the carob trees, almost guiltily; as if he were waiting for someone his own poor directions had made late.

When he came to the balustrade the street-boys gathered and serenaded him from the cover of the breccia wall. Abd Abd. Yimi Hundruq. BabMarlin. To silence them he threw down piastres and slips of gum.

In my room I no longer smelt the drying drains. The deep cope of the verandah made it difficult to read for long. When my eyes tired I lay back on the hammock and turned between court beauties and pale madonnas.

Lady Sykes, Nell Gwyn. Lady Hamilton, Adelina Patti; Mrs Siddons as the tragic muse. And I would always find her again in the sudden drop of a fringe and in a moue of sour lips and it was then I would return to the consoling abstractions of the perspective grids and villa groundplans.

At night I tried to keep her from my thoughts by remembering only those sitters that had least resembled her.

During those summer months I never went down into the city; only on the day Jaffer came. I did not leave the house until we needed food, and then always in the early mornings, and no further than the stalls up Abdul-Aziz. In the weeks my father had wired through my allowance I crouched on the floor of the taxi on the short drive to the bank on Hamra where all the telexes had been moved down into the re-inforced-concrete basement.

There had never been so much food in the shops. The guards lolling outside on their velveteen armchairs. The aisles blocked with pyramids of crates and cartons, the shelves so swollen with looted stocks that one had to walk sidewise through narrow crevices the way the fellahin moved as if in ancient relief among the closely planted sunflower fields below the river.

I brought back only what would keep; my garner in the cool of the cellars under the sawdust in the crates where the antique glass lay.

At Smiths-Stores I found pots of peanut butter and catering-size packets of all those American cereals made from candy and chocolate and marshmallow I had been forbidden as a boy.

From Spinneys-Supermarket I bought the last supplies of those staples I had developed a taste for at boarding-school which like the apples of Harun seemed mysteriously to augment in flavour the further from England they travelled. Marmite, digestive biscuits, Cadbury's Drinking Chocolate.

When Leighton and Verger had been up all night with their pipes they would buy from the wheelbarrow-men. The soft fruit and aubergines mushed with mountain yoghurt and sucked up through straws.

I would wake to the staccato slurping like the sounds of the cattlebirds watering down on the river, and afterwards through the slats I would watch Verger loping out to the lower gardens to squat in the tall grass below the cedar that had never liked the sea.

The day Jaffer came I was out under the wisterias that had overgrown the campus wall attaching lengths of garden hose to the tap there to bring fresh water back to the house. There were low, flat clouds again that day, but no rain, the air was close. He could not see me watching as he stood on the steps of the verandah and waited for Verger to rise from his recliner.

126

I had never witnessed Jaffer shaking hands before, his oustretched arm ceremonial and stiff as a prosthetic. Under the balustrade they sat together, Leighton squatting between them, translating as Jaffer scribbled on one of those square notepads they used in the village to tally the sheaves, throwing up his arms, holding the open page above his head as if to heavenly witnesses.

From across the lawns there was something of the prophet in this gesture, his tablets raised to an unanswering sky, but when I reached the house the notepad had been put away, and Verger had gone in to try his luck on the spirit-medium of the telephone.

The crotch of his tartan slacks and the neck of his leatherette mackintosh sheeny with his sweat. He avoided my eyes and seemed anxious to leave. But as he walked back to the steps he beckoned me after him, and it was only when we embraced that I saw the grazes on his cheeks and the deep black pouches under his eyes.

I did not want to go out on to the streets, not that late in the day, but I could think of no ready excuse for staying that did not sound altogether cowardly, and so I followed between the carob trees to the gate. As we wove between the broadened rubbish mounds he would only tell me he had come to the city to find his mother and Abu Musa though at the time I did not know whether to believe him, and he seemed reluctant to talk of what had happened in the village.

Later he would claim that the family had escaped down the orchard paths to join the refugee column heading north along the coastal highway after Fawzi and his cousins had fired shots over their roof on the day the Bey had left the village. From my last telephone conversation with my father I had already learnt that Uncle Samir and Aunt Mona had departed with the

Bey in the Dido-Sidonia from the north harbour when the fighting had reached the hills east of the village.

The cousins of Khalil who had remained to guard the house had reported that for over a month the road down to the coast had been blockaded by the Palestinians from Ein Helweh, and no produce from the village had reached the markets in Sidon, though some was now being taken by the mountain road to Nabatiyeh and the regis at Marjayoun.

Many of the fellahin had gone over to the Imam. There were rumours that many shebab had crossed the mountains to train with the new Shi'i militias in the camps in the Bekaa.

That week I had read in *An-Nahar* that the Bey had returned again from France; Jaffer had heard he had garrisoned the house above the almond hill with forty hunters from the high pastures, and sat alone all day with the curtains drawn watching old English films projected on to the high east wall of the diwan.

I thought at first Jaffer must have needed me as a guide, but already he seemed to know his way about the neighbourhood. On the sidewalks up from rue Clemenceau he strutted ahead like a typical country boy on his spree in town, following the girls with his eyes, clicking his tongue as they passed, relighting his joint with a flourish from a bulbous silver desk-lighter, the flame turned up high.

Along rue du Rome he began calling at the Christian girls in their tight jeans, waving, making the gesture of the thumb and palm, and I lagged behind not wishing to seem a part of it though most of the families I knew in that neighbourhood had left long before the summer and still not returned, and as we neared the park I could see there were country boys on every street and few city people.

On the approaches to Senayegh the families from the south

had taken shelter on the porches of the locked apartment buildings and under plastic sheets hung between the gate-posts; the old women squatting over butagaz-stoves, the younger boys begging from the steps.

Few shops had remained open, and those that had were guarded by militia deserters with fold-stock kalashins, but down on the edge of the park there was still the row of stalls selling fruit and vegetables and looted goods from the port, and around them more country women in white headscarves looking on in silence as if at a stranger's wedding feast.

These refugees were now trapped in the central districts by the ring of violence on the outskirts which in turn prevented those who had left the city from returning. All week we had heard reports on Channel Seven of outlaws from the mountains setting up ambushes on every approach to the city.

That morning while I had worked under the wisterias Monsieur Tannous had come out and told me he had heard Christian families had been tortured and mutilated at road-blocks in the southern suburbs, the women raped in front of their husbands, the children forced to watch what was done to their parents.

One rumour had it that a Christian doctor whose office overlooked a bridge from the west had turned sniper; he had killed and wounded over forty pedestrians, many of whom were then brought up to his surgery, and when captured had claimed that even at such a distance he had been able to distinguish the Palestinians and the leftists from all the others who crossed by that bridge.

Few of those city parks left behind by the French Mandate had survived the unruly domino game of the developers; those that had were soon stripped of their remaining trees for firewood and building purposes, and it was to these dust arenas that those refugees straying into the central districts had now converged.

As we came through the stalls we could see the lines of tents, blue-and-white plastic sheets held up on broken planks and palm stumps, naked children playing under the trickle from the iron spouts that had once watered the park, and between the shelters sheep and goats cropping the strips of burnt grass. Down among the tents there was the stench of excrement, and flies on every surface, and we crossed quickly to the al-Din end of the gardens and back again, peering in to where the fellahin lay on mattresses around small fires where they warmed coffee and fuul beans, but there were no families Jaffer recognized.

After we had checked the outlying shelters I wanted to return directly to the house, but Jaffer insisted we go down to the encampment on the beach. It was the hour of the promenade, and when we descended into the fresher air of the corniche we found a drunken crowd had already gathered to watch the refugees from the balustrades as if around some new attraction at the lunapark, some taunting, others throwing down blankets, money, nuts, Chiclets.

The beach cabanas below had been extended with awnings of polythene sheeting, and there were lines of washing hung between the weatherboards, and fires burning on the shingle. Where the onlookers had massed we had to push our way to the front, but it was difficult to make out individual faces from above, and Jaffer went down and walked among the cabanas, and I waited at the shawarma stand as the sun set and the promenade began to empty.

When he returned it was too late to cross into the Karantina district in the east of the city where many of the refugee families had been taken on government buses, and so we walked back together up the hill to the shuttered house.

His car was still there by the gates; he had paid the sahlab-seller to watch over it. With the streets darkening I did not want to remain outside, but he insisted on showing me the vehicle in all its particulars, leaning in to turn up the radio, tooting a long falderal on the horn as the village cars did on the turns below the drive.

The old white van he had replaced with an even more ancient Mercedes. A veteran service-taxi of the coastal highway and mountain-resort runs, piebald from its black replacement wings, plastic tulips over the dashboard, tortoiseshell worry-beads dangling from the mirror, the leather seats patched with squares of tartan and gauze, the hubcaps long lost to the cratered roads.

While I pretended to admire the thing he assured me that this was now the safest vehicle for crossings into the eastern districts. With the war on many of the service-drivers had been selling cheap; there were no longer registration fees to be paid at the shelled-out Mécanique. After the fighting was over he intended to restore all the ancient Mercedes in the city and export them back to Europe.

That night he slept in the car, drawing to the sun-curtain in the rear. He would not come into the house for fear of what would happen if the car was not watched.

The following morning he asked if he could conceal the vehicle in the grounds while he moved around the city. He had heard rumours that at the roadblocks of burning tyres on the outskirts old cars were being held by gunmen to provide spare parts for the militia fleets.

At first we tried reversing it under the carob trees, but he complained the snails and sticky husks would damage the paintwork so we cleared the garage and stacked paint-pots and planks and dustsheets across the entrance until the high grille was entirely hidden.

And after he had gone I squirmed back through the screen we had built, and tried each of the doors. Around the sea-green glass the rubber had perished, and I was able to force the lock with a bent wire-hanger as we had done at school when wheeling the cars of the masters out on to the playing fields at night.

Inside there was the faint smell of liquorice and stale joints. With the lighter flame turned up I worked my way around the floor, the door sills, the glove compartment, over the patched seats with their resin of old stains. But Jaffer had been careful. I found dried wasps, spent matches, some pages from an Italian pornographic magazine, nothing that would have belonged to her.

I had a proof of sorts though. When I had asked after the others from the front, he had answered readily enough: Harun was now teaching at the camp school; Asad was to train as an orderly at the Red Crescent Clinic by the water-tower. But of her he had said nothing.

For weeks Jaffer did not return to the house. We had no word of him.

Verger believed he had not wished to risk his precious car over the fronts, and had crossed on foot to the east, and been trapped behind the fighting around the camps.

But most days Verger did not hear the news, and it seemed

nobody would ever call again, the house drifting silently away from the city that had forgotten it.

I preferred to read my art books on the duller days. The crisp shore-light showing up the poor quality of the reproductions.

The lines between objects kinky and doubled like the vision of a cartoon drunk. The tones all out, as through a tinted window.

The faces and gowns of the monarchs as if dipped in T-shirt dyes; block-printed; the colours seeping, viscous as rime.

In the dark I tried to imagine the originals, knowing that when I saw them they would seem to have betrayed themselves.

The sitters in turn betrayed by so much form and flattery. The suspicion of a wig, the emerald of a gown that surely never could have been that colour; cornflower eyes that seem too dark for vision.

III

Only with the westward spread of the sandstone apartment buildings in the second quarter of the century had the house found itself within the city.

Detached from the bay and the port by the outcrop of Ein Mreisse, the headland had long remained a scrubland of fireweed and wild figs with chalk lanes winding between walled orchards and market gardens, the beaches empty but for the small crowds gathering where the lantern-lit caïques landed with catches dynamited to the surface of the bay, on the shingle the fishermen in their baggy shirwal weighing out the hake and red mullet with their stone measures, and on the lower campus there still survived pockets of this old wilderness in whose bowers the students courted and smoked joints.

Although the wide corniche road now extended along the beachline to the embassy compound, and the original three-arched villas were barely visible among the staggered condominiums, this campus salient remained isolated from the sectarian tectonic plates of the outlying districts, and of little strategic value to those militias probing in from the suburbs to stake their claims to the central districts of the city, and it was for this reason that Jaffer had chosen the house as a hiding-place for his service-Mercedes.

That early autumn the streets around the house had never been quieter. Only two baskets were lowered to the wheelbarrow-men who no longer called as they passed beneath the shuttered apartment buildings.

On some mornings there were reports on the radio of daylight raids on the shops up on Hamra and Abdul-Aziz, but for weeks we saw nothing from the house, barely a single passer-by, though at night we still heard the distant hooting of the cars on their way up from the suburbs to the university hospital.

If it was too dark to read I would settle by the radio, or with Leighton in the study. When he spoke I did not miss the England I had known, the mildewed country houses, the schoolfriends on their year out poncing drinks off the old queens at the Colony Rooms and the Chelsea Arts Club and smoking themselves gaga in the pubs off Ladbroke Grove.

What I missed was the electricity and looking out at the snow from a hot bath and the spiteful tidiness of the pavements in that little square off the Brompton Road where the Bey owned the house he never used and when each night I took my second Nembutal I dreamt of a country I had never left behind, a bey's England of summer hats and swizzle-sticks and concinnous buttonholes and garden parties where Layla strolls between gilded frames in her bustle and bows as if born to it all smilingly charmingly through the crowds on the terrace and miming the attitudes of the moss-encrusted statues and I follow her out across the lawns and under the bell-shadow of her dress the specks of blood lead a trail deeper into the gardens.

By the second week of that October it was cool enough to sleep inside again. Two cold nights and the dead flies scored the dustsheets and the open books and the long ledges above the radiators like the discarded punctuation of the summer.

The mattresses and lamps were brought down from the

washroom. The poolhouse locked, chipboards nailed over the windows so the street-boys would not break in and start fires as they had the year of my father's last sabbatical.

We closed the french windows on to the verandahs, and stuck the panes over with crosses of gaffer-tape. What few sources of light we had left we burnt under the windows. The oil jars, naphtha lamps; the paraffin burners. The house would never seem empty to the refugees straying up from the encampments on the beach.

On his porch Monsieur Tannous left out a bowl for the cats that chased away the rats from the rubbish mounds along the street. He no longer went down with his can and stick. Fuel had become too expensive to waste on rubbish-burning, but the cold still muted the scents from the gardens.

The sandalwood and camphor-balls and clove-buds had been used up in the study. When the stronger winds off the sea carried in the fumes from the neighbourhood generators and the tang of the beach wrack on to our lips and tongues we lit the moon-tigers left from the summer in circles around us, and hung our chests with garlands of cut garlic as the matrons had insisted on during the influenza epidemics at school.

Though the flies were all dead Verger rubbed his arms with Autan when the patchouli had run out, his hair with Flit for its lingering aroma.

Sometimes the north-easterlies brought in the bitter smoke from the burning warehouses over at the port where on brighter days we could see the upturned boats that had failed to clear the breakwater lying belly-up like melons cooling in a stream, and we would all go into the study, and seal the door from inside with tape until the wind changed.

In the weeks we had water there was no power to work the pump to the tank on the roof. Our drinking water we boiled from the supplies brought in along the garden hoses from the tap under the wisterias on the campus wall.

We washed and shaved in the water reheated over the butagaz-burner, though since the summer Leighton had trimmed his beard by candlelight with nail scissors in front of the rocaille mirror in the study; when the fighting in the suburbs had first knocked out the substations supplying the headland we had all shared my electric razor, but now the remaining batteries in the house were husbanded for the radio, and as the stocks ran lower the use of the Grundig was rationed to news reports.

Sometimes the power came on for an hour in the early morning. We were woken by the sudden brightness and the whirring of the appliances in the kitchen. We filled all the Pyrex containers from the hosepipe, and crammed them into the upper compartment of the ancient fridge, and for three days afterwards we drank our beers cool from the buckets of iced water in the cellars.

We had little other use for the power, though Leighton would save himself a quawaji's labours with the pestle and mortar by sitting up with the coffee-grinder, the dub-dub beat from the record-player drifting out over the rubbish-strewn lawns and all the dogs barking in the gardens of the abandoned villas.

Only Monsieur Tannous was left to complain, and he was too deaf to be troubled by the sudden blaring.

By late that October there had been reports on the radio that the leftist militias had advanced to Senayegh Gardens, and units had begun crossing rue Clemenceau to drive the Maronites from their redoubts in the deserted seafront hotels.

The street was still quiet, but that week the shawarma-man did not come down with his generator to the beach encampment, and so we could no longer take turns to run out for the sticks of kubbeh pounded with basil and marjoram that had become our basic fare.

When the rations in the cellars began to run low, and the cats got to the cereals under the sawdust, we had no choice but to wait by the gates and tip street-boys to go up to Bliss and hail a taxi. We would crouch below the level of the doors until we reached the pavement stalls that still traded for a couple of hours each morning.

We brought back whatever the first stall sold. Unsalted jebneh, monkey nuts, stale Gandour biscuits.

Sometimes a wheelbarrow-man passed down the street without calling. But Verger believed they were spying out villas for the militias to loot. When we saw the man we all came out on to the verandah and argued rough-house about the respective merits of our imaginary kalashins.

A few days after the shawarma-man moved on the street-boys began to claim they could no longer find taxis on Bliss. We tried to pay the boys to bring back the supplies from the stalls, but they would just run off with the money, and by the end of the week they had stopped coming to the street.

Leighton barely had the strength to reach the door of the study, and so Verger and I had to take turns carrying back supplies from the first stall or wheelbarrow-man we could find on the streets. The mornings were still the safest time to leave the house, but we avoided the corniche for fear of the roving gangs of refugees, and did not walk up beyond Abdul-Aziz as we knew from the radio reports that the militiamen had already penetrated the adjacent blocks.

To the east in Ein Mreisse one small grocer stayed open

until noon, but we would hope to find a pavement stall before reaching that street as the seaward end was vulnerable to the snipers on the upper floors of the deserted hotels.

On his first forays Verger improvised a large cross out of twine and bamboo from the dead terrace below the house, and ran the clearing with the cross held high above his head, but he had to abandon this device when the street-boys pelted him with rubbish and the old Druz grocer refused to serve him.

We made as few of these expeditions as we could. If we tried to bring back too much we could not crouch on those exposed stretches where the sandstone walls were already pitted with round craters. In the end we learnt to use back-packs rather than plastic bags, and whatever the weather we always wore the two long overcoats my father had left behind, one over the other, the lining torn to hold additional bags of rice and chick-peas. Each bag carried postponed our return to the streets by two more days.

On the mornings we could hear gunfire we no longer went out on to the verandahs and down into the gardens. We stood at the windows and peered out between the shutters and saw nothing. The newspaper-folds of our faeces we hurled out into the lower gardens, betting cigarettes from our diminishing supplies on who could land a hit on the cedar that had never liked the sea.

Fear is a strong laxative, and in those weeks when the fighting passed close around the house Leighton grew suddenly animated, unfurling oil-skin charts over the floors weighted down with volumes of the *Nights*, crawling over the gradient-whirls with dividers and compasses, entering lines and coordinates into a hidebound notebook I had never seen him use before.

All night we could hear the staccato bark of the kalashins above rue Clemenceau, and from below the crisper reports of the Maronite M16s like thick cardboard being torn. Leighton did not follow the fighting, but Verger would sit up with his pipe on the sill in the kitchen and watch the lazy arcs of tracer from the rooftop gunners falling like giant welding-sparks to the unlit ribbon of the shore.

On the nights of advances the militiamen sent up phosphorus shells from the mortars around Senayegh, and the sky burnt white over the headland, and the roosters crowed, and the dogs barked in the gardens of all the deserted villas.

On those nights I took two Nembutals, and still did not sleep. Under the shelves I lay among the fallen pipes, Leighton scuttling across the maps like an uncaged pet, charcoal pencils behind both his ears, the ravelled turban trailing after like a fallen lead.

He plotted a path in stars between the villages, single Hebrew letters on the hills and wadis, and later he told me this was the route of the last expedition Burton had planned into the Druz mountains before his expulsion from Damascus, and that from the sky the markings formed the sign of the aleph, and though he hardly had the strength to cross the house every night he whispered to himself that when it was safe to leave the city again he would hitch that way into the hills.

By early November the fighting had drifted to the east. We sat around the Grundig, spinning the dial between stations until the pattern emerged, name-checking the streets in the reports against the city map above the dripping fridge; after his first pipe Verger would turn to short-wave, and listen to the only

Arabic he understood, the insults traded between the fighters on the crossed wavelengths.

During the day we could hear the militias still firing down from the Murr Tower on to the last Maronite positions in the ruined seafront hotels. By night the Christians retaliated with bombardments of the silk and vegetable souks. Through the morning we watched the fires still burning; the firemen harassed by snipers, no pressure in the water-mains to work their hoses.

For days a pall of smoke hung over the city like the great umbrella pine of paradise. When we could get a picture on the old fish-bowl television in the servant quarters we glimpsed the ruins of the souks, commando units in firefights with fifty-strong bands of looters, armed convoys of Jewish and Armenian gold dealers heading out to the banks in Bab Idriss.

But within hours of this evacuation makeshift souks had spread to all the quieter corners of the city, and on the promenade beneath the campus we saw men unloading racks and trestle tables from vans as the refugees sat silently and watched on the balustrades; from that distance we could not tell what goods had been brought to sell there.

When it rained hard I waited for Jaffer. I listened for the scrunch of his platforms, his leather mackintosh flitting bat-like between the carob trees, the glint of the gold trireme-pendant looted from the souks.

And sometimes he came in the lulls at the end of the month as the banks opened for the militiamen to withdraw their wages, over the museum crossing in a service-taxi from the camp in the east where his mother and Abu Musa had been housed by the government. Always he brought something to sell. Razor-blades, a car battery to run the television from, hashmay-oil to chase over foil.

For Verger and Leighton: diamorphine ampoules from a friend who worked shifts as an orderly at the university hospital, and always the coarse Bekaa opium which left the house smelling like the donkey in the fellahin quarter.

Before running back to the taxi he would check the garage and tell us the worst of what he had witnessed. On Hamra, the rich looting Spinneys-Supermarket, and coming out to find their cars stolen.

Through the eastern suburbs, Maronite militiamen with belts strung with the ears of their dead rivals, on the window-sills of Ashrafieh whole jars of ears like snails in oil.

The university hospital had run out of fuel for the incinerators, and in the morgue families waiting for funerals were having to bribe spaces for their dead.

He had heard nothing of Ali, nothing of the village, though from his friend at the hospital he had learnt that Asad had been posted to one of the hard-pressed camp hospitals in the southern suburbs, but if he knew which he did not tell me. There were several of these hospitals, Acre, Gaza, Haifa, all named after the lost cities of Palestine. He must have known I would never have the courage to go out into the camps and search them all.

For days after Jaffer came we did not see another car on the hill. On those mornings the militia trucks piled with looted furniture and candelabra used the street as a short-cut to the corniche we waited until the evening before venturing out for our supplies.

The houses with generators kept their lights low, but to the east the sky was lit with the glow above those souks still burning from the shelling of the previous night.

As darkness came and the snipers were unsighted I passed old women and children with shovels and dustpans and trowels from the rooftop gardens filing over to the abandoned building site, loading the sandbags held open by the youngest boys who wheeled them back on barrows to reinforce the barricades of cement sacks and concrete blocks. But by the time I returned from the stalls they had all gone inside again and only the young guards remained huddled over the low iron braziers, and at the head of the street my empty stomach would shrivel against itself as behind me the first rockets fell from the east around the base of the Murr Tower, the old-woman's hiss of the katyushas, the muted crump of the B102s that detonated not on impact but after they had nosed their way through the outer concrete walls.

By late November we only risked an expedition to the stalls on the days Jaffer came when we knew the streets must be passable. As the light became too weak to read by I joined them around the fish-bowl television Verger had brought through from the servant quarters.

Under the piers of the ring-road, the corpses hung close and grey as caterpillar hives; off the coast the arms ships waiting in the mist like phooey supernatural sightings.

The Palm Court, the Excelsior, the unfinished Hilton, the twin-towered Phoenicia, the St Georges. One by one the seafront hotels had fallen until only the snipers in the heights of the Holiday Inn held out against the militias.

The car battery to run the television we recharged from the Mercedes in the garage, and as with the radio we rationed its use to the news. In protest against the ban on cartoons and westerns Verger would give readings from *The Prophet*, a dog-eared copy of which he had found among the books my father had left behind. He would read from nothing else, and opened the text at random, as if cutting a deck of cards, always intoning the same passage three times over.

When Verger was too stoned to fight Leighton had tried to set fire to the book, and each time it was saved from the flames fewer pages became legible, the charring imposing its own anacoluthons so that by December we were subjected to the relentless repetition of the same broken verses.

If Jaffer did not return within two weeks we rationed what food we had left. When we had finished the last of the rice and chick-peas, we divided what remained in the cocktail cabinet; we counted out the sausages, olives, peanuts, crackers into three equal heaps at the centre of the oil-maps: each could feed at their own pace, no one could maintain a secret garner.

My stock always ran out first. Leighton would trade me nuts and crackers for pipe-cleaning and shoulder-rubs and recitations from the Qur'ān. When he smoked the afioun he would not eat for days, but when I chased the hashmay-oil my hunger became all the keener and I would search the cellars and every container in the pantry though I had been through them all before and risk the gardens for carob husks and bitter hyacinth-beans.

Sometimes I craved foods I had always hated, some I did not know I had ever eaten; all the puddings that had made me sick as a child: sugared almonds and camardin and the bowls of rose-water semolina in the shade of the spreading plane tree where the flies hovered on the day the pilgrims left in the coaches for the coast.

I needed to hold her betrayal close to me. If I lost my fear the city had trapped me.

I had not come back for her, and yet each sleepless night I could blame no one else for reeling me back into this underworld.

And I could not leave with nothing to part from.

'Bodies have been dragged here.'

In the middle of the road, a scrape of dried blood, like a brushstroke. Verger turns, but I hold his arm.

'It's just the sheep for the feast.'

'When they are tied to the bumpers the men are still alive.'

'In the suburbs perhaps, not here. This is a good neighbourhood.'

Verger looks down the cratered avenue, and he laughs, deep and sonorous as an opera-player. It is Christmas Day.

Until we reach Bliss we see only children. Beneath a broken water-main, boys with tubs, buckets, Nido tins. At the iron grille of the bakery, more boys, with scabby necks and faces, paid to wait in line.

On Abdul-Aziz all the usual vendors have been replaced by boys, their wares laid out on the pavement. A jar of mayonnaise, more expensive than a television; a candelabra less than a chocolate bar.

A woman in an evening gown runs down between the pitches. Searching among the junk, for a looted heirloom perhaps. As she weeps the boys laughing and pulling at the drag of her skirt.

On Hamra, no festoons of fairy-bulbs, no speakers playing carols as in previous years. On the railings of some Muslim homes, painted-glass angels hanging between the palm and pine branches, and none are broken.

As we near the corner of Jeanne D'Arc, we hear gunshots. But the pavement vendors do not pack up and run. The sound is coming from further down the street, inside the cinemas the young militiamen shooting up the ceilings.

We buy our rice, artichokes, biscuits, and with coats and backpacks filled cross back on to Bliss, and to the east the sky is clear for the first time in weeks, the disused tramlines winking in the low sun over the mountains.

IV

'Being a closed religion, there have been many rumours.

'The turreted head-dresses of their women, their fair skin, had fostered certain legends. It was said they were descended from the last of the crusaders; those who had retreated high into the fastness of the Shuf Mountains.

'Of their spiritual leader, the Caliph Al-Hakim, it was recorded only that he banished singers and public conjurers; ordered the burning of the Holy Sepulchre; forbade women the use of baths, kohl, face powders; Jews the eating of mallow; Christians the service of horses.

'On the appointed day the Caliph would return in triumph from his long occlusion. Then the Muhammadans were to be made mules and asses to feed on vetch and draw heavy mills. The Nazarenes to bear metal discs in their ears that would freeze in winter and burn in summer.

'It was known they held Thursday holy, and worshipped among rocks in the high places; they would be reincarnated only as Britons and Nipponese.'

In those first cold weeks of January Leighton would talk of nothing but the Druz Mountains. He had the study to himself again.

He claimed the religion of the Druz to be the last true mystery of the east, though in moments of despair he would confess that the most secret springs of knowledge rarely ran pure.

147

After the last charred pages of *The Prophet* had been committed to the butagaz-burner, Verger had retreated with the television and car battery to the servant quarters; he had blocked the door with Amstel crates and watched the cartoons and westerns until he could no longer see the screen for the smoke.

I had to give a coded rap before he would let me in for the news. Though the pictures would not let me sleep.

In the plague years of the last century the camp had been used to quarantine people and animals entering the city, then settled by each wave of refugees, Armenians, Palestinians, Kurds, Shi'i; the government had surrounded the shanty-town with a wall twenty metres high to hide the eyesore from the tourists driving north along the coast road, but the mortaring had brought much of the wall down.

Each night they showed the same reel, the same choice corpses: the rooms where the dead had killed each other out of mercy into a stillness more animated than all the din and fireworks of the siege.

No Pompeii here, they knew what was coming, and had not tried to hide. Fathers had shot their daughters to save them from dishonour, then turned the gun on themselves.

The corpses propped against the walls by the cheated besiegers to be shot again, others dragged through the streets behind service-taxis and dumped in the garbage wadis where the snipers wait for those who will come to claim them. In the background dust, the bulldozers that will raze all trace of the place, the flattened black outlines of the corpses like cartoon roadkills that will fill back again into wholeness.

I do not stay in the room any longer than I have to. I tell him the smoke gets in my eyes; I will not let him see how the pictures wither me.

Though we had not had a visit from Jaffer for six weeks I knew that he could not have remained in the camp as the siege tightened. Unlike most of the refugees from the south the family had the money from the last poppy harvest to buy their passage out to one of the new settlements in the Bekaa valley, though Jaffer had now begun to make his own way on the streets and would not have accompanied his mother and grandfather over the mountains.

But if he had not come to the house because he believed I would follow him back to his rented room he had over-estimated my desire to heap more wretchedness upon myself.

As it was each night I had to watch the porn-reel of their couplings, his pocked peasant slickness, her fish-on-slab convulsions; the butterfly kisses she gives afterwards. The paintings I inhabit will not save me that and though I longed to blight and curse her covert pleasures by telling her to her sad little face that I had always meant to take her with me I could not risk the memory that room would leave with me.

In the dark he waits for the busty homesteaders, the saloon-bar whores, the blonde announcer on Channel Seven.

He kneels, and licks the screen, his hand twitching below like a severed limb.

The picture changes suddenly. It is the Brigadier General again, sweating under the lights. He never looks up from his paper, as if frightened to lose his place.

. . . the hour of deliverance is come, the presidential palace is surrounded by forward units of the Lebanon Arab Army . . .

For weeks he has been disrupting the programming with this same message, but the factions know the territory of the Brigadier General extends no further than the two blocks around the Channel Seven studio, and ignore him.

His image fades into a garden at twilight. Pines and cypresses, violin music, a girl in slacks strolling through the mist.

Her gallant waiting by a swing, holding out a packet, a slim lighter.

It's always a good time for a Kent.

Since the shelling began we no longer went into the rooms overlooking the verandahs for fear of shrapnel.

As each room filled with rubbish and pipe-litter, the encampment of mattresses and books and radio had shifted inwards to the servant quarters, and only the wing of my mother had remained unoccupied.

We had used up the paraffin and naphtha on the window lamps, but kept the curtains closed, and read by the light of the screen. The white backgrounds of the old cartoons and the deserts of the westerns provided the strongest light.

Every three days we spun the knife to decide who went down to the garage to recharge the battery, and when the blade elected Leighton we had to go out and help him on the steps.

Each night I stayed with them until the news was over. In the basements of the Baabda Palace the presidential family had sheltered for weeks from the artillery bombardments of the maverick majors in the hills. The end came cinematically; as the militias neared the gates there was no time to pack belongings and call their salukis, the President running to the helicopter with a revolver in one hand, in the other his trictrac board raised towards the mountains as a preacher would the holy book to a feckless congregation.

When Verger turned the volume up to cover the rallentando from the east I returned to my room, and lay without earplugs in the dark; I needed to hear the pattern of the shelling to know we were safe.

But only the ranging shots came close, some landing short of the radio tower on the other side of the campus, some falling beyond the promenade like whales foundering in shallow water, the sudden tide flooding the refugee tents down on the beach.

With the last of the winter rains the fighting ebbed away from the headland. On the lawns of the deserted villas pale maids came out and raked away the rubbish. Along the garden walls they stood and clapped as the first garbage truck in months passed down the hill; in its train an escort of thin boys in ill-matched fatigues, the straps of their kalashins trailing in the dust.

And at dusk the shawarma-man and the sahlab-seller with his lantern returned to the street, and down on the promenade young couples and old men strolled among the new outdoor stands piled with cowboy boots, rhinestone belts, shoulder holsters.

In the week the Palestinians allowed a convoy of diesel oil to leave the refinery on the Sidon coast for the power station to the north there was electricity once more, and water was pumped back into the city. We kept the lights out in the rooms we had abandoned, and lay all day in the baths until our skin was as shrivelled as the ancient peel over the verandahs.

As petrol was exchanged for flour across the fronts the first taxis began to appear again up on Bliss. We brought back croissants and black chocolate and breaded drumsticks from

Samedi Patisserie where there was still a household account, and gorged all day in our spotlit baths, and at night I could not sleep for the silence.

In the hours before dawn I planned my route to Asad, but through the mornings I lay in bed smoking the last of the hashmay-oil, and by the time I rose it was too late to set out. Despite the calm on the headland, transport into the suburbs remained irregular and expensive; Monsieur Tannous had heard that the service-drivers crossing into the east exchanged the Qur'āns hung from their mirrors for crucifixes as they approached the inner roadblocks, and some would wear false beards through the Shi'i districts beyond the airport.

Few drivers along Bliss would venture further south than place Unesco. The artillery that had shelled the presidential palace remained in the hills above the airport road, and Palestinian units still guarded all the approaches to the camps. I had thought of hiring a fishing caïque to drop me at the north harbour, hiking up through the orchard paths to the village and pleading with the Bey to order a driver to take me into the camps from the south of the city, but when I went down to the corniche I saw the shingle beneath Ein Mreisse was empty of boats.

On the evenings of the rallentando from the eastern hills the promenade would suddenly empty. These were the hours when the thieves and kidnappers were at large. In a single night of shelling two hundred people disappeared; a gang broke through the wall of the Coptic church to the vaults in Bab Idriss where the gold from the souks had been stored.

On those nights I slept well again, and dreamt of the twisted petals of shrapnel I had collected as a boy and traded

152

for that hard currency of sweets and conkers that had bought pardons from wandings.

In the lulls between the shelling Jaffer visited again, with Bekaa opium for the boys, a new prop-shaft for the Mercedes, a scribbled note from Ali. They had met at the offices of the Shi'i council in Baalbeck; before the siege of the camp in the east had tightened Ali had arranged for supporters of the Imam to drive Abu Musa and his mother across the mountains to the new settlement north of the town funded by the Iranians; on the day the cousins of Fawzi had fired on the house their father Musa-al-Tango had not joined the column of refugees on the coast road, but had gone into hiding up on the jurd near the old cave by the falls at Jazzin.

Jaffer did not leave the garage until the late afternoon; I never tried to follow him. The note from Ali, a quotation from the Sura of the Moon, I slipped among my art books and could not find again, and when I searched the house for the Qom-Qur'ān to check the reference by it too had disappeared; I suspected Verger must have sold it.

Each time I brought cooled Amstels out to Jaffer in the garage, and stood at the door watching the queue for visas ouside the embassy compound he would always offer to see me safely out for only fifty lira to the airport or the Jounieh Docks. At this price it would have been an insult to refuse the favour though I knew he just wanted to be rid of me. In the end I agreed to go with him to the airport reckoning that once he had left I would find another taxi there to take me out to the camp hospitals. But by the weekend the shelling had begun again from the hills above Baabda, and all the taxis disappeared from the streets.

For some months Middle East Airlines had been running irregular flights out of the city, refuelling their 707s in

Amman by night, but as the shelling worsened the airport closed again and I was left with no choice but to cross into the eastern sector, and take the Larnaca ferry from Jounieh.

The telephones had begun to work again. My father called each night. He complained about how much he had to wire through to cover my travelling costs. I had wilfully exaggerated so as to use the additional money on books and drawings in London.

It is raining hard. I wait under the garage, with my cases, the antique glass wrapped into the hollows of the rolled bokharas. In my pockets: both passports, the fold of dollars, the three letters Verger has asked me to post.

He waves from the verandah, but Leighton stays inside with his maps.

In his shiny suit and thin black tie, Jaffer tying the black crepe streamers to the wing-mirrors and aerial. The marble urn nestling in my crotch, both my hands on the scrolled lid; my fingertips numb from the three Nembutals.

The air in the front seat is heavy with a scent like over-ripe nectarines I had once bought at the airport for Layla.

Through the carob trees, Veger's arm outstretched high on the balustrade, as if from a parting liner. I wave back, but he cannot see me; the scent wafting up from the lining of the old black jacket I have put on for the crossing.

There is little sign of shelling along Basta and Ouzai, though all the women walking on the pavements are wearing black, and when we reach the museum-crossing the two cars in front are also flying mourning pennants from their wing-mirrors.

I hold my olive passport to the window, and the two kalashin-shebab on the hurj side whose uniforms I do not

154

recognize wave us through, and it is only when we reach the middle of the square that we can see the barricades a hundred metres down rue Damas, and behind the boys with large wooden crucifixes hanging over their padded chests, and I bring out the other passport and press it against the windscreen so they will see the navy-blue rectangle long before we reach the revetment.

The lack of rubbish in the front-line square seems almost a curse, like a land blighted of its vegetation.

As we make the turn Jaffer points up to the last plane tree where they string the spies who radio over the ranging coordinates, a middle-aged woman in a well-cut worsted suit hanging in the branches like a forgotten decoration; he does not look himself.

The eyes are gone, but I recognize the drawn cheeks, the high brow, and later in the ferry bar I will see her again picking through the pavement pitches on Christmas morning.

As we turn into Ashrafieh the clouds part over the mountains and the streets are drowned in sunlight. From the porches the rich kids in their rhinestone holsters are bringing out deckchairs, and under the shop tannoys blaring disco the blonde girls saunter along in their tight jeans, the glass crunching under their heels, the stallholders peeling back the covers from the apples and aubergines on the wide pavements of Independence where he leaves me at a taxi and reverses back towards Sioufi to deliver the contents of the urn.

From the bar I watch the last passengers out on the gangway, the little girls in tartan skirts and puffy white blouses, the mothers perspiring in fur coats.

Down along the quai the two smiling Phalange amputees with their collection box, between the antiquated Wehrmacht launch and the *Antony Quinn* which makes the night crossing.

It is exactly where I had stood as a boy when we had shipped the Plymouth to Brindisi for our summer motoring-holidays in Europe, my mother resting downstairs in the cabin as I scanned for our roof along the haze of the shoreline.

The old view is still there among the other framed photographs over the walls, but beyond the bar the peeling hoop-arena has been blocked off with high containers; on the side-decks the women dressed as if for the Lagon Club in lamé bikinis and captain's hats, catching the last of the sun, their eyes closed under their sunglasses, the city hidden by the smoke drifting across the bay from the pine fires high on the bright-clouded flanks of Sannine.

England–Beirut

... 1982

I

I had missed the first two terms; the college authorities insisted I wait until the autumn, and begin a year late.

Dismayed at this prospect my father contacted former colleagues who had found work in England; I was offered immediate places on several courses.

The university I chose was in Yorkshire, only a half-hour drive from the house where my mother had been brought up.

A sixties campus, on a hill above the fog-vale of the city, the low-rise blocks separated by concrete-lipped duck ponds, with windy walkways across the black waters which froze in winter; though never hard enough to skate on.

As all the student accommodation had been occupied I rented the wing of a manor house on the edge of the moors, driving across the Vale of York in a clapped-out Alfasud that lost its grip in the icy lanes.

That first bitter winter the snow kept me from the campus for weeks on end, crouching on the storage-heaters, reading books not on the syllabus.

I no longer took the papers, watched the news. Mecca and Medina could have vanished under the sands; I would not have known. The only Arabic I ever saw: the tourra on the slabs of hashish from the student dealer who operated from a cottage in the grounds of a prep-school on the Hull Road.

The city smelt of hops and cocoa beans from the factories on the outskirts.

Beyond the pedestrian precinct of half-timbered souvenir shops and tea-rooms the pubs with live bands where the Socialist Workers and students into Heavy Metal drank.

Some had no money to buy food, and roasted ducks from the campus ponds in their corridor kitchens.

On clement weekends I would drive with a girl from my seminar group to pick magic mushrooms below the mausoleum at Castle Howard, across the moors to Whitby Bay.

Down to London through the slipstream blizzards of the motorway canyons; below Wetherby the bare cube of the house on a windswept hill, the once-wooded grounds built over with the capillary closes of Leeds commuter homes.

She had Layla's fringe, her cold grey eyes.

Every couple of months mail was left by a representative from the Palestine Red Crescent at the house off the Brompton Road. Stoned scrawls from Asad on drug-company notepaper, long letters in English from Harun; he had returned to the university, applied for a Ford Grant to continue his graduate research at an American university.

I wrote back via the Red Crescent offices in Holborn, but

my letters seemed never to get through; my enquiries about Layla all unanswered.

The house off the Brompton Road remained empty. Every month a man I never saw came to clean and mow the grass in the narrow back garden.

Sometimes Aunt Mona stayed for two days when she flew in from Nice to shop at Harrods and Peter Jones; Uncle Samir was not well enough to travel.

She told me the Bey no longer left the house above the village, and saw nobody, and slept only in the afternoons. The grounds garrisoned with forty hunstmen from the high pastures, he sat alone all night in the diwan; watching films from the forties, dancing across the marble floors to big-band records in his boater and striped blazer, and in the first light over the mountains he wandered naked among the almond groves.

My father had arranged for doctors from the Ashrafieh clinic to go down to the village, but none had managed to reach the house.

In the summer holidays I joined him in the South of Spain. He had bought a condominium for his retirement in a pueblo-style marina built on land reclaimed from the sea.

On his bedside table, a photograph in an ivory frame of one of his graduate students; the face different each time I crept back to it.

At night we walked together beyond the chiringuitos into the quiet of the quays; the sea slopping against the hulls, the wind fretting in the stretched canvas; through the rigging and radar poles the avenue of moonshine across the straits; the dust of the desert on our gums.

By early July there had been reports in the week-late *Times* that Israel was mobilizing on the southern border; in October he had arranged for me to begin work at the offices of an English auction-house in Madrid.

That year Spain was hosting the World Cup, and a hooligan invasion had been anticipated along the coast. I told him I would spend the summer in England; on the day I left I reminded him the telephone in Yorkshire had been cut off, but I had already moved out; my few possessions stored at the house in London.

I go through each room with the torch. Under the beds and tables, into the deep drawers of the pantry, behind the bunched velvet curtains; my eyes watering in the whirls of dust.

I must make this round each night before I sleep; to check no one has climbed in from the streets. Tomorrow I will bring in tallow candles, kerosene and naphtha for the lamps; moon-tigers; a car battery.

Efforts had been made to tidy up before they left. The upper lawn and the verandahs swept, dustsheets draped over the divans and low tables, the tiles sheeny with disinfectant; the weeds cut away from the steps through the carob trees; the pool covered in polythene sheeting weighted down with rocks.

But the cleaning had ended abruptly at the inner corridor, mops and pails lying over the frowsty runner. At the end it seemed they had gone in some haste, abandoning all that was too cumbersome to fit into their travelling cases.

In the study all the longer sishas and hookahs remained under the depleted shelves, the oil-skin charts of the Druz Mountains rolled behind the door, the portrait of Burton turned against the rocaille mirror; the lower parts of the smoke-foxed walls covered in charcoal drawings of fantastical winged beasts; hippogryphs and rocs; the lonely Phoenix; Barwaq with his plumed tails; others I did not recognize.

In the servant quarters, the Qur'ānic inscriptions still hanging from the drawer-knobs; a prayer mat facing east towards the black hulk of the Murr Tower. This must have been Verger's bedroom at the end; I slept there as it was the cleanest of the inner rooms.

As night falls I take the overgrown path through the kitchen garden that avoids the street up to the rubbish-strewn porch of the house of Monsieur Tannous.

There are no lights visible, but I smell the cardamom coffee through the vines and wisteria over the wooden stoa; among the leaves my fingers feel for the Hand-of-Fatima.

When I knock he does not come to the door, but calls back faintly from somewhere inside.

For months he had heard no movements from the house, and fearing refugees would break in he had contacted the university authorities, but they had been unwilling to permit their old guards to leave the security of the campus.

I had missed them by little more than a week. On the morning the Israeli columns had crossed the Litani after months of silence he had seen the English lord and his negro servant and a girl with cropped blonde hair all running down with their cases to a waiting taxi.

I leave him to his coughing, and turn back down the path, staying close to the wall so as not to be seen from the road; through the stubby branches of the carobs the arcs of tracer and the white puffs of the decoy flares like the old-fashioned flashes of a wedding photographer as the first Israeli raids of the night begin over the camps to the south.

There had been only seven passengers on the flight in from Barajas; all reporters and cameramen. We had arrived in the heat of the afternoon, the terminal a camp-site for families waiting for a flight out, a stench of urine and curcum in the corridors, the old men in their white keffieh like sea-birds on the nesting-rocks of luggage, and everywhere the screaming of children and the calling of mothers, but I had found a telephone that worked; through the hubbub his sobbing like false laughter.

We had met an hour later at the Socrates on Bliss. His unit had been transferred from the southern suburbs to the three basement floors of the Near Eastern School of Theology on the corner of Hamra, but he had not wanted me to come there.

Of the thirteen Palestinian hospitals only the Gaza where three Israeli prisoners were chained to the upper storey had not been destroyed by the air-raids, but all the surviving staff and patients and equipment had been moved into underground facilities within the residential districts on the headland.

From the taxi along the corniche, the promenade empty of stalls and souks, iron grilles over the entrances of the shuttered apartment buildings, in every alley and garage and unguarded porch the refugees huddled over their stoves; on the campus wall along Bliss the faces of a hundred black-

164

turbaned imams among the spray-painted slogans of defiance. *All roads lead to Jerusalem. Sharon: Nero. Hatta al Nasr.*

But through the martyr graffiti, the broken plaster, the chicken-wire over the patio against shrapnel, the interior of the restaurant uncannily preserved like the dining-room of some long-drifting yacht; still the painted wooden chairs, the brass triremes and long-spouted coffee-pots over the walls, behind the aquamarine-tinted windows that inner courtyard of dwarf palmettos and cacti, all as it always had been on those wet winter Sundays when the gunpowder-black clouds over Sannine had discouraged my father from driving up to our favoured picnic-spots among the mountain ruins and the surviving cedar groves.

At the back of the empty courtyard Asad was waiting alone; a fried egg, a whipped yoghurt, both untouched on the paper tablecloth.

His head down in his hands, racoon-rings around his eyes, his pale scalp through the thinned hair like a bulb newly wrested from the earth.

As we embaced, my flesh cushioning his bones; against my lips his dried tears; the familiar tang I could not wipe away.

There had been no more news of Harun. He had left the camp in Sidon the previous week, but had never reached the university. Every day Asad had been to the crowded offices of the Red Crescent and the UNWRA building in Fakhani, but all Palestinian men between sixteen and sixty were being arrested on sight as the Israelis and their proxy militias advanced northwards up the coast, and little accurate information was reaching the city.

As he spoke I had tried not to listen; if I began to cry he would lose a little more hope. All the time I was holding the plastic bag of presents I had brought from London, the Clint

Eastwood videos, the country-music tapes he had asked for in his last letter, the journals for Harun.

Silently he had taken the bag, but had not opened it.

He had already risen from the table, and went out towards the portico without looking back; his shift had begun, and generator time at the Lahut was limited.

'And Layla?' At the mirrored sweet-trolley he had paused, his fingers over the dust-laden glass that had once held in tidy lines the frosted bowls of mochlabiyeh and crème caramel.

'It is as if she was never born.' He had walked away under the chicken-wire, not turning to face me again, and for one vile moment I had thought of running after him into the deserted street and offering him money to tell me all that had happened.

All week I waited for the airport to open again. I stayed inside during the days, eating what I had bought on the way in from the airport; acadiniah, cold felafel, canned beef.

Through the shutters the turbans of smoke rising above the camps in the south; down on the corniche the lonely promenaders watching the distant fireworks like paupers at the gate of a ball; when the Phantoms flew north over Mazraa they dropped only small squares of coloured paper that drifted sparkling like a shower of pantomime snow through the humid air on to the roofs and dusty hedgerows and wild wisteria over the walls and into the branches of the dying cedars in the lower gardens.

Each evening I took the Grundig out to the verandah, and listened to the commentaries on the first round of the World Cup though they did not interest me, ringing the results through to Asad in his basement-shelter so that night he would know he did not have to risk the journey down across Bliss to watch over me.

And if I slept I saw nothing of Layla, but sat again in the hut above the dead mulberry terraces with Abu Musa, the grid of sunlight through the walls of reed, his peasant whispering parched as the dry scuttling of the lizards over the warm earth floor.

'A young shabb who goes into the city is as one who drinks from water that no longer flows.'

'He is the caravan that follows the mist-lights on the marshes.'

'The rat who visits the wicker basket in the cellars of the Bey, the wide funnel narrowing to the cage that holds the offal bait.'

Each morning I tried to telephone the house above the village, but the advances of the Israeli forces north of Sidon had brought down the lines; the network within the city had been deliberately spared so internal calls could be monitored.

At the end of the week the airport was still closed, as were the crossings to the eastern sector at the port and Sodeco, the museum-crossing passable only to journalists and aid-workers. I did not have the courage to venture up there alone, though Asad had offered to walk with me along Basta. Through the mountains the road to Damascus remained a turkey-shoot for the Israeli fighters circling back over the Metn Ridge: I did not have the ready cash to part a way through the peasant-soldiers at the Syrian checkpoints who examined passports upside-down, the shake-down officials at Damascus Airport chain-smoking and sipping their demitasses under that large sign I had once photographed as a boy. *Please Enter Customs Before Parting The Cuntry.*

The corpses of those who had displeased the Syrians were uncovered by the rag-pickers on the tips along the airport boulevard; that week on the radio I had heard they had found the body of the writer Selim Louzey, both eyes burnt out, his writing hand withered to a stub from the acid.

Before turning to the football I compared the reports of the Israeli advance; on Kol Israel, Radio Monaco, the World Service; on the local stations the 'victories' groped closer to the city by the day.

The Israeli lines now reaching from the highway to the south through the mountains to the Christian sector in the east, the names of former students of my father among the rolls of those who had died defending the strongholds in Tyre and Beaufort Castle, but no word of our own village, though another by the same name to the north had been razed for harbouring Palestinian guerrillas.

The refugees who had fled into Sidon had become trapped without shelter among the ruined reed-bars on the beaches, the Israeli informers with hessian sacks over their heads passing silently among the lines, their fingers twitching like divining rods beside the Palestinians, and those who had sheltered them.

On the day of this report I had gone from room to room, carrying the radio with me like a suitcase, searching all the old hiding-places for the keys to my mother's wing. When I could not find them I had forced the door with a crow-bar from the cellars.

The wing had originally been locked so the maids would not be tempted by the long ranks of dresses and shoe-trees and hat-boxes, and the rooms still smelt of naphthalene and damp wool, but most of the wardrobes and dressing-tables had been cleared long before my father had left for Stamford.

Working my way through what remained I filled a drawer with all that might disclose her birthplace; diaries, maps, old packing labels; newspaper-cuttings; photographs of windy beaches near Haifa, of picnics among the groves of holm-oaks in the hills of Galilee.

I carried the papers out to the verandah steps, soaked in benzene from Leighton's last fuel-cache. Those coloured squares which had drifted down to catch among the upturned piles of rattan chairs I added to the low fire; the same message on all the flyers: Merry Christmas – in Hebrew, French, Arabic.

On the telephone Asad had claimed this was the Israeli way of saying they intended to visit rather longer this time. That night I had asked him to stay with me at the house, but he had been reluctant to leave his patients and the security of his camp-bed in the underground shelter, and it was only when I had lied and told him that refugees from the beach-encampments had tried to force the kitchen windows that he had agreed to come.

At first I barely saw him. He returned late from his long shifts, too tired to talk; shuffling to his room with head bowed, falling face-down on the bed without closing the door.

In the early mornings I woke to the single-engine drone of the mosqitoes, the thump of a rolled periodical against the wall, the drag of his flares over the tiles, the bitter scent of the cardamom and coffee.

And sometimes I opened my eyes in the night to see the glow of his cigarette, the outline of his hunched shoulders still as a crouching lizard against the shelves.

In the windowless basements of the Lahut where there was

only a three-hour supply of diesel-oil for the lights and respirators he had learnt to move silently among things; to draw the laundry, surgical-trolleys and bodies through unlit passages; to keep serene vigils at the bedside of the cases the doctors could do nothing further for, the casualties of the cluster-shells which lay dormant on the streets until triggered by footfalls, the shrapnel tearing through face, eyes, bones, viscera, of the phosphorus-bombs that burnt through muscle to bone and smoked from the lungs of the dying, the barbiturate-suicides revived to be told they had destroyed their livers and had no more than a day to live; the dark wards dependent on the meagre supply of analgesics salvaged from the ruins of the camp hospitals, the anaesthetic-machines functioning only in the hours the generators were on.

On his first night in the house I had offered my Nembutals, old clothes and toys for the children in the shrapnel-wards, but he told me the corridors were already blocked with all the unopened boxes of dolls and teddy-bears and electric cars looted by the guerrillas from the Hamra toystores, and he would not risk being seen on the streets with a suitcase.

We did not speak again of his work. In the night sometimes I heard cries from his room, and he came to sit and smoke by my bed, not meaning to wake me.

Often I could not sleep for the heat and the mosquitoes, and he would talk on in the darkness of the old days on the front; in the hospital he had heard rumours that Jaffer had grown rich as a glazier and that Ali had joined a new legion of martyrs in the Bekaa who called themselves the Party of God. *Hizbol-Allah.*

He did not speak of Harun, nor ever of Layla, but each week he risked the shrapnel to the relief offices in Fakhani to check the lists of the dead and the captured, though he could not cover the further six blocks to the south where his mother and blind uncle had taken refuge with their cousins in the Shatila district. The roads to the camp were under constant shelling from Israeli gunboats and artillery-positions in the Baabda Hills, and impassable to all but military vehicles.

If Layla was free of Jaffer she would be there also, with what remained of her family, in one of the communal shelters under the ruins of the camp.

Her mole eyes; in the closeness her mask smudging as if she had moved during a photograph.

Each night, his words, breathless in the narrow room, but patient always; the voice he must have used with his damaged children.

And through his words: the groundswell of their voices. I hear the old grandiloquence of Harun. I hear again her short words; wheedling, mocking.

II

Along that shore there had been nothing but an empty scrubland when her father and mother and the others from their village had first come to the place that would later be named Shatila.

A ridge of dunes where couples from the city courted in the shade of the umbrella pines, the sandblown walls of an abandoned cemetery under which the government had pitched the rows of canvas tents; above the beach the ruins of a fort where the children played.

What the families had rescued from their houses they had discarded and sold on the long march from Galilee; their pots, grain sacks, wrist-watches. They told the time by the clock on the tower of the monastery on the hill.

In that first winter they could hear the waves slapping on the rocks below the dunes and the cries of the jackals in the pine forest where nobody ventured after dark for fear of robbers and djinns.

The wind blew the sand down the wadis into their burghul and stews, the winter storms carried away their tents. When they covered the canvas with tar there were fires; the hospitals in the city would not treat those who were brought from the camp with burns.

On the roadsides the young men dug up paving-stones to weigh down the tents; the old women went out into the scrubland and picked sage, mint, oregano, hyssop, and made balms and compresses for those who had been burnt.

Many families could not afford the oil to heat their tents, and at dawn the women were sent out to bring firewood from the pine forest, and water from the tanks on the goat tracks, though there was never enough water and the guardians appointed to the tanks expected favours from the carriers.

The girls laughed when they saw the city women who did not know how to balance the wood and pitchers on their heads and staggered on their heels in the damp sands.

When Layla's mother and father were married that first winter a quilt and sheets made up the trousseau of the bride, sweets and cakes were offered in place of a sheep and curcum-rice at the wedding feast; a small white tent hired for their private use for three nights.

The government forbade the families the use of stone or cement and to build barakiyat of more than one storey. In those first years they lived within walls made from wooden planks and flattened petrol cans, under roofs of corrugated-iron. When the summer heat made the shacks unbearable they camped out under the pine trees.

But the families did not resent the building restrictions. They did not want to forget even for an hour the villages and orchards and hills of Galilee; at night the young men were forbidden by their elders to go into the city, the water-guardians patrolling the alleys between the barakiyat.

The households were not permitted to lay pipes for sewage and dig private cesspools and sluices for drainage. Public latrines were erected beyond the last line of barakiyat, the slops emptied in rotation by the boys of the camp who would peek in at the rows of squatting women.

For a week's wages electricity could be rented for six hours in the evening from the camp boss to run a radio and a single bulb under which the children could read their schoolbooks. The older students studied in the quiet of the cemetery where on feast days the women brought palm-fronds and wild flowers to cover the newly dug graves.

At dawn the plantation-owners sent lorries to take the women to pick oranges and lemons in the groves along the coast. Layla's mother was thankful for the darkness; those women who went to work out alone brought dishonour on their families: the proudest women in the camp were those who only left their barakiyat the day they were carried out on a bier.

Layla's father went with the other men to Barbir at the edge of the city where they waited to be hired by the day; the men would learn to be plumbers, joiners, tilers, electricians, and put these skills to use improving the barakiyat.

Layla's father became a tiler. She remembered cutting her fingers on the bright shards he brought as presents for the boys hidden in the lining of his jacket.

The men not chosen at the roadside were too ashamed to return until the end of the day. They loitered in the back rooms of the coffee-houses where the drug-dealers and prostitutes gathered among the shanty-towns of migrant workers that had begun to encircle the camp as the new airport and hotels and beach-clubs were constructed along the coast.

By the mid-sixties the family barakiyeh had walls of cinderblock and cement, and a small garden lined with geraniums in Nido tins. In winter they hung polythene beneath the corrugated-iron roof to stop the water dripping on their beds. The government police still forbade the families to build roofs, to cast water to cool the paths between the shacks, to visit friends at night.

Those who wished to improve their barakiyeh were expected to inform on their neighbours. She remembered the wooden yoke that had stood in the camp yard waiting for the necks of the young men who had joined political parties; their bare feet placed in frozen and scalding water. The women who smuggled guns into the camp swaddled like babies were tied upside-down in the public square and beaten on the soles of their feet; many were renounced by their families, and turned to prostitution in the shanty-towns.

She remembered bringing back ashes from the public oven for the hearth-brazier; her plastic sandals; on the alley corners the first men with watches always telling the time; the first refrigerators blocking the doorways of their proud households.

She remembered the one television, seats rented out for the nightly viewings by the shopkeeper, the boys boring holes in his walls which they hid with gum in the daytime.

She remembered the long tin trays gliding like magic carpets down the alleys; namoora, sfoof, sweet hareesh.

She remembered a pedlar with a Persian Box; through the peep-hole visions of places, tigers, houris.

She remembered the funfairs which came on feast days, five piastres each attraction. Donkey-rides, swings, pickles; a trick cyclist; a man who ate razor-blades; another who pulled eggs from his ears.

The year Layla went to school the people of the camp expelled the government police. For the first time names were given to the dirt paths between the barakiyat, the names of the streets of the villages and towns of Galilee, the order of the old neighbourhoods having been retained in the layout of the alleys.

Flags were hoisted over the new roofs of brick and concrete, sewage-pipes dug, asphalt roads laid. Work began on the Gaza and Acre hospitals, on a sports club to keep the young men away from the drugs and prostitutes in the shanty-towns; a diwan at the end of their alley built for the shuyyuk, with straw mats on the floor, bolsters along the walls, a brazier of bitter coffee for the old huntsmen who always brought a rabbit or a hare for the boys on the morning of Al'Fitr.

It was from the roof of the diwan that Layla had watched the wedding feast of the son of the camp boss which had lasted for three nights; she had seen whole lambs stuffed with rice, bowls of lebneh deep as Jayita, salvers of okra wide as the Bekaa; the high dais smothered in roses and asphodels.

When in her room I had no appetite for the bamia she had heated up on the ring she would throw up her hands and say: What, do I have to stand on the roof before you will eat?

This was the last memory of Shatila, the last she had shared. After her father had died at the accident on the construction-site at Ramlet al'Baida her mother had gone out to work at the house in the Sursuq quarter, Harun to the American University on a scholarship, Layla and Asad sent to live with their uncle at the camp above Sidon.

He said he remembered little of those years. In the early mornings he no longer left the house. The ways to the hospital had become too dangerous to walk alone.

A rumour had circulated that the Israelis would not target the embassy compound and the university, and armed refugees had converged on the streets around the campus, huddling under palm-shelters and plastic sheeting at makeshift toll-barricades on Abdul-Aziz and Jeanne D'Arc.

From the deserted seafront apartment buildings across the

gardens of the empty villas, lines of black and olive-green tents had suddenly appeared, three packing-case bivouacs down between the poolhouse and the dying cedars, in the patchy shade a semicircle of men in baggy fatigues and wide-brimmed straw hats, watching the football on a television run off a car battery, the set covered in a staggered cardboard visor, like an old-fashioned slide-viewer.

Those first days we exchanged waves across the gardens. We did not go down from the verandah. But when our supply of tins had run low every morning Asad crossed through the beds of dead storks and waist-high grass and nettles with cigarettes and chocolate, and returned with burghul, sardines, sometimes watermelons.

The men refused to take money for the food. They claimed to be Kurds, day-labourers from Bir-Hassan, but Asad said they spoke with Palestinian accents, and were probably deserters, from one of the units that had been holed up on the southern outskirts under constant bombardment.

The men told Asad what they had seen on their journey up across the wastegrounds of Fakhani and Mazraa, ducking into ditches and rubbish mounds and the entrances of under-ground garages as the Kfirs and F16s circled like swallows high in the cloudless sky above the city; beyond the environs of the campus the streets silent and deserted, on the corners lone gunboys selling their kalashins for five lira to buy a bowl of burghul, cats scurrying between the rubbish, the roofs of the occasional speeding cars smeared with mud so they would not catch the sun.

Along Hamra and Abdul-Aziz all the bakery-hatches had been down, no stalls selling food, just cigarettes and candles; the surviving shops emptied in the panic-buying of the first days of the siege.

At the passes the Israeli soldiers were selling flour, but no diesel for the bread-ovens; their gunboats shelling the Red Crescent convoys as they crossed the bay from Jounieh. Near the museum square they had seen shebab bribing the soldiers with slabs of hashish to let through single tanks of diesel, fresh fruit, vegetables. Some families had begun to burn their own furniture for fuel.

In the mornings the men came up to wash under the garden hose leading out from the wisterias along the wall, splashing and giggling in the spray like little boys. They would leave offerings in plastic bags hung on the balustrade. Two stale ghif; an apple; a giant cucumber; a melon as large as an American football.

Asad said the enormous fruits were kibbutzim produce, spiked, but down among the black tents on the corniche there was an old woman who claimed she had tasted apples from her own orchard in Galilee.

The gifts of fruit we ate as slowly as we could. We made a game of it, cutting transparent slices as if for a microscope-slide, letting them dissolve on the tongue; a bolus of rind and skin kept back to suck on.

In the cellars, behind the grilles of the air-conditioners, behind books on the study shelves still lay concealed the most deftly hidden of the old tin caches, but we were too lethargic from the nights of shelling to make further searches.

The artillery salvos continued until dawn from the south like a drunkard dancing in heavy boots, and to the east the deeper thumps of the vacuum-bombs falling like medicine-balls too heavy to bounce.

In the morning as Asad went down to the men the fires were still burning across the sky, no water-pressure in the mains to tame the wind-drawn flames, tall pillars of smoke over Mazraa and Fakhani; as if it were the depths of winter the mountains lost under the dark clouds.

On the truce days Asad went down to the Lahut, and to visit his mother and cousins in the camp shelters by the long way round the Raoche to avoid the inner toll-blocks.

Sometimes I tried to follow him, but would lose my nerve beyond the Commodore where through the broken wall I could see the pool had been filled again for the foreign journalists.

On the last day of Ramadan I had followed him as far as the northern edge of Fakhani. Customarily the day was celebrated with rockets and fusillades, but that morning the streets were silent, not a single firework, the children sweating and pale in their bright new clothes.

Despite making the journey on many occasions he still did not know the roads beyond the Red Crescent buildings, and several times he had turned abruptly in his tracks, and on rue Daouk I thought he had seen me as I had ducked below the drapes set up under the water-main for the women to wash behind, but that night he had said nothing.

We had spent the usual after-truce evening, listening to the bulletins and the football commentaries while we cooked whatever he had picked up from the pavement stalls; through the french windows the dusk lit up by the air-raids that had begun once more to the south over the camps; a garish festivity to the blue Bengals and the slowly descending parachute-flares, like a spectacle over one of the downshore lunaparks, the antiquated anti-aircraft guns only showering more shrapnel over the city streets.

179

The sky too bright to see the bombers and the distant impact-flashes, though we could just make out the decoy phosphorus trails like the cotton-wool clouds puffed out by picture-book biplanes as the Phantoms swept lower over the ruins.

Later as the spectacle brightened and Asad closed the shutters I had heard the short bark of a kalashin from the lower gardens. I had gone down to find the men hunched close around the television, the cardboard visor off in the grass, one of the men waving his gun at the sky; through their shoulders the blue shirt of Bossis as he stepped up to take the penalty.

I ran back to the house to listen on the radio, but as I reached the verandah he was already out on the steps, his eyes swollen with tears. When I caught up with him among the carob trees he was screaming in a voice I had never heard before; he said he was going to take the kalashin from the deserters and go out alone to defend the camp. I had to hold him down by the neck to stop him running out into the street.

All that night I sat on cushions outside his door. The next morning he did not speak of what had happened. As he practised his kung-fu kicks and jabs on the verandah I searched the room for hidden bottles, ampoules, drug-sachets, but there was nothing there; on the shelves only dog-eared martial-arts magazines and country tapes, a tin of family photographs: his father as a moustached gallant, Harun un-smiling on his graduation day, several of his mother in the same handed-down deerskin coat; none of Layla.

With the football over he returned to his old ways. His kung-fu exercises alternating with the languor of smoke-rings and fruit-sucking; he would no longer listen to the bulletins, leaving the room whenever the radio was on.

The Israelis had now taken the port, and advanced through the southern suburbs as far as the Golf Club. Each night the Kol Israel broadcasts from the mountain ruins of the Lebanese School of the Deaf and Blind declared that the city would fall the following day, but as the weeks passed the guerrillas held their cratered lines of fox-holes and rubble revetments.

Each night Arafat slept in a different shelter, and travelled between the fronts in a service-taxi, his face covered by a white headscarf.

So many had died on the outskirts and wood was in such short supply that coffins were having to be shared and dug up again; many of the bodies went down into the crowded plots still smouldering; water did not extinguish the burning of the phosphorus.

The old woman of the apple orchard I took in to clean the kitchens and our rooms; in the deserted streets above Hamra she had seen dazed men in striped dungarees picking through the mounds of rubbish; the guards from the city prison and asylum had abandoned their posts, but after an hour on the streets many of the inmates had returned to their cells. She told me the rats and pie-dogs came out only on truce days.

Each morning we woke to find the sun obscured by the pillars of smoke, and each night the sky to the south was day-bright with the flares, but a strange calm like that of a public holiday had settled over the streets of the headland.

In the cool of the evening Monsieur Tannous wandered out in his sun-hat and clipped the wisterias along the wall. We could see through over the campus, on the tennis-court a doubles in whites, a man walking his dog, women with prams. Between the black tents the old men sitting out on stools around their narghiles and trictrac.

On the verandah Asad elaborated his exercises, leaping

between chalk lines, over a course of hurdles made from the rattan chairs, pretend-kicking me whenever I came out with beers and news.

If I went down into the garden he came with me, his arm around my waist or across my shoulders. In the evening he would spring around my reading-chair like a restless puppy, and later when I would no longer talk he did not sleep but walked barefoot through the corridors, striking at mosquitoes, tapping on walls as if searching for hollows, humming those country standards whose words he would never understand; to the south the remote crump of the shells like the touching of moored boats in choppy waters.

On the broken pavements in those last weeks of the summer there suddenly appeared stalls selling every manner of suit-case; holdalls, sports-bags, fake sets of Louis Vuitton.

To the south the shelling had eased, and on the radio we heard reports that preparations had been made for an evacuation of the guerrillas from the port. Down among the tents there were rumours that those with the right papers were managing to walk over the Israeli lines, handing one half of a hundred-dollar bill to the soldiers at the checkpoint as they passed, the other half when they returned, but the local stations still carried reports of Muslims and Palestinians being shot down at Barbir and the other crossings to the eastern sector.

The airport remained closed, a ring of gunboats on the waters between the port and Damour, but on the morning of the first day of the evacuation I had got through to the caretaker at the house in the Sursuq quarter, and after convoluted haggling over the fare had been able to secure a ride on a boat bound for Larnaca from Sidon Harbour at the end of the week.

That afternoon I had followed Asad out towards the camps for the last time. Along the avenues to Fakhani all the lamps and hoardings and stumps of trees cut down for fuel had been stuck over with bright-red slogans. *Sharon: Hitler. All roads lead to Jerusalem. Beirut adieu.*

Up in the streets of Mazraa the people had come out from the shelters and underground garages to watch the evacuation, and from the shattered balconies and windows women threw down rice and rose-petals as a convoy of open trucks passed away towards the shell-toothed hulk of the Murr Tower like a series of carnival floats, the guerrillas in freshly pressed uniforms among the placards of Arafat and the Dome of the Rock, their faces tuber-pale from the months underground.

But when he saw all the commotion ahead Asad had turned down into the side-streets beneath the shadow of the sports stadium, and for some minutes I had followed him through the sudden peace of the ruins, the fallen cinderblocks rustling with lizards, the sea-breeze through the wild figs and fireweed, our footfalls in rhythm over the glass and rubble on paths without shade or cover between the fissured walls where he needed only to have turned once to see me treading alone behind him across the desolation.

The way led through the side of a building that must once have been some sort of hospital, the old men sitting silent on the steps, staring down over the fallen ruins to the thin line of the sea; in the puddles below two naked children chewing at the plastic bracelets on their wrists, Asad brushing at the flies on their lips and foreheads as he passed.

183

This was the last standing structure, beyond only a flattened wasteground leading on to the high piers of the stadium.

At the far edge, a row of old buses with tinted visors and wrought-iron roofracks, garlands of white lilies framing the sea-green windows; a long column of children and women in headscarves waiting as the soldiers checked their papers. Asad walking to the end of the line, the nearest soldiers nodding him through.

I called out, but he did not hear, the women turning to stare across the empty wasteground.

One hand raised against the glare over the sea, his head bowed, the dark band of sweat between his shoulders lost among the shadows under the piers.

That night he did not return. I slept out among the upturned recliners waking to the laughter of the deserters under the garden hose to find the house still empty.

At noon the car came to take me to the Kola flyover where the service-taxis departed for Sidon and the south. The boat would not embark until the end of the week, but the caretaker at the house in the Sursuq quarter had arranged for me to leave the city that day in case the truce did not hold.

I kept the car waiting two hours, the driver anxious he would not have time to return before the checkpoints closed.

We waited one hour more; when Asad still did not come I left as many dollars as I could spare, and a note telling him to bring his mother and Layla to the boat at the north harbour; promising we would try everything in our power to locate Harun through the Red Crescent offices in London.

The journey to Sidon normally took less than an hour. That day we did not arrive until late in the evening.

From the Palestinian roadblocks outside the ruins of the

Acre hospital the coastal highway was blocked all the way down to Damour by a solid column of cars held up at the succession of Lebanese Army, Haddad Militia and Israeli checkpoints.

The fine grey dust from the long-barrelled tanks levelling the former guerrilla positions along the verges lay over the lemon and jasmine and orange blooms in the roadside groves and over the men fishing and sunbathing out on the beach and over the helmets and tents of the soldiers at the checkpoints as if the entire landscape had just been brought down from an ancient attic.

Below the wreckage of the reed-hut bars where the jeeps and diggers had been parked in even squares, the old town in darkness, the streets unlit and empty, a flickering of kerosene lamps behind the beaded doorways; the hooded beams of the army headlights crossing above the marketplace.

The sense of people there but in hiding; as if the whole town were playing at sardines; no tanker-lights to the south; the front and the causeway not distinguishable at first from the black drape of the sea beyond.

The Armenian hostel had been taken over by families from the new town whose homes had been lost in the first days of the bombing.

I had bribed a room in the hotel on the front; the lobby telephone worked, but the lines to the western sector remained down.

In the morning I had tried to reach the village by taxi. The sandstone alleys above the arcade had not been touched by the shelling, but there were soldiers at all the turnings into the districts to the south.

The road through the hills had been closed at the lowest bend by two Mekava digger-tanks. At the far edges of the sunflower and zucchini fields, jeeps with tall aerials; tents and troop-carriers further up on the first level of the orchards.

We had returned by the old Ein Helweh road. There had been more tanks at all the entrances to the camp; through the broken walls I had glimpsed bulldozers pushing back the tangle of cables, pipes, cement-blocks.

Nothing had been left standing, only a small corrugated-iron shelter at the roadside; as we slowed the wide-eyed children waving in their cheerily coloured relief-agency smocks.

At nightfall I sat on the steps of the deserted arcade; I waited.

In the upper alleys families had begun to return to their houses; the Chiclet-boys calling; pie-dogs baying over on the lot.

Down on the beach the first fishermen carrying torches to the caïques, the moon on the foam, the low waves lapping on the causeway.

It would be a smooth crossing.

Madrid, London, Beirut

1982–1989

I

Beyond the edge of the park the cafés are almost empty now; only those who want to be alone or with time on their hands come in this far in the mornings, elderly couples sipping horchatas, some children in tartan scarves running with plastic propellers that whirl in the chilly breeze over the artificial lake; the line of pedal-boats drawn up under the iron-railings, the groundsmen clearing the leaves from the unpaved promenade above.

I sit at the last café open on the lakeside where the waiter knows me now and brings the silted cortados that keep me going through the doldrums of the siesta hour when as an English company we stay open while the rest of the city sleeps.

On these fine autumn days I often come up to the Retiro Park. There are many reasons to leave the office; catalogue-entries to be researched for the next sale, export-licences to be followed up at the labyrinthine Ministerio de Cultura.

When the news of the massacres at the camps had first broken in early September I had used these same excuses to return three times each day to my unfurnished flat on the other side of Castellano to telephone the Red Crescent offices in London; after the final Israeli push into the western sector the headquarters in Hamra had ceased to operate effectively, their files looted by the Maronite militiamen, the staff deported and car-bombed, but the Holborn section had

189

continued to receive updated rolls of the missing and dead from the other relief agencies. By the end of the week after the massacres there had been so many calls that only immediate relations had been permitted to make enquiries, but the staff had promised to keep monitoring all the data received from the camps in Beirut and Sidon on my behalf.

By early October I had learnt only that Layla had not been listed among the missing from Shatila and Ein Helweh; Asad and Harun had not been entered on the official register of detainees at the Ansar camp on the southern marches. Nobody of that surname had been ledgered on the roll of the living or the dead.

I walk to the end of the promenade, into the beech woods. Where the paths meet there are statues of antique heroes crusted with moss and bird-droppings, the crossed branches forming a tunnel overhead, the way coming out at a sandy spur circled by wire bins; the promontory from which the Habsburg court had once enjoyed the spectacle of the mock sea battles in the lake below.

I will make this short loop through all the coming seasons, the last of the Malvinas demonstrators huddled around their brazier on the square outside the office, a black mulch on the paths, the bitter winds from the plains of La Mancha through the bare branches. I will go there when the snowdrops and crocuses turn the banks white and the botany classes come up from Atocha in their long grey mackintoshes to collect specimens, and when the café tables are filled again with the old watching the young promenaders, and when lovers lie in the cool of the shadows as the children splash in the shallows of the lake, and as the nights draw out again, the twin glows of cigarettes at dusk across the waters, the lighted upper floors of the apartment buildings on Independencia hung like lanterns in the darkening canopy of the branches.

Each morning as I crossed Plaza Neptuno I saw the newspapers in the kiosks, and looked away. All the names that had played as refrains in the long song of my childhood returning like strange blooms to these foreign walls and hoardings, but the pictures only of ruins; the after-wrecks of suicide-bombings; sites of disappearances.

The city had become a dark star into which those blindly falling could send back no returning signals, their final images suspended as if in some immortal relief against the void horizon.

Across the squares and boulevards of Castellano the dark band of sweat between his shoulders lost to the shadows under the piers; Layla at her window still; for ever unconscious of that moment scored to eternity; through her fringe she peers down as the tanker-lights vanish with the dawn.

On first arriving in Madrid I had learnt that the Bey had left the village in the early days of the Israeli invasion, from the north harbour in the Dido-Sidonia; he had taken up residence in a sanatorium above Cap Ferrat.

Each month I had put off making my visit. The week I had finally bought the ticket for Nice the telegram came from Aunt Mona with details of the funeral.

We buried him at a windblown cemetery above the coast. My father came late, straight from the airport, with Elaine; on her back their first-born in a paisley-patterned carry-cot.

Uncle Samir was wheeled to the graveside; after the stroke he had hardly recognized me.

Aunt Mona had hired a line of poor Algerians and

Moroccans as mourners, and a white-turban headstone, like a giant blancmange.

Afterwards we went back to the flat in the hills. The African maid served up homespun versions of mloukieh and bamia; on the terrace the funeral cakes laid out under Cellophane.

Through the window, the rows of model triremes, a Pharaoh's fleet for the afterlife; some made from matches, others from balsa-wood, pipe-cleaners. On the chart-table, a smart new captain's hat; a telescope pointing down between the pins maritimes to the marina along the shore.

It was not until later the second winter in Madrid that I learnt what had happened in the village. Through one of the Red Crescent receptionists I had managed to contact the cousin of Khalil the cook who had stayed on as caretaker at the old house.

After the departure of the Bey, Fawzi-from-the-mountains and his followers from the high pastures had set up tolls on the paths through the orchards, looted food and clothing from those fellahin families who had remained. When a column of Israeli armour had approached across the jurd from Naba-tiyeh the younger huntsmen had opened fire with handguns in a show of bravado.

The Israelis had thought there were Palestinians sheltering in the village, and bombarded the hilltop from their Mekava tanks; later that evening a single Phantom had flown low over the house of the Bey, dropping two vacuum-bombs.

Many of the huntsmen garrisoned there had already fled to the mountain, but others had been trapped under the fallen masonry; each night the villagers had heard the cries grow gradually weaker.

For three weeks the sharqiyah over the mountain had blown the sweet stench of the rotting bodies down through the almond groves into the alleys of the fellahin quarter.

Only when the Israelis pulled back towards the gorge of the Litani had the black-veiled women come down from the high pastures to dig among the ruins.

That week Ali had returned with twenty bearded shebab from the Bekaa and planted the black standards of the martyrs over the graveyard of the beys and over the paths through the orchards, and when summer came again to the village grasses and wild poppies had grown among the fallen walls, and the children wore crowns of twisted glass and silver, and the goatherds let their flocks ramble over the ruins on the hill.

After a third year in Madrid I returned to London to take up a position as a junior curator at the Tate Gallery.

My days were spent escorting art-works between the different sections of the reserve collections, from the stacks beneath the exhibition halls, from the storehouse in Acton which for security reasons had never appeared on a map; the sculptures on the Jungheinrich forklift from the underground chambers built into the caissons that had once lain beneath Millbank Prison.

Solitary, archival, immured; a discipline in forgetting.

It must have been during that first winter in London that I met Leighton again. We had lunch at the gallery restaurant.

I hardly recognized him at first; the tailored suit, his hair cut short, feathery on top like the down of something just born.

His eyes faintly bloodshot through the heavy tints of his

glasses; he kept abruptly turning to stare at the murals on either side of the table, as if to catch the animals and hunting parties shifting their positions behind his back.

He told me he was staying at the house of the veteran Arabist Julian Crossley in South Kensington; his own flat in Notting Hill having been stripped of its collection of silks and bokharas and antique water-pipes by associates of Verger to whom he owed money.

He had spent the advance for his Burton biography, and was no longer able to call on Verger to curb the depredations of his colleagues; during his ramifying Druz researches he had persuaded Verger to penetrate the ranks of the Brixton chapter of the Nation of Islam whose curious theology was rumoured to have originated in thirties Chicago with a mysterious immigrant Druz pedlar, but Verger had gone over to the brotherhood and was now to be found every weekend on the Railton Road hawking the Last Trump in a long black mackintosh and bow-tie.

What had come down to me from the Bey, the portfolio of Swiss bonds, a dossier of worthless land-titles, the revenues from the final rents and harvests, all held in a private bank in Basle, had largely been dissipated in the succeeding legal disputations with Aunt Mona who had contested the will on grounds of insanity; in a codicil the Bey had named me as his true son and the entailed but the opposing lawyers had been unable to prove that this surprising instruction had been added in the final years of his decline.

What remained I spent on high living. I discovered that a lonely upbringing and the remote insouciance that comes to those who have survived a war in which they have not participated played well with women.

With those actresses and society girls whose features were the living image of the portraits which had succoured my boyhood I pursued brief and barren affairs. I held up a mirror to their frivolous vanities, but their illusions were too shallow for a man to drown in.

My self-disgust found consolation in antiquated radical posturings. From fashionable artists I commissioned grand homages to Leila Khaled and Carlos the Jackal. When coming down I dreamt of my fallen body in a dry wadi on the borderland; to those who pretended to consider me original I claimed there was more poetry in the bark of a kalashin than in all the stanzas of Christendom.

But I remember little of those times now, and what I remember is not fit matter to record, and the rigours of the pipe were to save me all such follies.

I would not see Leighton for a further two years. By then I had given up my position at the gallery and was trying to write at home; most of the furniture had been removed by Aunt Mona, but she had left the secretaire under the casement windows on the first floor.

The square was quiet during the day. Few cars came through the arch into the cobbled mews behind. In spring the pavements were white with the cherry-blossom. The children played on the en-tout-cas court, their nannies sitting on the bench across the rutted green.

The thick brocade curtains drawn; a single empty page under the hub of the anglepoise. I put down what I remembered from the years before the war; the mountain picnics, the roof-terrace parties; on the campus the carnival of student demonstrations; the cold exile of boarding-school.

One windy day in March I came back to find Leighton on the steps with a suitcase. I let him take the room under the stairs; he spent that first afternoon kneeling by the door, watching the square through the stained-glass surround.

Each morning he would walk out to a Citroën parked by the green, close all the curtains and blinds on the ground floor and shut himself in the kitchen.

The room would be thick with wreaths of grey smoke. Beside the hob: the wrecked origami of the wraps, the spilled tubs of bicarbonate of soda.

The pipe itself, a Heath-Robinson construction: an Evian bottle, the tube of a biro for a mouthpiece. The smoke white and eddying in the furred chamber like weather speeded-up, and afterwards the sensation of floating above oneself, the past laid out like a landscape; a single winged shadow flying westwards, then open sea.

Leighton came to believe the house was being watched. The nannies were in the pay of those he owed money to; keyhole-cameras hidden in the bay trees. He devised a system of mirrors so as to observe the square unseen from behind the drawn curtains.

By early June he had disappeared once more, leaving his suitcase and books, but the Citroën still waited each morning by the green. Through trial and error I learnt to bake the powder, and spent my days smoking in the study from the tall rosewood hookah that had stood as an ornament beside the firedog; each evening trying to transcribe the patterns of the wing-shadows over the jurd and the groves.

As the months passed I no longer remembered what I had

seen during the hours with the pipe. I grew thin, and in the mirror I seemed taller. In the mornings I would discover pages I did not remember writing, in a hand I barely recognized as my own.

Always there would be the brothel in the mansion block off the Edgware Road, a locale I knew only as the provenance of the meals I ordered on the telephone, and the girls who played the twelve wives of the Prophet; down the long corridors the swish of their diaphanous leggings, the tread of the tinsel-crested mules, the faint tinkle of ankle-bracelets.

Like a building growing under cover of darkness new annexes, towers and wings the text extended itself night after night. On the long leather divans, the clients with their scented worry-beads; sheikhs, merchant princes, contractors; beys, waasta-men, sons of ministers; a hooded-eyed novelist.

Veiled maids guide them down the low-lit passages to the black doors; to Aisha who was little more than a child and liked them to bring her candy and computer games; to Hafsah with her crop and shackles; to Rehara who was a genuine Jewess from Crouch End; to haughty Ramlah in her couture hosiery who was said to have pleased the Shah in his last days; to hard Maimunah who had worked her way up through the ranks at Madame Blanche; to shy Safia.

Not long after I had hidden this unbidden text among the mounting disorder of the first floor, I had received a visit from Julian Crossley who had come to recover certain volumes lent to Leighton.

Noticing the squalor into which the house was descending he had suggested over tea that I might consider returning to write in Beirut, the western sector having become a forbidden city to foreigners since the kidnappings, but it had been almost seven years since I had been home; I found it difficult

197

enough to make it out to the shops on the Brompton Road, and could no longer contemplate a life without the pipe.

Afterwards I would realize that Crossley had taken away my manuscript among his books. To my dismay the text found its way into the hands of his new lodger, a Yemeni radical, and was copied, and circulated first among dissident student groups, and then among the wider expatriate community.

But it was only later that year that I began to notice the house was under direct observation. At night the curtains twitched on the top floor of the house beside the court where the lights were always on. In the afternoons bearded men drove across the end of the square, and others loitered in the telephone-booth that had never worked.

I could watch them unseen through Leighton's mirrors. I kept the lights down, the flame low on the bowl.

One afternoon in October a bearded man came up the steps, but did not knock; earlier that month I had seen the same man on the porch of the neighbouring house.

That night I climbed out of the back window to a mini-cab waiting in the cobbled mews. After making sure we were not being followed, I took another taxi to the airport.

II

Nature had crept back that winter into the streets of the headland. Grasses and weeds had overgrown the promenade and the ruins of the embassy compound, and tumbles of wisteria and wild fig covered the walls of the deserted campus.

Hoopoes nested in the shells of cars and among the fallen railings, and flocks of screeching white storks and rose-winged starlings flew at dusk through the seafront palms and the gardens of the abandoned villas.

Those who had remained said they had never seen so many birds in the city. At night I heard the clattering of bats in the branches of the dead cedars. When I looked out between the cordite-impregnated curtains the darkness was broken only by the lanterns of the sahlab-sellers and the fires burning down on the shingle.

I had come in on the one hydrofoil still running from Larnaca, the cabins unlit, the windows blacked-out with paint and blankets; a line of cars along the shore, their headlamps dipped to mark the quay.

In Cyprus the newspapers had reported artillery-duels in the hills above the bay, and there had been no other traffic on the broken road as the service-taxi wound down past the derelict casinos into the ruins of the city, the streets around the crossings so grown over with creepers and bushes I had not recognized the way, pitch-dark canyons where once had

199

stood teeming avenues and squares, across the bay the half-moon through the hollow façades.

In the mornings I woke to the roosters down among the cabanas, the screeching of the storks, the teeming of the gulls over the promenade, the cries of the goatherds leading their flocks to the wild lots; on still days I could hear the call of the button-quail like dripping water carrying far over the empty fields of the campus.

In the rubble of rue Clemenceau I had seen cows tethered to the ruined blocks squatted by those few refugee families who had remained on the headland; under the fissured walls old men holding out in one hand single eggs, earth-encrusted beets, in the other a club to beat away the packs of dogs; on the tyre-strewn tip that had once been Senayegh Gardens, two thin white mares grazing in the dust.

A thin column of smoke rising from a line of black shelters on the sandy arena at the furthest edge of the park where I had walked with Jaffer all those years ago; the sheets of canvas hung on single ropes between the stumps of trees, the outer flanks held up on poles in the Bedouin manner.

As I came above the encampment the children playing with tyres ran away behind the rag walls dividing the interior of the tents, and I could hear the soft Galilean voices of the women crouched above the pots of burghul, and the coughing of the old men within.

I had returned to the place, and wandered among the tents with my most recent photographs of Asad and Harun, but the women had put on local accents and shook their heads without looking up; the old photographs of Layla were not suitable to be shown in public, with their sultry poses and misleading hairstyles, the deep fringe almost covering her eyes, but I had cut out what remained of the face and stuck it between the heads of the two boys.

As the weeks passed I had brought cigarettes, powdered milk and chocolate for the children. A few old men had claimed to recognize the photographs, but when I questioned them each described another young man, a cousin or a lost grandson; some who had emigrated and never been heard from again, others who had disappeared in the first years of the war, their bodies never recovered.

That winter the four-year siege of the camps by the proxy-militias of the Syrians had been partially lifted, and in my wanderings through the ruins beyond the headland I found other makeshift encampments; the inhabitants from Shatila and Sabra and Bourj al'Barajneh, all reluctant to talk about the final years of the sieges.

Each week I would watch the women walking in Indian-file through the desolation of Fakhani and Mazraa to the Syrian checkpoints around the camps, on their heads the straw panniers of supplies for the men who had remained. The women could take only what they could carry, no barrows or carts, no cement, breeze-blocks, corrugated-iron; those caught smuggling building materials were forced to eat the cement, their few bags of rice and vegetables trodden into the dirt.

At the checkpoints I had seen the soldiers confiscate coffee, cigarettes, medicines, batteries. Some of the women carried through tyres under their arms for the men to burn as fuel, and use as padding against the pressure of mortar-rounds; in the shelters I heard stories of butagaz-containers with false bottoms concealing ammunition, of single shells hidden under spinach leaves.

On Fridays along the airport boulevard the women brought palms and wild flowers to the mass graves. One rainy afternoon I had watched a wedding ceremony held at one of the checkpoints there, the Qadi standing under a lopsided umbrella with the bride, the muffled vows of the young man drifting back across the flooded wasteground.

The fighters who had survived the years of siege lived on under the rubble of the camps. Theirs was a world without trees, without bird-song; the only vegetation they saw was the mildew over the cinderblock walls of the broken bunkers.

The men slept and ate among the dead of fifteen years of war, the bodies seven-deep under the floor of the mosque, in the drains below the camp, under the foundations of the houses, the bones disturbed and rising with the rains; to the south the mass trenches, to the north the original walled cemetery; the pine forests a network of shallow graves, the deeper pits beneath the piers of the stadium, and under the rough and bunkers of the abandoned golf course where the crows circled.

With the siege partially lifted the fighters were more at risk from each other than the snipers in the five-storey shells of Sabra. Each week there were fatal burnings from butagaz explosions, anonymous executions in the alleys, firefights over supplies of morphine stolen from the clinic. The bodies of those who had tried to wander out at night between the Syrian checkpoints were uncovered later on the rubbish mounds along the airport boulevard; still dressed in their izaas and veils.

Between the rains I worked to clear the gardens. With a long-handled axe from the cellars I hacked down the weeds and

202

creepers that had grown over the balustrade and the shoulder-high hollyhocks that had covered the beds and rockeries, mashed the broken stalks into the damp earth.

The chicken-wire fence had fallen in several places above the wall, and the piles of rubbish burnt slowly, the sea-winds through the ruins of the embassy compound carrying the bitter smoke into every room.

The lower branches of the dead cedars had been cut down for fuel, and what remained I gave to the old men from the encampments who came out to forage on the headland. The sodden wood they loaded into their back harnesses, and on the carts and barrows they trundled in slow zigzags up the hill; one old man with sunken cheeks and proud eyes brought a shopping-trolley and dragged away the tins and bottles that had survived the bonfires.

Later that week when all the wood and rubbish had been taken one of the gatherers from the encampment in Senayegh Gardens had come back alone to the house. He claimed to have known a man who had worked with Asad at the Gaza hospital and was now hiding out from the Syrians in the ruins of Fakhani. The old gatherer promised to bring the man back to the house, but after three weeks he had not returned; I began to suspect the story may have been no more than a ploy to land more cigarettes and branches.

On the night they finally called I had closed all the shutters against the wind, and had not heard them shouting out on the drive.

They had both come in long-coped hoods, wet-through and shivering, the younger man with narrow shoulders, and wide, startled eyes, looking behind the doors as they followed me through to the study.

I remember I gave them the whisky I had brought back

from London, and mugs of instant coffee, and we smoked the last of the duty-free cigarettes. The wood had dried, the flame-shadows leaping among the fantastical birds over the walls.

The younger man sat close to the fire, and spoke softly, as if afraid of being overheard. All night I would listen in silence; not hearing the dawn-cries of the solitary fruit-sellers; the crowing of the roosters down among the cabanas.

The man said he had been with Asad in the autumn after the first massacres at Sabra and Shatila. Each day they had passed the survivors sitting out on mattresses and blankets in the streets around the camps, at crossroads, outside the stores in the shanty-towns.

From the upper floor of the hospital they had watched the women outside the coffee-house selling themselves to buy food for their children, the army bulldozers clearing the alleys, the camps beyond barely visible through the clouds of dust.

Each night some of those they had passed on the streets the previous day would disappear, picked off by the Israeli jeep-patrols.

For weeks the bodies would come up with the rains, from drains, from empty garages, from the sunken warehouses on the airport road. The visitors to the camp had all worn white gauze masks, but Asad and Aziz had grown used to the smell. In the air-conditioned basements they laid out the bodies for the relatives to identify. Many had been sprinkled with white lime to dissolve the flesh; a pendant, a bracelet, the only clue to who they had been.

In the afternoons the taxis called at the hospital, sent all the way from Damascus by the evacuated guerrillas, many returning empty over the mountain roads. Some families were too frightened to go back to their houses, and camped in the underground corridors and morgues.

Those children who had survived the shootings under the fallen bodies of their parents would not speak again for several months. On the flat roof Asad had held kung-fu classes, teaching the older boys to high-kick, to chop bricks and planks.

That year the winter storms came early. Each dark dawn along rue Sabra a line of women waited ankle-deep in the slough for the bread and powdered milk from the hatch of the ration-stores.

When they went down past rue Salameh they passed the cratered shelters that had survived the bulldozers, the women crouched down on the reed mats over the balls of dough and bowls of washing. The walls had been stripped of every hanging and picture; all the flags, photographs, pennants in the shape of Palestine hidden away from the roving patrols.

But sometimes at night from their beds on the upper floor they heard the high-pitched wail of pipes among the ruins, the distant drums and stomping of a debkeh from some chamber underground.

During the rains he remembered a blonde women in an expensive leather coat had come several times to the hospital asking for Asad, but he had always refused to see her; there were rumours that this women was his cousin or sister, the mistress of a wealthy Maronite collaborator who had fled to Europe after the Israeli retreat; he had watched the women in the line spit at her and kick the dirty water up at her face as she had hurried back across rue Sabra to her waiting taxi.

Aziz could recall nothing else about this visitor, and in all the years of the sieges Asad had never spoken of her, though after the first siege was lifted he remembered that one of the nurses at the camp clinic had triumphantly claimed to have seen the woman down among the soldiers on the front-line near Sahat al'Burj.

When Aziz had returned from the Bekaa two years later he had found much of the camp had been rebuilt, but every day the hospital was treating the wounded from firefights in the neighbouring shanty-towns.

A local hashmay-dealer known to the camp-dwellers as Nimrod had been driving his car into the narrow alleys during Friday prayers, butting children with the car door, blasting out disco music during a funeral procession, entering the mosque in his boots. His mutilated body had been found some weeks later by the rag-pickers along the beach at Ramlet al'Baida.

As the Amal militia of which he had been a member had laid siege to the camp many of the foreign doctors and aid-workers had fled, but Aziz and Asad had remained in the hospital until it had been overrun.

Many families had taken shelter in the basements and the morgues; the gunmen had set fire to the wounded in the upper wards, and fired their B7s at close range into the mortuary fridges. Those patients who could walk had been led out and shot against the walls of the lane behind Sabra market. From their hiding-place among the racks of artificial limbs on the upper floor they had watched the bulldozers edging backwards to the burial pits under the stadium, in the scoops the bodies stiff and light as pretzel-men.

For thirty days the militia had bombarded the camp with tank-shells, heavy-calibre rockets, mortar rounds filled with phosphorus and jet-fuel; dynamiting the homes on the boundaries to clear a path for direct fire into the central buildings.

There had been no lulls for the families in the shelters to fill and empty their cans, to wash their clothes; in the hours of darkness the snipers had operated with night-sights from the five-storey blocks of Sabra.

Some of the old men still remembered Asad as a boy from the years when he had stood on the roof of their diwan with his sister to watch the wedding feasts; on the darkest nights Asad and Aziz had helped the old men build barricades from the rubble and burnt-out cars and set blankets on washing-lines across the mouths of the alleys to unsight the snipers.

Aziz and Asad had helped the fighters excavate the tunnels and trenches that linked the outer defences of the camp, the shovels with sawn-off handles for digging at close quarters. The sandy soil made for easy digging under the pipes and electricity cables, but the tunnels would cave in during the rains, and had to be spragged with planks and broken doors.

When the tunnels had flooded they had worked with the water up to their chests, the deposits from the blocked drains bobbing along the underground tides; in some sections of the defence-ring the fighters had used the municipal sewers to shuttle between their forward positions.

The water-main had been blown up in an attempt to flood the camp, all the wells on the boundaries destroyed. It had been one of Asad's tasks to patch up the narrow-bore pipe that led up from an artesian well sunk below the sand-table. Without this water the camp would have fallen within three days.

If the shelling eased the two men went down into the communal shelters, aspirin, antibiotics, cough-syrup on trays strapped to their necks, passing among the huddled families like Chiclet-boys through a darkened auditorium.

Cigarettes and milk-powder had been rationed by the

camp committee, and there was no bread; the black smoke from the bakery had become a ranging-point for the surrounding gunners, as had the hum and diesel fumes of the generators. In the deepest shelter Aziz had witnessed single packets of cigarettes and bags of rice changing hands for a thousand lira.

In the dug-out they shared the two men had taught themselves English from the comics and thrillers they had saved from the hospital library and from the lyrics of the country tapes played on a cassette-recorder salvaged from the burnt remains of the shrapnel ward. The failed batteries they boiled in water on the fire, dried and cooled. When they had got through the wood from the roofing and the furniture in the bombed barakiyeh, and used up all the candles, they made lamps from halved tins; strips of denim soaked in oil as wicks; the kerosene smoke stung their eyes when they read, and as the months passed they turned black as miners from the soot.

The door of their barakiyeh also served as a stretcher to bring back the dead and wounded through the back alleys. The snipers had made excursions to the cemeteries too dangerous, and after the old graves under the mosque were filled, and the bodies left in the old feeding-centre eaten by feral cats, the dead were buried by night without light in the pine woods, the sheikh whispering the prayers.

For almost two years they had lived on together under the ruins, sleeping on damp mattresses, the water seeping up from the broken pipes, the livid fungus spreading over every wall.

Only the heavily sandbagged clinic run by the walrus-moustached Greek-Canadian doctor had remained above ground-level, the walls of the wards smeared with the faeces of the brain-damaged fighters.

The young men had starved so the women and children could be fed. When the underground supplies had run out the fighters had trapped rats and wild cats in cages baited with the flesh of the dead. The children ate grass and scavenged in the rubbish mounds.

On the short-wave they heard that in the neighbouring camp the sheikh had issued a fatwa permitting his people to eat the corpses of their relatives.

Old women in the shelters woke to find their feet lost to the rats. The old men who had built the barricades walked out in a procession with white handkerchiefs, and were gunned down on the boundary of the camp.

The young fighters smoked sawdust and green tea, wandered hallucinating into the ruins to be picked off by the snipers. Aziz had seen one shabb gnawing from his own arm. The children sat with fishing-lines beside the rank ditches, and hunted water-rats in the sewers, and fired the guns of the dead men at imaginary birds.

In the last weeks of the siege the relief agencies had sent convoys to the western border of the camp. From their dugout the men had watched the lorries burn, smelt the flaming sacks of rice and sugar; the hollow popping of the pressurized cans like corn on a griddle; the women crawling under the snipers to the sacks flung free of the fires.

Aziz had been too weak to remember what had happened at the end. They had carried him out with the wounded to the university hospital, but when the militiamen had broken into the lower wards he had stumbled back across the headland to the ruins of Fakhani.

There he had found other camp-dwellers in their

makeshift shelters, and in the following weeks had searched the black tents in the neighbouring squares and basements and garages, but he had found no one who had seen Asad since the siege had been lifted.

Beirut, 1990

January–April

When I returned from boarding-school for my holidays in the years before the war my father would sometimes drive me up to the Ashrafieh asylum in the pine hills above the city. While he chatted on the terrace with the other trustees I would sit on the railings and watch the patients walking in the garden with their watering-cans between the tidy rows of bright shrubs and flowerbeds.

It was only on my last visit when I had dared to climb down from the terrace that I had discovered the entire garden was made out of paper, the leaves from streamers, the rocks from papier mâché, the blooms from crepe and tinted foil. As the patients poured from the watering-cans, a fine white powder covered the coloured paper like icing-sugar and blew up over their boiler-suits and into the cracks in their faces and over their wild hair. It was as if they had all just climbed out from under the chalky soil, and I ran round to the front of the building without looking back, and locked myself in the Plymouth, and waited with my eyes closed for the rustle of his worry-beads.

Driving through the city that winter I saw many such gardens. Along the ruined avenues where the blasted palms and planes had been stripped away stood trees of discarded water-containers with fronds of plastic sheeting, groves of stacked tyres and twisted piping where once there had been lemon orchards and mulberry terraces, and of that wilderness of camomile and wild roses under the forests of snobar pines planted by the last emir to protect the city from the over-bearing easterly winds where families had come to picnic at weekends nothing remained but an expanse of charred stumps from which the street-boys hung tendrils of sacking and telephone cables and the black bunting of the martyrs.

Hearing that I had returned to the city Jaffer had sent a driver to watch over me, a slight man with heavily pocked cheeks and thick wire-framed spectacles who carried no visible arms, but having relations in both Amal and Hizbollah could negotiate most checkpoints within the western sector.

The man arrived later each morning with ever more florid excuses, his decrepit van mounted on to truck-axles and outsize tyres to clear the deeply rutted roads, the engine adapted to run on cooking oil, but fired with a tablespoon of kerosene which he kept in a flask chained to his belt.

On those wet afternoons he would drive me in this hybrid vehicle through Fakhani and Shiyah and down as far as the Tayuni roundabout and the airport boulevard to the south, but not to the camps themselves still ringed by the Syrians and the Amal snipers, and never out to the front line at Sahat al'Burj where desultory mortar exchanges continued through that winter.

I would wait in the van while he went down among the black tents with the polythene envelopes in which I had enclosed the photographs; the features gradually receding under the palimpsest of rain and thumb-prints like the faces of the drowned under ice.

Returning from the last encampments on the edges of the pine forest the tracks cut between sheer hills of rubbish, the

214

lines of rag-pickers in silhouette against the candy-rose dusk over the beaches, many with picks and spikes tied to the stumps of limbs lost to the butterfly-mines set in the mounds by rival gangs, thick spirals of gulls shrieking overhead. At the base of the tips we would pass the loading-bays, the convoys of barrows and trolleys piled high with hardboard, glass, tin cans.

From these rubbish hills the street-boys of Shiyah and Sabra would follow the fighting to every corner of the city, snatching watches and gold teeth from the fallen militiamen, hiring themselves out as corpses to the foreign-news crews too craven to shoot on the front line.

In a city of ruins there was little calling for beggars, but a corpse could make a decent wage; the amputees working at premium rates. During those wet weeks I had seen the same cast of histrionically splayed corpses in reports from as far apart as Sahat al'Burj and the foothills of the Shuf.

On some evenings as we drove back towards Jaffer's new apartment in Hamra we would hear gunfire from below the Kola roundabout, the alleys emptying within moments, the stalls and trictrac tables and fruit barrows vanishing from the pavements as if by some long-practised conjuring trick, the crates of apples and eggs reappearing as suddenly as they had vanished up on the surrounding balconies and rooftop arcades. In those alleys the snipers had turned magician also, toys and silk scarves and belts with silver buckles drawn by fine threads across the open lots to tempt passers-by into their line of fire.

Coming out from the maze of Fakhani into the avenues of the headland we passed the piled wreckage of green and rose tiles that had once been Ottoman villas; fragments of majolica embedded in the dark rubbish like glazed fruits on a cake. On either side the higher modern blocks had not taken so many direct hits, but these listed palazzos had been deliberately targeted by the gunners in the hills on the orders of the property speculators who were already dreaming of the new city they would build over the ruins.

Jaffer had taken over an apartment on what had once been the most fashionable strip of rue Hamra, the row of marble-porched mansion buildings with staggered cream terraces like the decks of an ocean liner where I had spent many tedious afternoons as a boy chasing though the interminable corridors with the children of my father's bridge partners.

Now plots of marrows and tomatoes grew on the terraces, and much of the marble and iron-work had gone from the façades, and from the shell-holes above the charred railings women in white headscarves lowered baskets to the wheel-barrow-men coming up from the corniche, and walking between those fruit and poultry stalls set into the blackened walls where once there had been the show-windows of boutiques and jewellers I had heard again the voices of the southern mountains, of Marjayoun and Nabatiyeh and of our own village, and of Tibnine and the village-with-no-name.

In the stairwell some of the original marble steps had survived; a few bent sections of the elaborate balustrade like fragments of a lost score. Inside the apartment the upper stems of the chandeliers still hung from the peeling stucco ceilings, along the walls between the scrolls that had once held mirrors and tapestries the Qur'ānic inscriptions looted from the walls of the shelled mosques; on the smoked-glass alcoves the straw bulls and sea-shell figurines from their old house above the village.

For weeks Jaffer had not returned from the south where he had been coordinating the mountain routes with Ali for the convoys of construction materials to reach the bombed villages below Tibnine. I would wait on the terrace as his young wife, a thin-limbed girl with the almond skin and kinky hair of the emigrant families of the fellahin quarter, brought through the sweet mint tea and stale baclava on a warped salver that had once hung in the Bey's manzul, and went in again without speaking.

On the long bolster over the reed matting she would squat down over her plastic bucket of washing; around the door the wide eyes of the two little boys peeping at the beardless stranger come among them; their bare feet slapping away across the marble floors.

And later when Jaffer did not come I would walk back through the dozen blocks I had grown up on, under the broken walls the lone cigarette-sellers and shawarma-stands, outside the few remaining grocers the tannoys announcing the currency prices, the furtive shoppers hurrying in with their knapsacks of bundled lira.

Over the gutted cinemas the high hoardings of Harb and Khomeini; beyond Hamra the streets empty apart from the few armour-bumpered cars swishing away into the winter night, and below towards the house the rain-muffled goatbells in the overgrown lots.

The hardboard-and-iron grille over the front door had not been disturbed, but for three days I had seen smoke rising from the back of the Tannous villa.

I cut my way through the thickets over the wall, and clamber down on to the rear terrace. On the french windows all the crosses of tape and puckered sheets of polythene are

217

still in place, but there are tracks leading through the high grass to the tarred shed down by the campus wall.

I step off the terrace, sinking waist-deep into the grass; below me a hunched figure flitting away behind the frangipani. I follow through the nettles and self-sown sunflowers, and in one of the burrows under the wall I find the old man crouching with his face hidden in his hands.

The squatter has long white hair and a ragged forked beard, like those of the patriarchs in Gothic cathedrals. There are mattresses on the floor of the shed, a small butagaz-ring, shirts and blankets hung along a cord from the water-spout.

When he sees I do not mean to harm him he gestures me into the cabin, and brings down a plastic mug and a container of benzene from a dug-out under the wall, and I shiver as I hear his voice, soft and erudite, the shock of it like the taste of fine wine from a broken mains-spout. I push some bills into the pocket of one of the hanging shirts, and run back to the terrace.

Out through the carob trees I tread lightly, my head lowered under the verandah where the driver slumps on the recliner sleeping off the whisky and Nembutals. The van free-wheeling on the hill, almost down at the corniche before I let the engine catch.

This was to be my last day in the city. All week there had been reports of the fighting between Amal and Hizbollah for control of the drug passes through the Shuf spreading down into the headland, and Jaffer had arranged that I should leave that evening with the convoy of construction materials for the safety of the Jihad al-Binaa complex in the hills east of Sidon.

It was already midday by the time I reached the waste-ground below the stadium, and the soldiers eating burghul behind their tarpaulins paid me no attention as I drove under the shadows of the shattered piers.

The road beyond had been smoothed over with poured concrete, across the marketplace the high façade of the Gaza hospital, less damaged than I had expected; the flooded craters of rue Sabra leading down to the camp. Halfway along beside the gutted frontage of the Ali-Handar coffee-house the street was blocked with sandhills and rubble revetments, and I had no choice but to leave the van, and walk out into the ruins.

Through the three-storey buildings on the periphery of the camp, some hollow shells, others collapsed in upon themselves like houses of playing-cards, the winding alleys had been cleaned and repainted, on the cinderblock ledges loops of bright washing and tins of pink geraniums. But before I could reach the clearing beyond the way came out beside an Amal outpost in the basement of a roofless storehouse, on the wall a portrait of Nabih Berri in younger days, the militiamen in their green armbands lolling on sacks of grain and flour, pipes and beer cans over the concrete floor.

Through the open doorway they called up to me, but when I said I had come to speak with a nurse at the camp clinic two of the soldiers climbed out with their kalashins, and stood across the mouth of the alley laughing. I saw the viscous sheen of sweat over their faces, their dead-fish eyes. I ran back into the ruins.

In the van my shoulders still shuddering, my mind emptied of everything but animal fear, a spreading dampness between my legs as I reversed between the flooded craters; to the left another outpost I had not seen before, at the front the soldiers in their black headbands bowing towards the foothills of the Shuf, over the roof the black flags of the martyrs.

The sky had begun to lose its light as I passed the blackened hulk of the Murr Tower, over the bay the remaining skeletons of the seafront hotels like carious teeth in an ancient gum, through the gutted shells the pink swabs of the clouds, and there alone on the ridge the jagged cromlech that had been the Holiday Inn, the charred crown once the eagle's nest of the revolving restaurant from which as a boy I had looked out across the lights of the city, the shimmering boulevards like spun sugar down along the coastline where now there was only darkness.

In these streets there had always been long and noisy traffic-jams, a hubbub of hooting and the calling of the Chiclet-boys and peanut-sellers weaving between the high fins of the American saloons, but as I came down into the overgrown scarps of rubble and the silence the road ran off into a series of fosses and sandhills, and once more I had to leave the van and walk out into the wilderness.

Palmettos, ground elder and bindweed had grown up over the ruins from the earth revetments and shell-craters, but I kept my bearings by the band of sea still visible at the end of each gulley, and climbed between the mounds to the tracks that led eastwards towards the front line at Sahat al'Burj.

Through a sequence of shell-holes in the broken walls that had been enlarged by the soldiers who had once used this route I came down into a dank chamber, creepers hanging from the ceiling and thick grass growing up through the tiled floor, the final blocks of the front line already showing through the breaks in the further wall.

As I rested against the parapet I noticed the faint outline of the keyhole arches behind my head and painted lozenges and stellae over the crumbled ceilings, and it was only then I realized where I was standing. This had once been the most famous restaurant in all the city where we had sometimes come as a treat on those dreary Sunday afternoons in the years before the war, the tables laid out as if on either side of a souk, each with its centrepiece of beets, white plums, almonds in ice, my mother always in a simple cream slip-dress and an extravagant hat, my father slapping my hands as I flicked pistachios over at the politicos on the other tables.

The street above must have been partially cleared in an earlier truce, and the going was easier through the following three blocks, the peeling yellow paintwork of the Fattal Building rising over the pitted façades; across the grassed-over square the upper storey of what was once the Rivoli Cinema, the faded lettering of the billboard still advertising a film from the mid-seventies, *The Divorced with Jack Lemmon and* . . .

From behind the square I could see down the overgrown avenue, across the gap at the end a single figure slowly staggering towards the sea, an old man dragging behind him a manhole-cover as broad and heavy as a stone tablet.

Beyond the lanes narrowed again into thickets over the rubble and trenches, and from somewhere up the line towards the mountains there was the distant thump of shells falling like a carpet being beaten out over a balcony.

From the last trench I came up into a level clearing, tidy rectangles of vegetable plots over the earth redoubts on the far side, and in their lee the tents and dug-outs of the soldiers, and there on the opposite corner the girls standing in their short, bright skirts, and I knew then this must be the place the camp nurse had described.

I walked out across the clearing, but as I got closer I saw the group at the corner were old women wearing platinum wigs; short, threadbare fur coats above their shiny skirts. The women did not come over to me, but waited at equal intervals apart from each other, as if set in invisible niches on a colonnade.

Along the line there were the mixing scents of heavy perfumes and cordite and damp fur, and when I held out the photograph they all laughed, ruffling my hair with a stagy motherliness, gesturing towards a woman with a soldier walking away through a fallen wall into the ruins.

I followed the couple back along the overgrown trenches and up between groves of saplings and low fissured façades to a dark portico, a flickering of kerosene lamps in the triple-arched windows above. All these surrounding ruins would have once formed the brothel quarter, but now all that remained was this single corner-building rising like an anvil above the wilderness.

Stumbling in the half-light of the hallway I call out her name, and the woman with the soldier half-turns, and points upwards to a blue glow at the head of the stairwell. There are no railings up the steep stone steps, and I keep one hand on the damp tiles until I reach the first landing; over each doorway bead curtains and plastic drapes, low divans on the linoleum floors, the soldiers reclining with their water-pipes as the women bend over them.

On the landing at the top, three soldiers sharing a bottle of Arak, squatting down in the blue light from the room beyond. I push past them through the jangling beads over the door.

The room is larger than the others, with looted armchairs along the wall, a large bed with a mother-of-pearl headboard and straps tied to the corners. At the window, her back to the

222

door, a silk shawl over her skinny shoulders, a girl with a dyed-blonde bob looking down at the few lit streets in the eastern sector.

I call her name again, and she turns. She comes towards me with her little hands outstretched, a girl of no more than fourteen, her gown open, the garters loose over her thin thighs; her lips bruised, the kohl smudged under her eyes. And rising from behind the bed like string puppets lifted suddenly from their boxes two gangling soldiers in ill-fitting fatigues, at their feet a trail of broken glass and stubs across the tiles to the pocked parapet that had once been a balcony.

The sky is turning dark above the bay. I go down slowly, one hand still on the wall. Through the ruins I follow the shrieking of the gulls back to the sandhills above the breakwater.

HOMECOMING

'The martyr will be given again what he has lost in this world.'

– Sheikh Naim Qassem

South Lebanon, 1990

April–May

From the narrow camp-bed I cannot see the gardens.

All the balconies on this second floor have been stacked with sacks of grain, drums of Nido and Mazola. It is quiet here at the back, the windows high but blocked by the crates and sacks.

The partition to the bathroom cut away, the wall beyond still crossed with tiles bearing nautical motifs. Anchors, scallop-shells, tritons.

Each morning I read in the niche I have made among the sacks, across the lawns below the lines of pepper and acacia trees, buddleia and lilac, the lower reaches turned over to the villagers to grow tobacco and zucchini.

All through the night the convoy of construction materials had travelled by wadis and on mountain tracks between the abandoned hotel resorts where the Druz militias controlled the passes into the higher Shuf. We came down at first light across the frothing waters of the Awali among the tobacco plots and olive groves, on the hillside of burnt pines and cypresses at the head of the valley the complex of four-storey buildings, the flat roofs lost under the dawn mist over Jazzin.

The place was on that ridge of hills immmediately to the south of our village, up a turning off the old road that criss-crossed over the jurd to Nabatiyeh. The original L-shaped block had been built in the late fifties as a hotel retraite for those tourists making the round of the surviving cedar groves and crusader castles, but the spot had never caught on and the buildings had already fallen into disrepair when the Jihad al-Binaa had established their headquarters there after the Israelis had pulled back south of the Litani.

On the cracked esplanande under the balconies from which the guests would have once enjoyed the prospect down to the coast sodden tarpaulins now covered rolls of cable, piping and mobile generators; alongside the earthed-in pool planted over with cousa and cabbages radio-masts rose up behind the sunken solarium. It was in the cabanas and bungalows in the gardens on the far side of this pool that the fighters would sleep on the last night of their journey down to the border; sometimes in the evenings as I sat out among the sacks I would smell the bitter smoke from their pipes drifting up through the pepper trees.

On the lower edge of these gardens among the burnt pines, a further row of tarpaulins covered water-tanks, mobile generators, bore-tripods for drilling artesian wells, and it was in a small cabin below this second depot that Ali spent his days, the lorries disguised as ambulances and fruit-trucks backing up the lane to be loaded with the plant that would be driven by night along the back roads to the devasted villages below the Litani.

It was beside this second depot that the convoy of construction materials had pulled up in the mist of that first morning, but Ali had already gone up to meet me at the front of the building, and as the hamals had begun to unload the drums of cable and piping I had watched him wander down between the burnt pines, his figure stooped, his long and unkempt beard lifting like toadflax in the wind off the mountains.

When we embraced I saw how he had aged, the sagging

230

skin over his hollow cheeks, the rifts and chapping covering all his brow and forehead, his hair thinned into antic wisps, but as he drew back there was the old ellipsis of his smile, and in his eyes the level light of faith, and he held me tightly to him again, and pounded my back with his fist, and with his thin arm over my shoulders and with tears in his sunken eyes he had led me up through the debris of the lobby to the room on the second floor that would be my home for the next five months.

When all the trucks had been unloaded we had sat together on the terrace over the earthed-in pool, between us the dishes of fried eggplant, warmed ghifs of mountain bread, garlic rice with almonds and lemon brought out by a girl who veiled her face with a white dishcloth as she crossed to the low table.

Ali had eaten in silence, with one hand scooping the rice into strange cones and spirals, with the other reaching to clasp my own fingers as if they were something he would pull out by the root, and as the bitter coffee was brought I had told him of my wish to go to the village and search for the picture of my mother among the remains of the house. But he had warned me the road was closed by fighting between the rival Druz militias and that it would be another week before he returned from an irrigation project below the Litani, and only then could we make the journey in safety over the hills with an escort from the complex.

As the jeep juddered down from the last ridge on the jurd into the tracks between the groves I could barely recognize the old valley below. On every side the olive orchards had been torched, the ground between the black stumps left fallow, and higher up many of the tobacco terraces had been resown with poppies, some covered with long hooped tunnels of silver-green sheeting.

From the track we joined the road up from the coast at the upper bridge, the black flags of the martyrs fluttering from the reed poles at every turn above the silent press, and as we climbed the final bend we passed the old driveway, the gate blocked by sacks of concrete, along the eucalyptus windbreak a double row of refugee tents, the wilderness of palmettos and wisteria from which I had once clambered down to the river-bed levelled into a promontory built over with prefabs and barakiyat.

The lower parts of the village were deserted, all the trictrac tables and kiosks gone from the square around the plane tree, the shutters stuck over with posters of martyrs garlanded with black tulips and lilies, but further up towards the mosque a buttress of sandbags marked the entrance of a new shop run by the party, on the lane from the fellahin quarter a queue of women in white headscarves and in the alleys behind black chadors flitting like stork shadows low against the adobe walls.

I had hoped to search among the remains on the hill, but when the jeep reached the road above the cemetery I could already see this would be an impossible task. The ruins of the central hall and diwans had been ploughed over and planted with smallholdings, those walls still standing in the outer wings now used as lairages by the goatherds from the jurd, all the bossed sandstone blocks from the upper promontory slid down on pallets to build the new mosque on the clearing in the almond groves where the villagers had seen the Bey wander naked in the year of the invasion, the unplastered nozzle of the minaret rising above the bank of trees.

Ali gently took my hand and we walked through the cemetery into the fellahin quarter, the men knocking on each door along the lanes, and in every home we entered I saw some object or ornament I recognized, in one house the hunting prints from the study, in another the brass coffee-pot that had hung in the manzul, over the hearth of a long barakiyeh the heads of the lions that had stood guard below the front steps, their mouths stuffed with coloured bulbs connected to the new mains the Jihad al-Binaa had laid throughout the quarter.

Like a great ark broken up against rocks, its contents washed up on every cove and beach along the shoreline, the treasures of the house had found their way into each lane and lairage in the village, but though we searched throughout the fellahin and emigrant quarters and the outlying tents and barakiyat of the refugees we found no trace of the painting.

It was late afternoon when we returned to the road above the cemetery, through the hills the sun already sinking into the sea. Up ahead beside the jeep a group of elderly men and women had gathered, each bearing bundles of varying sizes, some wrapped in newspaper, others in canvas bound with string; two of the shuyyuk loading these parcels with difficulty on to the raised tailgate.

As we came closer I recognized some of the faces. The uncle of our cook Khalil was there, and old Yusef from the kiosk who had served me gasouzas after my long climbs up the dry river-bed, and Elias the gardener and former hunting companion of Abu Musa who each year had cut away all the pollen-bearing plants from around the wing of Aunt Mona.

Some lurched out to kiss my hand, and others from behind called out blessings on the house of the beys, and I held out what money I had but they would not take it, and the old men took me in their arms and announced they had prepared a homecoming feast at the manzul of Umm Khalil, but our

233

armed escorts were anxious to cross the jurd before nightfall, and pushed back the old people with the butts of their kalashins, one beardless youth firing into the air, and once I had mounted the jeep pulled away abruptly down the hill, the trail of dust suddenly obscuring the small crowd by the wall and the ruins on the hill.

It was dark when we arrived at the complex. Before we reached the main building Ali was called to join a night convoy carrying water-tanks to a village east of Jibsheet, the bundles were carried up by the men to the room on the second floor, most no larger than orange-crates, one rectangular and broader than the rest, the dirty sheeting tied over with trellis-twine.

I sat alone and unwrapped what the fellahin had saved, majolica chargers, decanters of painted glass, caskets in mother-of-pearl, for the most part gaudy and worthless objects not one of which I could remember from my boyhood wanderings through the halls and diwans.

In the large rectangular parcel, a gilded rocaille frame, but the canvas burnt away; in its place a tartly coloured map of the city from the years before the war. With all these glittering objects arrayed along the walls, the room like a brocante-stall from the arcade above the front, and leaving the map over the bed I packed everything back into the canvas and newspaper and called up two of the shebab and ordered them to distribute the packages to the old fellahin when crossing north over the jurd.

The map was of the type that might have once hung in the lobby of one of the fashionable seafront hotels. Stylized caïques and water-skiers among the ruffles of the waves, minarets and umbrella pines inland, belly-dancers marking the nightclub districts, plump waiters in fezzes the famous restaurants of the day; over the hippodrome the figure of a piebald jockey puffing on a narghile.

The lower districts of the city, the southern suburbs and the hinterland of Shiyah, had been omitted from the map, but all the principal boulevards fell in broad lubricious glissades between each pleasure zone, and lying in the cool air off the mountain I let my eyes play over the ribald contours of that fallen city and remembered the nights as a boy when I had crept up the corridor and hidden behind the cabinet of Phoenician vases which shuddered with the stomping and laughter of the guests beyond and pictured in the veins and crevices of the ancient glass my own imaginary cities though later I would know that the mountain beys and merchant princes at those parties had inscribed their names across all the streets of the headland and the city of their memories was already as lost and forgotten as the chimeras in those time-clouded glasses.

When the revving of the last night trucks has died I fall asleep to the low-intoned suras across the wild gardens, the sky raven-black above the ridges of Jazzin.

Dawn comes stealthily here, a pale aureole on the mountain, but I woke into a sudden brilliant light as the new sun flashed in a floodlit instant over the level steppes of the Syrian desert, and when I looked away from the glare I saw the dunes were sown with skulls and ribcages and the jawbones of camels, and beneath on the level waste tumbleweed blew between the sun-blanched bones of the martyrs, and in the clear sky over the plain of Kerbala two angels bore away my heart, and the angels washed the heart in the snows of Jazzin, and the sun was shrouded by the wings of the angels, but when I raised my head again I saw these were the cranes of Numidia that flew higher across the deserts than all other migrant birds, and as I followed the shadows over the wastes I passed above a city buried in the sands, and recognized half-sunken entablatures from the rooftop gardens of the seafront hotels, and in those crumbling cones the pinnacles of the minarets of Basta and Museitbeh, and beyond that land of buried stones I came upon a ring of palms and a well, and lay down in the shade of the grove, and from the trees spiders spun silken threads that sutured the wound over my heart, and through the grove a woman came with a pail of water and balms, and her golden hair covered her face like a veil, and her gown was the green of lizards among vines, and through those palms I glimpsed the rising of a greater tree and the spreading boughs covered all the earth from the sands to the sea in a fragrant and eternal darkness.

South Lebanon, 1990

May–July

'In the Holy Book was written every word in the language.'

You told me it was enough for an unbeliever to hear the words though they did not understand them. Many were converted by the beauty of the words alone.

'When subject peoples heard the words they abandoned their own tongues. The bards of the tribes and the kahin who spoke from under their cloaks were as the jabberings of apes to the barakah of the book.'

You told me that when the pilgrims came to Mecca to circumnavigate the Ka'bah, Abu Jahl posted guards at all seven gates for he knew that those who heard the recitations of the Prophet would be lost to him.

Ibn Amr, the poet of the tribe of Daws, would only enter the city with his ears stuffed with wool.

'In the oasis of Medina the clansmen Usayd and Sa'd came with their lances to attack a gathering of believers hidden in a walled garden, but when they heard the beauty of the words they prostrated themselves before the book.'

You told me the Prophet walked alone through the valley of the sands and when the band of djinns behind the dunes heard his recitations they flew away like startled geese and proclaimed their faith in the quarter of the desert that is empty.

On the nights when the cabins across the gardens were silent you came to my room and recited suras.

The Elephant. The Mantled One. The Moon. Qaf. The Spiders.

And the army of the Elephant became like the withered stalks of plants which cattle have destroyed.

On that day the sky shall become like molten brass, and the mountains like tufts of wool scattered in the wind. Friends will meet, but shall not speak to each other.

Those who serve other masters beside God may be compared to the spider which builds a cobweb for itself.

On the crux of your lap the Qur'ān you had rescued from the burning mosque in Kfar Tebnit.

On the north bank of the Litani we had driven through the seven deserted villages, on the heights the minarets bent and splayed like spent fireworks, over the abandoned squares and alleys the calling of long-dead martyrs from the muezzin-tannoys, the voices of Harb and Jarradi.

Along the hills the shattered water-towers and aqueducts, the flooded terraces of sunflowers and plum trees, on rafts bands of fellahin cutting down the fruit on those boughs above the water.

On the lower bank you took me through a ravaged land-scape, groves torched; bridges, silos, water-towers all in ruins; the harvests rotting in the fields.

We passed columns of refugees coming north along the cratered roads from Qana and Museitbeh. Donkeys pulling traps, whole families clinging to tractors, some walking with sacks and suitcases, the few cars loaded with sheep and chickens.

Further south we found villages more recently abandoned, along the walls the sacks of grain soaked in oil and kerosene by the militiamen, ripped pages of the Qur'ān riding up in the dirt of the squares, and from the empty mosques and Husseinyas the barking of dogs.

You drove faster now, your head below the steering-wheel, after the villages leaving the road and coming down into the borderland of the Jabal Amil through tracks and dry wadis.

We passed only solitary travellers here; above the ridge the darkening sky towards Mount Hermonn, a faint sgraffito of vapour-trails. You told me no families risked journeying together through these hills.

You told me to watch for the shadows of the silent spy-gliders, like the shadows of the buzzards over the jurd, and to listen for the buzz of the Hueys from behind the hills.

From the air every car and motorcycle and donkey a potential suicide-bomb crawling like a viper through the vines. You pointed to the valley where the boys had volunteered to walk across the fields ahead of the guerrillas as human minesweepers, and to the turning in the road where a teenage virgin had driven her white Peugeot laden with Hexogen into an Israeli convoy.

Down at the head of that valley, the dust trails of the Yamahas we had seen parked outside the hotel two nights before, and your eyes filled with tears, and you knelt in the dust and prayed for their families; as you started the jeep again I brushed the barwaq pollen and reed-strands from your beard.

Between the hills we climbed to the clearing in the orchards above the bombed village overlooking the Occupied Zone, but the men had not come up to meet us. You would not wait for them, and we unloaded the generator and the

241

water-tank, and laid them under the olive trees. Once we had worked our way back up the wadi you had followed a different track, eastwards, knowing the direction of our incoming dust-trail had already been sighted by one of the militia outposts in the ridge to the south.

The previous day there had been rumours of Amal check-points along the road south to Nabatiyeh, and so we had taken a detour up across the jurd, spending the night in a cave below the falls at Jazzin before descending through the deserted villages to the gorge of the Litani.

You had forgotten the path to the caves, but Musa-al-Tango still knew every crevice of the jurd from the years he had hidden on the mountain and worked the plots of poppies in the land above the ruined kilns.

He walked ahead of the jeep, rolling away the rocks and branches that had fallen across the track into the ravine below, the dry wind down the hollows wrapping his baggy shirwal around his thick calves, his bony ankles dancing between the stones, across the path the shadow of his wide-brimmed straw hat against the bear sun over the ridge.

It was already late afternoon when we reached the cave, along a track that led above the silted mouths of the abandoned quarries. In the years before the war certain village families had jealously protected their knowledge of the route to the cave, but there seemed little to see now, just a low hollow, the entrance hidden by a thicket of stunted juniper and barberry, the smooth floor strewn with ash and rusted cans, the ceiling blackened by the smoke of previous bonfires, at the back the beginnings of a passage lost in the narrowing folds of the crannies.

At the edge of the hollow we had made our fire, and Musa-al-Tango had recalled how his father had hunted gazelle and boar with the beys in these mountains, but the firs and cedars had long been cut down to build the railways and feed the charcoal kilns, and even in the late afternoon light we could see right down the deep erosion grooves across the barrenness of the jurd and the sahel to Jabal Amil, the plains of the south rolled out before us like a creased paper bag lying as they had for centuries a dry expanse without roads or networks of irrigation, the fellahin reduced to sharecroppers, woodcutters, caravan-guides while high above the sahel the beys of the mountains had intrigued and built their palaces with walls of cedar, their fountains of basalt, their pavilions set within imitations of the four gardens of paradise, their days spent hunting in the forests, their nights feasting on the livers of bears and gazelles stewed in mountain wines.

Of all the mountain emirs only the dwarf Fakr-al-Din had brought water and fruits to the dry lands of the south, building terraces of mulberries for the silk trade; plum orchards and olive groves; bridges over the Awali; moles and watchtowers to protect the caravanserais of Tyre and Sidon against the Italian pirates.

In the village it was said that the emir was so small that if an egg dropped from his pocket it would not break. When one of the tall beys of the village had insulted Fakr with the words, 'Why, I could put you in my pocket with my keys and carry you away,' the emir had answered, 'You are the poplar but I am the saw,' and his army had carried away the stones from the diwan of the village bey to heighten the walls of his own mountain palace at Dayr al'Qamar.

But the Turks had grown jealous of the emir's trade in silk, soap, wine and olive-oil, and sent a fleet of twenty-two galleys to destroy the fortifications on the coast, and an army drawn from every corner of the empire, from Aleppo, Gaza, Damascus and Cairo had converged upon the mountain.

After his own troops had been defeated down on the plain, his palace laid waste, the head and seal-finger of his son dispatched to Istanbul, he had retreated with a small following into the upper reaches of the mountain and it was many months before his underground refuge was finally discovered, the drinking water polluted with the blood of slaughtered animals.

The dwarf emir was led in chains to the Ottoman court and there his eloquence before the Grand Sultan bought him some passing favour though only months later he was strangled in the square of the mosque by two mutes, and it was in the labyrinth beneath this hill that the villagers believed the emir had spent his final year dreaming in the darkness of the paradise that would be his kingdom when he emerged into the light, and those families who guarded the secret of the route to the place had come each year to light fires in his memory and leave offerings of coins and barwaq-petals, though we had seen none during our stay in the hollow, and all night I had listened to the rushing of the falls only to discover as we descended the following morning that the sound had been the droning of a generator from a lower encampment.

From the wadi above the village on the border we took another route northwards through the three valleys of ruined villages abandoned decades before the present war.

These were the villages of which the fellahin had always said that the fox could go in and nobody would drive it out.

The chalk walls overgrown with ivy and toadflax, the

rotten roof-beams open to the sky, on the hills the terraces of dead mulberries below which before the war there would be roadside stalls selling watermelons and white plums, and I would be frightened to look into the ruins.

The maid Zainab had always told me the valleys were haunted by djinns and by the wandering spirit of a beautiful girl with the ink-black eyes of a houri, her feet and hands dyed not with hennna, but with the blood of her tribe.

In the village it was said that at the merest hint of infidelity Al-Jazzar the tyrant of Sidon had ordered his eunuchs to drag all thirty-seven of his harem on to a burning pyre, and when it was discovered later that the girl on whom suspicion had fallen was a native of these valleys his army had poisoned the wells, burnt the cotton fields, cut down the mulberry groves. Such was the quantity of books pillaged from the mosques and learned ulama of these villages that the smoke had risen from the ovens of Sidon for six days and six nights.

And if I brought reeds and flowers into the house Zainab would warn that Al-Jazzar would come tapping at night on my shutters, with Shaitan, and Yezid of the bleeding heads.

The three valleys fell into such desolation that godless clansmen rode down from the north and stabled their cattle and beasts of burden in the ruins of the mosques, and if merchants passed that way and came into the mosques to pray the Nusayri would call down to them, 'Bray not, and your fodder will be brought you.'

So isolated had those valleys become that the European travellers who ventured up from the coast to visit the ancient remains were thought to be conjurers of spirits; the surviving villagers believed their pale skin a sign of leprosy and fled into the hills.

But the valleys had still been populated at the beginning of the century. Musa-al-Tango remembered his father telling of busy markets there in the years before the Great War and of the merchants going into the villages garlanded with nosegays to ward off the stench from the silkworms.

'It was the conscription that emptied the villages of their men.

'Those the Turks took, we never saw again.'

With the ports blockaded by French and British warships, the silk industry collapsed. The wood, grain and fruit harvests were plundered by the Turks, and what remained was consumed in the year of the locusts.

That was the year his father had worked as a rat-catcher in the cellars of the old Bey; he remembered wading thigh-deep in the hoarded grain as the villagers starved down in the valleys.

Such was the famine that one farmer sold his entire olive grove to the Bey for a single lemon; another his house and ass for three sacks of wheat; fellahin were sold for single pails of milk.

As we climbed again towards the gorge Musa-al-Tango had told me that it was in that same year that his father had travelled with the Bey into the three valleys and seen whole families writhing in agony on the bare floors of their huts, all the furniture sold, and the tiles from the roof; in the rubbish heaps at the roadside women scavenging for old bones, peel, canes of sugar; when the heavy rains stopped the children ran out and filled their stomachs with the weeds which had sprouted in the fields.

And Abu Musa would have been no older then than I had been during that long and dry summer when I had clambered up the river-bed to his hut and sat in the cage of sunlight through the matted straw to hear his tales of the lost caravans under the marshes and the land of the locusts.

And after the famine and the blood-feuds that followed men of his clan went out into the fields not knowing if they would return alive that night to their homes.

Many of those who had saved for the passage to Al Na-Yuk were rooked by the travel agents at Marseilles and sent on ships to Haiti, Brazil, Argentina, Sierra Leone; in the village they said this was the land where rubber tyres grew from trees.

There were men long believed lost who returned decades later with fortunes made in the diamond trade and built the sandstone diwans above the fellahin quarter, but many more did not return.

These were the faces in the old photographs kept in the folder Uncle Samir had always shown to the tourists from the buses that used to stop to take in the view on the turn above the house.

For years the nights in the village had been filled with the voices of the departed singing out of the empty cisterns and exhausted wells.

But many men went no further than the southern suburbs of the city. There they found lodgings in the shanty-towns; they worked as porters, street-cleaners, boot-blacks.

Sometimes Musa would hitch a lift up on a fruit-lorry and work the week in one of the Shi'i teams asphalting the first runway. When he went into the city and spoke with the accent of the south the shebab would spit on him in the street and call him 'Metawili with a tail' and give him the order 'Shamil', 'Turn leftwards'.

Even in the years before the war the boot-blacks from the

south who worked the tables at Faisals outside the main gate of the campus did not dare to kiss the hands of their clients, but by proxy kissed their own hands before looking upwards and calling on Allah to bless their young benefactors.

At election-time Musa returned to the city with his father, in the convoys of buses sent by the Bey to collect the Shi'i from the shanty-towns to register their votes in the villages of their birth. The parliament of the new republic had allowed thirteen seats to the people of the south, and in his diwan the old Bey boasted that if he wished he could have his walking-stick elected to the House and the other twelve deputies would come riding in on his coat-tails.

The young Musa had been among that retinue accompanying the Bey to the opening of parliament, but the ceremonials were interupted when the Bey engaged in fisticuffs with those who had dared stand against him and without waiting to hear a word of the debate set out on a thorough tour of the brothel quarter, his followers mounting armed raids as they passed through the districts of his political opponents before finally being chased out of the city by the gendarmerie.

Again I remembered the photograph facing out to sea in the dining-room we never used, the moustached Bey in his cream linen suit and tall fez, the murafiqin and other retainers a pace behind, some in lesser fezzes, others in loose keffieh, all posing stiffly, as if lined up before a firing-squad.

When the son of the old Bey returned from his studies at Cambridge Musa was among the three hundred followers who had travelled north to receive him at the new airport. At the edge of the runway he had helped to build he had added his hunting-shot to the welcoming fusillades from the Enfield and Berber rifles before they were seen off once more by the gendarmerie.

Like his father Musa had worked as a rat-catcher in the cellars of the Bey before taking his place as a murafiq at the doors of the great diwan.

The fellahin who waited on favours from the Bey were not permitted to wear neckties in his presence, nor any other article of European dress, and were served the dishes of the Bey cold, after he had sampled them and walked away.

Musa remembered that every year an old fellahin brought a lamb to slaughter for the pleasure of the Bey, and when one year the Bey honoured the peasant by offering him a small cut of the meat the old man did not eat it but took the morsel back to his village where he kept it as a trophy to show to all the shuyyuk of the neighbourhood and would not throw out the rotting meat even when his house was swarming with flies.

But for reasons that would never become clear in the week that the old Bey lay dying in the university hospital his son had appointed Fawzi-from-the-mountains and his cousins to the household. After the night of the shooting of the mastiff and the discovery of the body of the cousin of Fawzi in the dry wadi off the coast road there had been blood between the two houses.

Abu Musa had been dismissed from his position as bailiff on the sahel, and Musa-al-Tango had fled to Argentina. He had returned an outcast to tend his plots of poppies hidden in the ravines and gulleys of the jurd through which he guided us on that fine May evening back down on to the uppermost stretch of the Nabatiyeh road.

Ahead the charred pine hill, the hotel-complex above in the lee of the mountain.

This is the empire of liquor, and the Blasphemer is the Grand Signor here.

His solarium strewn on every side with ancient bottles and flasks. Demijohns, jeroboams, greybeards, carboys.

Beyond the deck the ripple-pools and jacuzzis brimming with wine, on recliners over the tessellated paving his harem of playbirds, full-figured Bollywood beauties in platinum wigs and diamanté thongs, the Blasphemer Puppet got up like some seventies playboy in mirror glasses and a cream safari-suit with gross epaulettes and lapels, stumbling among the bottles, fulminating against the Prophet and Imam Ali, riding bare-back on a great pot-bellied boar towards the gilded serail at the end of the pool, on the divan within Shaitan awaiting his loyal servant in striped pantaloons and an elongated stovepipe hat which rides up like a wind-sock into the Bombay noon.

Across the screen drifting the smoke from the afioun-pipes and hashmay-oil brought down from the city by the boys on the last convoy of construction materials. This is the largest room in the complex, the bridge-hall and small ballroom below the lobby knocked into one long chamber with a makeshift mizrab on the podium for the sheikh who comes up from the coast to take the Friday prayers.

When they have finished their work at the depots the boys come in and sit around the card tables playing trictrac and arguing over the out-of-date copies of *Al-Safir* and *An-Nahar*; at the back on the Al-Manar channel the loop-tape of martyr videos and scrolled quotes from the Qur'ān.

And do not speak of those who are slain in Allah's name as dead, for they are alive, but you do not perceive them.

We belong to God, and to God we shall return.

In the weekday evenings there are the Iranian martyr plays

dubbed into Arabic, and later the theological broadcasts which nobody watches except Ali when he cannot sleep.

(I come down to find you squatting beneath golden ladders and pyramids and trees; a jerky radiance spilling from the turban of the faquieh through the shroud of the mujtahid down to the open hands of the ulama and into the light over your face.)

But at the weekends when the convoys arrived we had Cairene soap-operas and the Bollywood religious sagas of which the Blasphemer Playboy was always the favourite due to the playbirds, and afterwards those who had been smoking wandered out into the gardens and danced around the earthed-in pool to old numbers by Fairouz and the Supremes, a city shabb dressed in what remained of the concierge's uniform riding on the back of another down among the bungalows, on the rotten palliasse in the poolhouse Jawad reclining in the guise of Shaitan, with striped shentian for trousers, and a long night-cap that rose up above the rafters of the broken roof in the wind off the heights.

Those were the nights you went alone to your room, drawing a drape over the window to cover the view to the gardens, on your crossed legs the book you had saved from the burning mosque.

You would not read the suras aloud and I returned to my nest in the sacks on the balcony below and when the wailing of the gramophone had ended I looked down and saw in the clearing beyond the cabins an old man dancing alone by the light of the moon, one arm out-stretched, the other turning his invisible partner towards the black wall of the mountains.

In the shade of the sandstone porch. Your thin length on the plane-wood bier. The white sheet; unwound to your knees.

Up the lane on the hill they carried you over their heads as light as a tray of ma'amoul.

Through the newly paned windows I saw for the last time the dark swirls of the bokharas over which I had crept so often as a boy to disturb you under the gallery where there had never seemed light enough to read.

The accident had happened on the Nabatiyeh road. The water-tower had collapsed as the jeep had drawn up underneath; the others had already got out to lay the pipe. There had not been time for Jaffer and his young wife to arrange all the passes for the roadblocks through the Shuf, but representatives of the Jihad al-Binaa had driven up from the coast, black cloaks thrown over their khaki jackets; the older men perspiring in the late spring sunshine.

On the lane the boys from your depot jostle for a touch of the planks. The place is too narrow, but those left behind keep their hands raised to the sky, as if they were still carrying you.

At the front Musa-al-Tango walks erect; he pushes back those women in black headscarves who cling to his arms.

The column climbs between the stone turbans of the beys, some warped in the heat of a past explosion, drawn out like the torch of Liberty, others slipped in on themselves like cones of ice-cream half-melted in the sun.

In the small space left at the top of the yard they have already dug the trench. Over the mounds of your mother, and Abu Musa, hexagonal wedges of unpainted wood; in black print, the names, the years of death, but not of birth.

Above the almond groves white with blossom, the newly plastered minaret, on the tower the speaker that will carry the inzah out over the alleys of the fellahin quarter and rooftop

252

terraces of the emigrant houses and down among the orchards and tobacco plots.

As the mourners leave I wait for the car that will take me to the harbour, in my clutch bags the few books from your room; never having learnt to read your father had insisted I keep them.

Under the sandstone porch the old man had embraced me with all the village looking on, in his rough Sudaco-Spanish telling me how he had always known it was written that the last of the beys would redeem the crimes of all his forefathers; not recognizing the low hissing syllables and believing perhaps that grief had addled his wits the women in their headscarves had gently led the old man back into the shade of the porch.

London, 1992

February 3rd, Nightfall

'He must be late.'

A ring of condensation against the pane. He wipes it away. He peers out to the mouth of the drive.

Across the road the scaffolding is empty now; above the rank of containers the still heads of the gantries like giant croquet-hoops.

'Or not going to show.'

Verger does not move from the fire, the hood of his puffer-jacket down to his chin. Leighton comes away from the window, crouches on the tiles below the fire, his back to the tea-chest.

'You could phone, a call-out. A couple of joeys to tide us over.'

Verger makes no reply, the khaki fabric lifting and sinking over the hidden face like an undersea anemone.

The room is close, airless. I pull myself up from the garden chair and go down into the yard; through the keen air of the late winter afternoon the mingling smells of the coal fires and the exhausts of the standing traffic and the tar from the workmen on the hill.

In the trickle from the melting slush in the guttering above I wet my hands, my eyes. On the crazy-paving, the rectangular outline of where the mat had last lain. I unroll it there again.

The mist thinning beyond the allotments, above the

skeletal beeches the brewery tower at the bend in the river, and as I bow again into the slough the fingers of the Prophet lift me out above the terraces and bridges and the sky is the fathomless sea in which I am washed and below floats all the city light and airy as the clouds in that winter sky.

Their backs over the fire; his hood up; Leighton glancing from his bare wrist to the window.

A pewter dullness on the hill, under the depot wall the winking tail-lights, those trying to get home before the rush-hour in a single unmoving line down from the roundabout.

It is too cold to go to the yard again. I need all my strength now for the final drive.

Over the bare boards of the upper landing I spread out the mat, above the stairwell the last light of the day through the dusty glass. In the hall below, a shaky glare over the black-and-white tiles from the inner passage where the striplight is never turned off.

I lift my head, and beyond the rim of brightness a figure is standing on the stairs, the face covered by the shadow of a shroud. I try to look into the face, but see only a mirror there, and in the mirror the face of Ali, and in his eyes a dance of flames.

The wind draws the fire across the square, and the snow under the porch is puckered by a fall of pebbles, and the broken heads of the bays drift out in the wind.

There through the charred windows are the chambers where the writer betrayed the religion of the Prophet and mocked the customs of his fathers and aped the manners of his conquerors, each attitude of kayf and blasphemy and lechery frozen into a separate body, the house teeming with the horde of bodies, and all are burning.

High over the unreal city and the walls of fire I am rising light as a cinder on your warm breath.

Outside on the drive I can hear an engine idling, the crunching of tyres on the loose shale. I go to the window, but I can see nothing through the creepers over the pane, only the blur from the tail-lights beyond the wall and lower down the hill the yellow glow from the Shell sign where later I will find my own car.

I had bought the old Mercedes during my first month back in London. When he heard I had joined the brotherhood my father had finally cut off my allowance, but Salah from the Ealing Husseinya had found me shifts at Excelsior Cars in Turnham Green where the other boys at the communal house worked to supplement their benefit payments.

The regular drivers were Sudanese, Algerians, Somalis. Over the glass-fronted controller's office there was a small room with a tawny kelim over the hardboard flooring and framed sura-inscriptions over the unplastered walls. Between shifts the men knelt to recite the Salat; on the withered carpet the rub-prints of their knees and foreheads as if heavy statues had once stood there.

I returned to my room in the early mornings to find my possessions disturbed. The spines of Ali's Qom commentaries and martyr plays ripped and twisted, the collection of art-historical postcards stolen and defaced, the kings and courtesans covered with hastily scribbled moustaches and phalluses. Many of the boys' families had suffered under the beys, but I did not put a lock on the door.

Six weeks after I had begun the night-shifts Jawad arrived at the house in Ealing to raise funds for the Jihad al-Binaa among the expatriate community. The room was no longer disturbed.

In the evenings I rarely joined Jawad and Salah at the Al-Bustan and the other Lebanese restaurants in the area, and when they went out with plastic buckets to collect at the Regent's Park Mosque and the new universities I stayed alone in the house.

Behind the communal kitchen there was a small, blind yard, the concrete cut open into troughs, fallen stakes and chicken-wire over the black earth. It was here I burnt the ruined books and cards, washing down the stone afterwards so no trace of the fire remained.

The week Jawad arrived I had received a call from the Red Crescent. The woman at the Holborn office had not wanted to tell me the circumstances of his death, but I had snatched the file from her hands. The body had been found half-eaten by dogs under the Kola flyover; Asad had only been identified from photographs hidden in the lining of his jacket.

When I returned that afternoon I burnt all that was left in the room and began a new regime of washing. I cleaned the bathroom, and wiped the surfaces with disinfectant.

Under the water my skin puckered like coral. I scrubbed with the pumice and the nailbrush, but still I saw the rifts of dirt in the veins, and I worked until the skin bloomed.

The clothes I had worn before washing I took to the fire in the yard; turning them over the white embers with a stake from the trough.

In the flames I looked for the faces war and time had stolen as I had in the abstract ruins of the city, but the flames danced only into the butterfly-wings of the wash behind the ferry on the last crossing to Larnaca, and when the fire had died I ploughed the ashes under the damp earth.

In the autumn Jawad returned home and I moved to the room in Leighton's house. My skin grew dry and white, and fell away, the sunken veins no longer visible.

Each week I burnt the clothes in the yard. I woke in the afternoons, the clock upside-down on the table, the sky darkening over the hill. When I had washed I read the Book and saw the city grow small beneath my shadow.

It was not until early in the new year that I received the news from Palo Alto. I had returned to Ealing to go through the room to make sure I had left nothing behind. The letter from Elaine was computer-typed, unsigned. He had died the night before they were to travel back to Spain.

There was no mention of a will, nor an account of the funeral. Amid the ranks of sun-blanched crosses and weeping angels I pictured the white mushroom of the turban. With his death, the last weight had been lifted, the inevitable symmetry joined.

That was the week Ali appeared outside the cemetery. I knew the place from the summer months when Leighton camped out under Burton's tomb.

We drove through the snow to the house on the square, and he cast the pebbles beneath the porch, and the broken bays tumbled out in the wind. Above the square I saw again that which I had already dreamed, the ladder over the furnace to the spreading tree and the spring in the hollow where the boys lie naked in the stream while she waits under the willow with her comics over the road through the orchards.

Below I can hear a scraping on the ice, a dull rapping.

Verger is standing at the head of the stairs, his laces loose behind him on the floor; as he goes down the parquet clacking like a domino game.

My head bowed, eyes closed. Nothing will end the fear of the pain, from the stomach through the cold boards, without muscle and cartilage and bones rending and melting the spirit will never fly back to its beginning.

On the upturned chest he lays the packet down. The man talks of checks at the docks, the one lane open on the motorway.

Verger cuts through the bandaged cellophane. On the blade he lifts the powder to the purity-tube, the solution turning the blue of tempera skies.

In the corner Leighton crouches, and over the foil the Brown runs easy as quicksilver, and for the last time I am lying at night in the mountains among the sacks on the balcony and the smoke drifts through the gardens from the cabins.

I kneel over the chest, Leighton passes the lighter, the blackened spinnaker of foil.

To begin with the road into town is clear, the Ka'bah swinging from the mirror as I pass the drainage works and cross by Chiswick Bridge.

Over Mortlake and the brewery tower hang the shadows of a great tree, in the locked park grow the thornless sidr and the talh, on the recreation-grounds it is balmy summer. In the closes and the rat-runs I hear the streams and the four fountains, among the low-rises of Stamford Brook the wind against the high pavilions.

But on King Street the traffic slows as always, on the pavement outside the corner of the Al-Bustan I see a crowd has gathered. On the ground two figures tumble in each other's arms and then the woman breaks free and staggers on her broken heels along the wall, her face hidden under her heavy fringe, her shiny raincoat reflecting back the lights of the slowing cars.

I turn the Mercedes on to the pavement, the fender hard up against the wall, the two staring at each other over the bonnet, the man bowed, gasping for breath, a dribble of saliva over his bushy moustache.

When she closes the door there is the rustle of the fringes and beaded tassels under the raincoat. She sees me looking at the blood from the scratches on her forearm, and pulls up the sleeve.

The sweat dripping into my crotch and my hands shaking on the wheel as I stop outside the mansion block in West Kensington where I had dropped her after her last show in Soho only the week before.

She tells me she does not want me to come up, but under the porch she crouches down on the steps, and I take her arm, and guide her up the five flights to a door with a brass horseshoe knocker.

Inside a dog is barking. She goes through to the kitchen to feed it, I stand at the window where I can watch the car. Along the shelves and covered radiators photographs of the woman in old revues alternate with more homely touches, furry pierrots, embroidered samplers in Spanish. Through the open bedroom door, more photographs in a small shrine with a plastic-flower surround; I recognize the wavy hair and thick moustache of the man outside the restaurant.

When she comes out of the kitchen she is wearing a track-suit top, and in the light I see the fault-lines under her make-up, a dark blotching under the eyes. The large lacquer tray of lemon tea and almond pastries she places over the armchair blocking my way back to the door.

Without speaking she sits over the tray, and as she pours I try not to stare at the ladder of welts and bruises on her thighs.

I drink the tea quickly, scalding the floor of my mouth, the pastry I swallow catches in my throat, but still she does not lift the tray. She follows my eyes through the doorway to the photographs, her voice remote and wistful as if recalling a novel that had once touched her deeply though her memory of the plot had faltered with the years.

The man in the photographs had been her lover in Buenos Aires in the last years of the Generals. The daughter of poor immigrants, she had met him at the university, the youngest son of one of the leading families of the city.

This was a time when many of their radical friends had been arrested and disappeared, and he had spent increasingly long periods away in London, promising to take her back each time, but always returning without her.

I stare towards the front door, and down at my wrist, but she talks on without the slightest attention to my reactions.

Within six months she had saved enough money for the journey, and come to the city, and when she could not find him she had worked as a waitress and a dancer in hostess bars. The two had met by chance years later, and he had been unable to hide his contempt for what she had become.

She knew he would never love her again, but for a decade she had followed him all over the country, and hurt herself to win his pity, and the violence had only made him shun her, and she had resorted to ever more desperate acts to capture his attention.

She was tearful now, and clutching at my knee, her false nails drawing up and dropping one by one to the floor. She cried out that she no longer knew who he was, but still she followed him knowing that without the pursuit her life would be drained of its last purpose, yet there were other times when the madness passed, and she saw that he was no more than a false light within the marshes that were her city, and the brighter his light shone the more impenetrable seemed the walls of mist about her.

She opens the window; the pane heavy with condensation. Down in the street the roof of the car has frosted over; through the sodium pall above the darkened plains of the city a dim crest over the Cromwell Road and on the squares behind where the house waits.

The cold air fills the room, ruffling the paper napkins we had not touched, lifting the leafs of the calendar as time passes in old films.

I push away the tray, stagger to the door; out on the unlit landing the warmth spreading back to my feet and fingers.

On the stairs the cool, hard angles through my thinned soles. The warm armour of the Brown beginning to wear off now. And on every step her voice tears through the visions, bringing them down, empty flaps, perished canvas, one after the other until nothing remains but sand and wind.

Out on the street I take my time to reach the car, play my feet over the bars of the railings, drink deep of the air scented with coal fires and the mulch of long-dead leaves, follow the swirling clouds of my breath, run my fingers on the pumice face of the brickwork, over the convoluted stellae of the frost.

For years the dwarf emir had hidden in his cave, and peopled the walls with his imaginings, and though he remembered the world he had no longer trusted his memories, and when at last the Turks brought him out into the light he had forgotten the brightness of the sun and the hues of the firs and myrtles and mulberries, and on the long journey to Istanbul his captors could not but wonder at all the joy that was in their little prisoner.

It is snowing as I reach the square. Light flurries over the telephone-booth, low drifts on the court and the green where the nannies bring the children in summer.

I park under the arch into the mews. The snow lies thick on the steps, the door half-covered by the untrimmed branches of the bays.

In the locks both keys turn easily; the door catching on the pile of letters and papers. I try the switches, but there is no light.

In the kitchen, a huddle of foil and broken bottles over the table, the water from the open fridge frozen over the tiles. On the shelf I find some tins, a jar of instant coffee.

Upstairs the scents of acetone and stale milk, and in the darkness I stumble on the litter of broken pipes and stems in those rooms where I had dreamt through the years of the war.

I pull back the brocade curtains, on the desk the crusted plates and ashtrays, the winter dawn breaking to the east.

In the stand the inkpots have dried, but behind the twisted lamps slumps the old Underwood on which I had once forged the tourist-card I had never used.

I lift the plastic hood.

The keys are stiff; the letters faint, legible.

As always I had dreamt of Layla.

From under her thick, damp fringe she looks down at the land she has never left as if at the first view of a foreign shore . . .

APPENDICES

Chronology of the Lebanese Civil War

1948 *the creation of the state of Israel. 800,000 Palestinians flee to refugee camps in Egypt, Jordan and Lebanon.*

1970 *after expulsion from Jordan, the Palestine Liberation Organisation establishes its headquarters in Beirut.*

1976–1981 *the Syrian military occupation of Lebanon fails to contain repeated armed conflict between the Palestinian refugee population and Christian Lebanese militias. Israeli reprisals against Palestinian guerrilla raids launched from South Lebanon displace the indigenous Shia population into the suburbs of Beirut.*

1982 *Israel invades Lebanon with the co-operation of the Christian militias. UN oversees evacuation of 11,000 Palestinian guerrillas from Beirut. The Palestinian camps are destroyed, civilian refugees in Tyre, Sidon and Beirut detained and massacred.*

1983–1985 *US and French Marine bases destroyed by suicide-bombers. As Israeli forces withdraw south of the Litani River, two Shia militias fill the power vacuum, the Islamist Hizbollah, and the Syrian-backed Amal. Hizbollah abduct Western journalists including John McCarthy and Terry Anderson.*

1985–1990 *the reconstructed Palestinian refugee camps are besieged by Amal. Christian, Druz and Shia militias fight for control of Beirut and the Lebanon mountains. Christian separatists led by General Aoun are defeated by Syria.*

Beirut Airport

The Village

Awali River

Sidon

Ein Helweh

Jezzine

Nabatiyeh

Jibsheet

Litani River

Tyre

Maarakeh

ISRAELI SECURITY ZONE

Qana

N

River Jordan

MAP OF
SOUTH
LEBANON

Naqoura

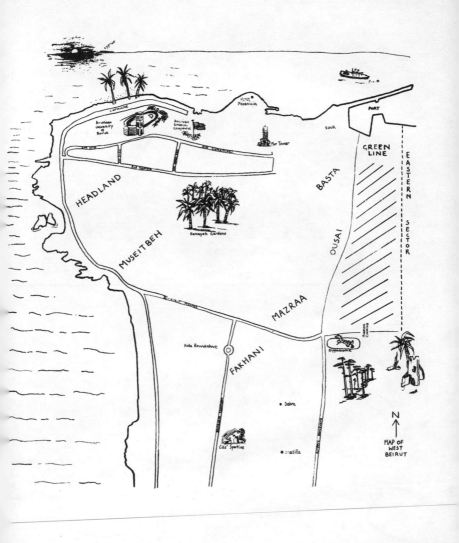

MAP OF
WEST
BEIRUT

Acknowledgements

I wish to thank the London Arts Board for the grant that supported the writing of the later parts of this novel.

My special thanks to Liz Calder for her courage in editing and publishing this book; to Omar Al-Qattan, Mary Furness, UNWRA and Beyt Hanania for their logistical assistance; to Becky Shaw, Mary Tomlinson and their colleagues for their patience and understanding; and to Isobel Brigham for the maps.

Finally I owe a particular debt of gratitude to the work of Rosemary Sayigh in confirming my worst suspicions.

This book pretends neither to be an accurate nor inclusive account of the tragedy of Lebanon; in war the first casualty is always truth.

Before her testimony, Sayigh recalled these lines by the poet Mahmoud Darwish:

'But should we not have some other work,
Than writing exequics
So they will seem unlike those we have just written.
How small are these flowers,
How deep is all this blood.'

A Note on the Author

Born in Beirut, Tony Hanania was brought up in the Lebanon and educated in England. He now lives in West London. He is the author of *Homesick*, shortlisted for the John Llewellyn Rhys Prize and recipient of the London Arts Board New Writers' Award. His novel, *Eros Island*, is also published by Bloomsbury.